PLACE

HUSSEY PLACE

LEOLA CHARLES

URBAN BOOKS

http://www.urbanbooks.net

This is a work of fiction. Any references or similarities to actual events, real people, living or dead, or to real locales are intended to give the novel a sense of reality. Any similarity in other names, characters, places, and incidents is entirely coincidental.

URBAN SOUL is published by

Urban Books
1199 Straight Path
West Babylon, NY 11704

ISBN-13: 978-1-59983-083-4
ISBN-10: 1-59983-083-3

First Printing: March 2009

10 9 8 7 6 5 4 3 2 1

Printed in the United States of America

Acknowledgments

Acknowledgment to you, Almighty Father, for the gift to discern the pain and struggles of others, showing me how to step outside the box, and for an always praying mother (E. Bess), who taught her children to hold on to their integrity.

My sons, Darrek and Dashante, Reverends and Prophetesses Eloise Hunter, and Loretta Smith, who supported me through even the minuscule steps of writing.

My husband, Roosevelt, who helped me with my very first novel *The Truth About Lies*. Maxine Thompson, my agent, and an author whom I greatly admire.

Tony Lindsay and Carl Weber, whose novels were a great inspiration, and I have read them all.

Curtis Rivers, owner of Mood Makers Books, the only African American bookstore in Rochester, and the best bookstore in Rochester, New York.

I also give praise to all the rappers and urban writers who first opened up our voices through their pain, struggles, and sufferings. May God bless them all. They have been pioneers for black voices and all voices that have messages to relay. There are so many whose writings I find incredible but would need to write another novel to list them all. Well done, for everything is done for a purpose.

Hussey Place,
Rochester, NY,
1967

Chapter 1

During cold weather, in upstate Rochester, New York, Lena sat in her living room on her tattered cloth love seat that faced the window. Every summer morning, weather permitting, at 5 o'clock, Lena sat in the frayed wicker lounger situated on her one-riser wooden porch of her shacklike bungalow, with the chipping paint and broken shudders that were in desperate need of cosmetic attention. The paint was so worn and faded, there was no longer any distinct color—just a faint distinction of the shudders being a darker shade than the house. The same house she had birthed her baby Gweneth in by the hands of a midwife, on January 19, 1930.

It was a time when even the North was still somewhat rural in areas, very much separated by black and white, and older housing existed for mostly the poor or those of color. Gweneth was born during these times—times when many people of color lived on what was called camps while migrating to the

North from the South. Camps were considered their temporary homes. To Lena, in some ways, Hussey Place was a slight reminder of those times, those temporary homes. The housing was shabby and so was the landscape. The only difference was that her husband, Kenneth, actually bought their home a few months before Gweneth was born, and it was more than a tent or one-bedroom shack. But Lena was happy to be with Kenneth. She would have lived with him in a shoe. He had done right by her and took her as his wife while she was pregnant in order to give her baby girl a name. Lena felt blessed.

In her time, being unwed and pregnant was frowned upon. Lena felt that she had no other recourse at the early age of fifteen but to marry Kenneth Galloway. Not only did Lena believe that Kenneth was a very handsome man—but a very honorable one—until the day he up and left her and Gweneth and never returned. Lena waited with patience and hope in her heart for Kenneth's return, but as time went on, circumstances surrounding her at age twenty caused her to become so bitter that when Gweneth finished School of Home Design, Gweneth quickly left old upstate New York for California, to pursue her career in architecture and design.

Hussey Place had always been too seedy for her, anyway. Oh, it could have looked brighter, much brighter, if someone had just taken the initiative to plant more flowers, trees, and add some decorative outdoor benches and remove all the raggedy seating that crowded most of the porches. A fresh coat of paint wouldn't have hurt the houses, either, but no one seemed to care or think that there was a chance of improving the old alley, and Gweneth couldn't bear looking at the place any longer.

If only Gweneth knew. Her mother and most of their neighbors were the former children of share-croppers, who had never owned anything, including the land they seeked a living from, when they'd lived in the South. Most of them didn't know how to do any better, because they had never had any better. Although interior cleanliness was important to the people of Hussey Place, exterior appearances was an option. They were just happy to have their own plot of land.

Kingdome Synthe was a resident of the neighborhood, but not of Hussey Place. He had full custody of his daughter, Kyanna. Kyanna and Gweneth had been friends before their parents met. Kingdome would take the girls out and acted as a father figure. Lena was their mother figure, braiding and styling hair, dressing the girls and herself in all sorts of pretty things, and cooking for everyone. As far as Lena was concerned, her life was full again, although she and Kingdome had never taken a romantic interest in each other. But Lena deemed him to be her true friend because of their similar circumstances, his faithfulness and dedication as a friend, and the understanding they had for each other's situations. Kingdome's wife had also left him with his baby girl. Not only did Kingdome love to cook, he loved to eat. He and Lena sometimes fought playfully over the kitchen and who would do the cooking. The two would play cards, checkers, and other games with the children for hours at a time, almost every day, and things had been good. But when Kingdome found a real love interest, he and Lena drifted apart. This caused Lena to grow bitter again, and this time, more hateful, allowing herself to become overweight and dowdy over time, and become drawn to the seedy look of the alley.

She sat on her porch in her special chair. With her long, willowy fingers, she scooped up a hunk of watermelon into a hand that did not match the large arm and body that it was attached to. However, it agreed with the thin, dark face that usually scowled— a face that would have been more than pretty if she hadn't scowled so frequently. Lena was only in her early fifties; the dark skin and wavy hair she inherited from the Charles clan, who were of Native American descent, were very distinct, down to her cheekbones and her skin, which looked leathery and wrinkled but was so smooth it crinkled with her facial expressions.

Lena spat a stream of snuff over her banister as she held a raggedy fan in her other bony hand, fanned, and warded off the flies and other insects that were attracted to the sweet nectar of her fruit. Snuff was a form of smokeless tobacco that she started dipping when she was a young woman. She would tuck the coffee-colored wad into her lower jaw and chew until all the bitterness came out. After a comfortable time would pass, she would spit out the brown rivulet, sometimes skeeting it through her teeth. Many women who lived in Hussey Place dipped snuff. Some hid in the house and spit their remnants into a tin can, but not Lena. She didn't care who saw her. She slowly and lazily rocked back and forth in the old wicker lounger with the lumpy, stuffed pillows while watching, like a devoted spectator at a sports arena, each tacky-looking, but neatly tucked-away, house in the neglected circle.

Lena wouldn't leave her spot until way after the sun went down—no matter what the season. At times, neighbors didn't know that Lena sat in her window for hours on bad days. Others forgot that she sat on her porch far into the night during mild weather, and some just didn't pay her that much attention at all. She was no more to them than a wave, a nod, or a brief hello. She was just a nosey old woman who was jealous and watched others going on with their lives, because she'd chosen not to live out her own. It was as if the one man she'd lost was the last.

After spitting her snuff out, Lena chewed her fruit slowly, and wickedly watched her neighbor exit her front door and take the one step down onto her front porch.

The beautiful brown woman turned and smiled. "Hey, Lena!"

She had the same long, thick black hair, figure, and beauty as her twin sister. Her even brown skin was still flawless. The same as Lena remembered Venn's twin sister's to be.

Lena allowed her chuckle to roar within her stomach so that no one else could hear. Each encounter with Venn Bazedale was just a taunt. She had no real interest in the pretty young woman. Lena held a straight face, "Hey, Venn, suga. How are you today?"

"Just fine, Lena! Fine!"

Venn was one of the few people on Hussey Place who worked or took up any time with Lena. Lena had poisoned pets, sprinkled vegetable gardens with ingredients to stump the growth, and had shooed away children who were barely near her door. No one could ever prove that it was Lena who had poisoned pets or killed their gardens, but everyone knew how nasty Lena could act and therefore kept their distance.

As Venn turned to lock her door, Lena cut her eyes wickedly and smiled as she remembered Chell—Venn's twin sister. Each time she saw Venn, she'd please herself with the same thoughts.

Venn walked over to Lena's worn-down fence. "Lena. Did you know about the new center that's opening?"

Lena took a deep breath. She didn't want to scare Venn away altogether; she loved her secret game. She gave Venn a fake smile and crossed her arms. "No, baby, I sure didn't."

"Yeah. That's where I'm headed. I'll be working there part-time—evenings. They got some of everything down there for everybody—kids and all, Lena."

Lena stared at Venn blankly. Why would she want to associate with any of the people from around her way? She barely talked to them as they passed by. And Venn was the last person she wanted to get close to. Venn was the only one who didn't know it.

Lena almost chuckled as she spoke. "Well, you go ahead and enjoy your new job."

Venn could hear the cynical, venomlike tone of Lena's voice. She cleared the embarrassment from her throat. "Uh-hum. Okay, Lena. Have a nice day."

Lena laughed inwardly but grinned outwardly. She enjoyed Venn's uncomfortable stride and watched her until she was out of view. Mission accomplished.

Lena finished feeding her mind with the thoughts she loved as she leaned back, closed her eyes, and relaxed.

She and Chell had gone out together to one of the old hole-in-the-wall clubs. Lena had gotten close to Chell and pretended to be her friend, allowing her constant visits to her home, but only when Lena's husband was away for long periods of time. Lena couldn't let Kenneth know that Chell was coming over, or that she had seen him offer the young girl money. That would mess up her entire plan. Lena couldn't let that happen, but pretending to be Chell's friend was inwardly eating away at Lena.

Lena was desperate. She felt that she had to do whatever it took to keep her man—and tried to never shy away from her plan—of pretending that she and Chell were equals and best of friends. It was a struggle for her, but she endured. When she felt that she and Chell were close enough, she successfully helped Chell to get out of the house by lying to her parents so that they could hang out together like two old friends. Chell would be spending the night and helping her out with some odd jobs. Chell almost had to cover her mouth so that she wouldn't grin and giggle as she listened to Lena lie for her.

Lena dressed Chell in the prettiest outfit that she could find, made up her face, and did her hair. Every now and then, she'd purposely snatch or comb Chell's hair a little too hard, causing Chell's sentences to break up, or her to say, "Ouch, Lena. That hurt, Lena. Lena!"

Lena would only halfheartedly apologize, but Chell hadn't noticed. She had still giggled and chattered through the whole ordeal. She was so excited, and hadn't quieted down until they were seated at their destination and the band began to play at the old hole-in-the-wall.

Lena had remained quiet the entire time, not really hearing a word Chell said or the band. She was going through her plan, over and over again, in her mind. It had to work or she'd be without her man. She'd even caught her man a few times talking about Chell in his sleep and moaning. Sure. The twins were pretty, even beautiful, but Lena had been quite a looker herself. And she'd done more for that man than the average woman would have back then.

Chell was only seventeen at the time; Lena was twenty-eight and was to look out for Chell. Instead, she'd set her up. When the band began to play, Jay Mocker called to Chell. Chell looked over at Lena, then back to Jay Mocker, who was now shushing her with his finger.

Chell shook Lena's shoulder. "Jay Mocker callin' me—"

Lena quickly turned to her and snapped, "Then go see what he want, girl! I ain't goin' no place!"

As soon as Chell got close enough, Jay Mocker pulled Chell into the men's room, where several men began to attack her. Her clothes shouldn't be torn or soiled. Lena wanted it that way. She had to seem genuinely shocked by Chell's story. Chell had to look like a liar when she returned to Lena. Lena had paid good money for things to look a certain way, and had spent a lot of uncomfortable time with Chell. It all had better work, or she'd report them with Chell if she had to.

Lena remembered watching the scene through the battered and cracked door. Sonny was muffling Chell's screams while two men held her arms. Mack Dolin lifted her up by the legs. She was dropped to the floor and left on the men's room floor when they thought they'd heard an unfamiliar sound. They slowly and cautiously exited the bathroom, looking around before doing so. They were all too frightened to complete their mission.

Lena stood on the other side of the wall so that she couldn't be seen.

Jay Mocker remained near the bathroom. When he saw that the hallway was clear, he went back to Chell. He stood over her dazed body. "You sho is pretty, Chell."

Chell reached up for help.

Jay Mocker pushed her hand aside. "Not till me and you get better acquainted."

Chell tried unsuccessfully to make her screams be heard over the band.

Lena wiped the sweat from her face and forehead as she watched her prey being tortured. The hurtful sounds Chell made excited, and satisfied, her. But Jay Mocker moaning out about her attractiveness angered Lena more; it seemed to make her ears ache, made her wish that Chell would be damaged for life when he was done with her. How could Chell have been so naïve as to believe that she could mess around with her man and she'd forgive her so easily? She'd pay for that, and Lena wanted her to pay in the worst way . . . shamefully. She remembered how she pretended to be on her way to

the bathroom when she saw Chell staggering out of
the men's room. How she quickly helped Chell
back inside, helped her to clean up, and lectured
Chell after Chell told her what had happened. Neither one was to speak another word about the incident to anyone—and from Lena's point of view, she
suggested maybe an older man wasn't what Chell
needed, and she should stay away from all of them.

Chell never perceived that Lena knew all about her
husband giving her money. At first like a father
figure, then to woo her. And although Chell had
turned him down, Lena was angry. She was going to
make sure that Chell wouldn't want her husband or
anyone else's. But none of that had mattered. As
soon as Lena's husband sought Chell out again, she
ran off with him, believing no other man would want
her. She was sure if she had stayed in Rochester,
someone was soon to find out about her being raped,
and then not even Lena's husband would touch her.

When comforted by Venn, Chell's twin sister,
Lena pretended not to care that her husband had
run off with a mere child, but she did. She cared
every day.

That had been twenty years ago—back in 1947.
She was still making Venn pay today for her twin
sister Chell's mistake. Venn remained in that for-
saken house that reminded Lena of her sister. The
comfortable house that always had a mother that
adored her children and made sure that they always
looked perfect and ate well. And a father that kept
that house in tip-top shape, and now Venn's little
prize was still taking care of their house.

But where was Lena's man? Yeah, Venn would pay until the day she or Lena died—no matter how much Venn sided with her or apologized for her twin sister's indiscretion. Lena sometimes wouldn't say a word to Venn; at other times very little when Venn tried comforting her out of a guilt that she had no business owning. But each day, as long as Lena could breathe, she'd make sure Venn paid for her hurt and loss.

Lena allowed the aromas of the stews, meat loaf, chicken, pork chops, and boiled corn that wafted through the air to caress her nostrils and draw her attention away from her old memories. The houses were so close Lena chuckled secretly and shook her head. The thought of being able to tell what was going on in each home, right down to the flavor of Kool-Aid that she knew was being mixed in large generic containers and being poured into mason jars loaded with ice, made her take a deep breath.

She closed her eyes and imagined those aromas— *Grape, orange, cherry?*—then continued feasting on her watermelon. The snuff would have to wait, the watermelon would be her only meal for the day. She couldn't dip and eat. She had never been able to maneuver the snuff under her lip, like she had seen others do. She scooped and smiled impishly until she saw Thomas, Venn's son, back out of their front door, pulling their lawn mower along with him.

Thomas allowed the screen door to slam as he and the mower made contact with the porch. He'd already begun to sweat from the struggle. He pulled his T-shirt over his head. His upper body glistened. It was an unpleasantly warm summer's evening. He'd complete the yard work as usual before he lost all light.

But Thomas also had other intentions. He glanced over at Lena's porch. She gleamed at him. Thomas checked his watch. Lena stood up and lifted the corners of her long skirt as she rose. Thomas, using one of their signals, slightly nodded in her direction. In an hour or so, he'd be with her. It all had to be calculated just right. Like all of the older women from her day, no one else was to know about their ventures. They had to be discreet or become bigger outcasts than they already were.

Their ventures began when Lena summoned Thomas seven years ago, shortly after his birthday. Using her sweet charm, Lena had gotten him drunk, and made him feel at home. The handsome, brown-skinned, slightly over six-feet-tall seventeen-year-old became instantly hooked, and constantly ignored the flirtatious gestures of females his own age to be with Lena.

Thomas had always noticed Lena's pretty face, skin, and hair. He had even thought of her as attractive when he was younger—had fantasized about her. Lena was groomed then and hadn't taken up snuff dipping. When Lena began to allow her upkeep to spiral downward, so did Thomas's interest. After being with Lena a few times, he had eventually crawled into her bed on his own, forgetting about her extra weight, snuff dipping, nasty attitude, and age. Lena could do more than any young girl of his era— and she cooked for him. Lena learned at an early age that food wasn't the only way to a man's heart and had educated herself on how to have more control over the opposite sex. If her parents or anyone

else had found out about some of the things she'd
read and practiced, she would have definitely been
an outcast—not only in their eyes, but the entire
community's.

Thomas sat in the freshly cut yard with his knees
up, T-shirt across his thighs, picking his teeth with
a twig, slapping mosquitoes and knocking bugs
out of his low-cut Afro while secretly watching Lena's
house. He could see her looking back at him
through her favorite spying window. He grinned
broadly, showing his perfect white teeth, which Lena
always swore she could see a sparkle in. Thomas
knew how anxious she was. They hadn't been together for almost two weeks. He would keep her in
suspense.

Thomas slipped up behind Lena as she continued staring out the window, searching for him.
"What you lookin' for?"

Lena almost fell as she spun around. "Which way
did you go? I didn't see you leave the yard."

"Don't worry about that. Just worry about me."

Thomas sat down in the wood-legged chair far
away from the window where Lena usually started
with him. He gave her a serious look. "Come on."

Lena walked over to Thomas. "Ain't you going to
bathe first?"

"You want me, Lena, or you want me gone?"

Lena was now tied in. She couldn't afford to lose
Thomas, and Thomas knew that she didn't want to.
He knew that his youth and what little he did for
her had her too attached, and he stared at Lena
with no emotion, letting her know his thoughts.

Chapter 2

Lena stood with her mouth open as she rubbed her eyes in disbelief. Gweneth was standing at her door with a young girl that was the spitting image of Gweneth, beauty and all. Before Gweneth could speak, Lena grabbed Gweneth and hugged her. "I thought I'd never see you again!" As she wiped the tears that wouldn't stop flowing, she turned to acknowledge the young lady next to her daughter. "And who is this, Gweneth?"

"This is your granddaughter!"

"How old is she?"

"She can talk, Ma! Tell Mama how old you are, Kerrissy?"

"Um, seventeen. Turned seventeen three days ago."

Lena smiled. "Well, Kerrissy, I'm glad to finally get to meet my granddaughter. Y'all come on in and stop standing in the doorway!"

Kerrissy stepped inside and immediately turned up her nose. She'd gotten past the faded exterior. She'd assumed that the interior, like many houses, would look nicer than the exterior. The house was clean, but the furniture definitely needed to be replaced, and the walls needed paint and patching.

Lena took Gweneth's hand. They walked over to the sofa and sat down. Kerrissy reluctantly followed them and sat next to her mother.

"So you got a job doing what you went to school for, Gweneth?"

"Mmm, got my own business. Run it out of my house. Got so many clients, I can barely handle them all."

Lena smiled broadly. She was proud of her one and only daughter.

Gweneth could see her mother's admiration. She lowered her head and blushed.

"How long you here for, Gweneth? Is Kerrissy's father—I mean, is your husband—"

"Thought I'd stay about three months if you want me to—got the time. Figured you could use some help fixing up, and I wanted to buy you some new furniture. Wanted to make up to you for being gone so long without calling. Just want to make up to you, Ma—especially for keeping your only grandchild away from you for so long, and use some of my experience helping the woman who put me through school to get it. . . . And no, my husband won't be coming. We split up a while ago and I don't want to talk about that man." Gweneth growled in a high pitch with frustration.

Lena hugged Gweneth. "It's okay, baby, we together now. When it's time, you'll get another husband."

Gweneth rolled her eyes toward her mother, then up at the ceiling. She wondered why her mother always thought it was so important to have a man. She'd met the jerk and married him while in California after knowing him for only a few months and progressed more without him. Gweneth soon found out that Eugene was only willing to take chances when he wanted to cheat on her. If it wasn't for the job given to him by Kodak, through a special program for African American males fresh out of college, Eugene would have never done much of anything with his life. He remained at Kodak in film development and never used his degree in architecture to pursue any specific dream.

Kerrissy was still slowly looking around.

Gweneth stood up. "So, is my old room still vacant?"

"Just like you left it!"

Gweneth was happy. She knew that Kerrissy would be more at ease once she saw that the old room her mother once occupied was in better condition than the rest of the house, and it was. A smile instantly crossed Kerrissy's face when she saw the room. Lena had been changing the bedcovers weekly and washing them since Gweneth's departure.

"Come on in and put your things away, Kerrissy."

Kerrissy did as her mother ordered.

Lena had gone into the kitchen to prepare dinner.

Kerrissy quietly asked her mother, "Why your old room look so much better than the rest of this house?"

"Probably because Mama ain't been in here except to change the bed."

Kerrissy tilted her head and replied, "Oh"; then she proceeded to remove the items from her suitcase and store them in the drawer that her mother had specified to be hers.

Lena and Gweneth chatted away at the table. Lena asked about Kerrissy's father again. Gweneth informed her mother that they'd gotten married, soon after she arrived in California only knowing him a short while and like most men, when he'd gotten tired of the "husband and father" routine, he'd found him another woman. He and Gweneth divorced. Not only did Gweneth have a prosperous business, but her ex-husband had to pay her spousal and child support. She and Kerrissy weren't hurting for anything, except for a man around the house— although Gweneth's ex-husband, Eugene, visited Kerrissy regularly. That put Lena at ease.

Kerrissy indulged in the collard greens, corn bread, roast beef, rice, gravy, macaroni and cheese, and the Kool-Aid that her grandmother had prepared. Gweneth was a good cook, but not as good as Lena.

Although Gweneth rolled right along with the flow of things, she wondered why her mother hadn't lost her touch, only cooking for herself. She wasn't aware of her mother feeding her young lover—in more ways than one.

After dinner Lena pulled her shade down, giving Thomas the signal that all was not well, just in case this was one of the nights he'd seek her company.

Chapter 3

Lena, Gweneth, and Kerrissy laughed merrily as they all carried bags into the house. They were going to make Lena's house the envy of the circle. The makeover was going to be a fun project. They'd all get to know each other; Lena and Gweneth would become reacquainted.

The first two weeks were promising. The inside had been completely done. Kerrissy didn't want to stop. She became infatuated with the way the house transformed. She'd even discussed doing interior design with Lena and her mother. They were all closer than ever. Lena was even speaking to people more freely and sincerely, and she'd been too busy to really spy on anyone, wreak havoc, or dip her snuff.

Being with Thomas had crossed her mind—he'd even been watching her window. But where would they go? She hadn't planned on her daughter's visit; she hadn't even planned on her *ever* returning home—the girl had only written and called every blue moon since she left. Lena had made up her mind. She and Thomas would have to rearrange things for a while. At least until they could decide on an alternate meeting place. She'd slipped off and told him so, but he hadn't taken the news too well. He'd even begged her to do things near the shed he'd just built for his mother, anxiously urging her, "Can't nobody see us between this shed and fence, Lena! That's why I put it there, to give you view of me in more privacy, just in case somebody else was outside and saw you at your window calling me. . . ."

Lena refused, and Thomas had gone into his house without another word.

Chapter 4

The day had arrived for the exterior painting of Lena's house. All three ladies began to paint the house a light blue. The trim and fence, of course, were to be white. The neighbors observed the project.

Thomas stood in his yard and watched, too, as he leaned across his chain-link fence, with both arms dangling over it, his fingers looped into the holes of it. He stood upright and walked over to Lena's. She became tense and prayed that he wouldn't say anything distasteful. To her surprise, he picked up a brush and began helping. Lena relaxed. Thomas continued to paint the house without giving Lena any eye contact. As if there had never been anything between them.

Kerrissy began to play with her mother, slapping her backside with the paintbrush. Gweneth slapped Kerrissy on the back. Lena and Thomas stood back, smiling. Gweneth drew a line down Lena's arm. Lena tried to catch her, but was unsuccessful. Kerrissy dipped her brush and slung paint at Thomas. Unlike her mother, she was unsuccessful at getting away. Thomas grabbed her around the waist and painted her backside. This shook Lena, but she remained expressionless. She'd speak to Thomas later.

Through all of the playing, the front and sides of the house had been completed, and it looked good. When darkness hit, everyone was ready to fall out. Thomas and Lena pretended to continue painting.

"What was that all about, Thomas?"

"I don't know what you're talking about."

"You know what um talkin' 'bout. Was you tryin' to mess with my granddaughter?"

"Lena, you hallucinatin'. You know them young girls can't do nothin' for me. That's unless you tired."

"You know what my situation is, Thomas—"

"Then you'd better hurry up and fix it! If you don't, I just might have to teach somebody to do what I need! You hear me, Lena!"

Lena dropped her head.

"I said. Do you hear me?"

"Yes, Thomas, yes. I hear you."

Thomas gently lay the brush down and casually walked away.

By the time Lena woke the next morning, the exterior of the house was complete. Thomas was doing small touch-ups when Lena walked outside.

Lena's eyes brightened. "Thank you, Thomas! Thank you!"

Thomas continued to paint. When he was done, he closed the paint can, laid the brush on top of it, and walked away.

Chapter 5

Lena was happy. Her furniture had arrived and it was beautiful. The striped satin sofa, love seat, ottoman, and two solid colored chairs were gorgeous. The dark wood tables with clawed feet were sensational, and the marble tops made them look exquisite. Her new bedroom set was white, and so was the dining-room furniture. The colors that her daughter had picked out for her walls matched everything to a tee, including her delicate kitchen set. Lena would treasure it all forever.

She'd even been blessed with a new wicker porch set with a swing. Thomas had bought her the pictures she'd been admiring, stating that it was sort of a neighborly party to celebrate her renovation. Lena was definitely in heaven. The house was so beautiful that she'd planted flowers and bushes. All of the hard work had encouraged the entire circle to do the same. The old alley was looking better than ever and much brighter. To benefit all, the circle had gotten together, chipped in, and hard-surfaced the once-dust-ridden area where cars pulled in.

* * *

Gweneth looked around the circle in admiration. She'd never seen it look so good and bright. She actually thought about staying. Even Kerrisy seemed to be happier here than she'd been at home. She'd seemed so withdrawn in California; spending the summer with her grandmother seemed to change her entire personality. But how would Gweneth do business from her mother's house? It was impossible. In another week she and Kerrissy would have to hit the road. That made her sad. Gweneth's eyes became teary. She and Kerrissy had already missed more than fifteen years of her mother's life. Now she wished she'd tried to come back earlier, but soon remembered how her mother had cursed her with everything she had within and told her that she was no good like her father. Gweneth closed her teary eyes, then opened them. The trip had been well worth it, but she and Kerrissy would be on the road in two weeks.

Chapter 6

Gweneth and Lena shopped for everything. Kerrissy knew how her mother was. She knew that her mother would be gone all day if she wasn't shopping for anything specific, so she chose to stay behind.

Gweneth decided that she and Lena would get something to eat while they were out and take in a movie. Kerrissy loved her grandmother's cooking so much she refused to eat anything else and would warm up the leftovers and watch the television that Gweneth had purchased to put in her old bedroom. Gweneth wasn't aware of it, but two televisions made Lena feel like the richest resident on Hussey Place.

It was almost midnight when Gweneth and Lena arrived back at the house. It was dark—all but the light that shone from underneath Gweneth's bedroom door. Gweneth could hear the television playing. She set her bags by the front door and put her hands on her hips. "Why does Kerrissy always go to sleep with that television on? And so loud? I know she ain't deaf!"

Gweneth headed for her bedroom. Lena set her bags down, chuckled softly, and followed her.

Gweneth gently pushed the door open so that she wouldn't wake her daughter. Her hand went over her mouth. Kerrissy and Thomas were naked and entwined, kissing like they had so much passion they couldn't wait for the magic moment.

Lena almost passed out when she took in the sight, but soon recovered and quickly went into a cackling rage. "That's why I took care of your aunt! You look and act just like her, you filthy, no-good, bastard!

"Gweneth! Gweneth! Get this nasty little heffa out of my house! *Now!*"

"Don't you call my daughter no heffa! You da heffa! Come on, Kerrissy! We shouldn'ta come here no way! I told you how this old piece of nothin' is! And now you see it for yourself!"

Kerrissy was now cowering near the headboard under the sheet she held up to shelter her naked body. Thomas was still on the bed, staring at the two women arguing in the doorway.

Gweneth marched over to the bed and grabbed Kerrissy by the wrist, slinging her into a standing position. Kerrissy was still holding on to the sheet. Gweneth scowled at her. "As soon as we get packed, we're outta here!" Kerrissy scurried out the door, but Gweneth made sure she left last, to leave Thomas with some parting words. Pointing at the young pervert, Gweneth promised, *"If I see you near my daughter ever again, Thomas, or even look at her, I swear to God I'll kill you!"*

Lena stood at the door, chest heaving, waiting for Gweneth to pack and get out.

Thomas continued to watch the scene in disbelief from the bed. What did Lena mean by she'd "taken care" of his aunt? He wouldn't be leaving until he found out.

Gweneth called a cab without bothering to see what time the next flight left for Los Angeles and hustled Kerrissy outside as she argued with her. Tears were streaming down Kerrissy's face. This had to be the worst day of her life—a nightmare! How would she ever live this down? She'd been caught getting ready to commit what many considered was one of the most despicable acts ever, and it had been witnessed by her mother and grandmother.

Thomas had eased off the bed and was now standing. His eyes were squinted and evil, his fists were clenched.

Lena stared at him with a deep scowl for a long time, checking out the similarities of him and his aunt. Although Venn and Chell were identical twins, Lena had always recognized a distinction. Thomas looked more like Chell than his own mother, Venn.

She'd noticed it the first time she'd seen what she'd privately called "the Little Yellow Bastard of Hussey Place" when Venn presented him to her. As far as Lena was concerned, Venn was a bigger whore than that slutty sister of hers. She'd willingly had sex with Thomas's father and had gotten pregnant. Although he was lying, Thomas's father had pretended that he was going into the service. The upshot was that he never came back. Didn't the little stupid child know what day and age it was? That men in their time wooed you so that they could lay up? Lena had reveled in that, too. Both the pretty little whores had gotten what they'd deserved. *Now look at um!*

Lena threw up her arm and pointed at the door. "You get out, too!" She now detested the fact that she'd taught Thomas how to be a night creeper.

Thomas who was now twenty-four and had been secretly sleeping with Lena for seven years, stood flexing his fists. His voice was deep and angry. "What did you mean by, that's why you 'took care' of my aunt?"

Lena crossed her arms in defiance.

Thomas punched the bedroom wall near her head. Lena yelped and jumped simultaneously.

Thomas put both arms against the wall to lock her in. His voice was low and sinister. "What did you mean by that? And I ain't goin' ask you again."

Lena backed into the wall. "You just get out my house!"

Thomas grabbed her throat with one hand. "Tell me, you old witch, or you'll be dyin' even sooner than you think!"

Lena tried to free herself by placing both her hands on his and forcing his away.

Thomas shook her, causing her stringy hair to tousle. "Are you going to tell me what you meant, or am I gonna have to squeeze the little life out of you that you got left?"

Lena closed her eyes and chuckled wickedly. Tears were running down her face. She was now holding Thomas's hand tighter around her neck. Thomas looked confused.

She lifted his other and put it around her neck, too. "Go ahead. Do it. Kill me, Thomas."

Thomas stared at her. "You think I won't do it?"

Lena became irritated. "Just do it if you goan do it!"

Thomas pulled her away from the wall without releasing his grip, threw her down on the bed, and straddled her. He drew back a fist, then thought again. She was still weak for him. If she wasn't, the scene wouldn't have made her so angry. He ripped the front of her dress and planted kisses on her flesh. "You goan tell me, or is it over?"

Lena gasped as Thomas murmured on her skin. She swallowed loudly. She was happy that it wasn't really over. When she'd ordered him to get out, she was hoping that he'd come crawling back to her and apologize, and she'd be ready to accept it.

Thomas knew that she was weakening. He caressed her.

Lena moaned. "You won't be back if I tell you. Besides, it was a long time ago, Thomas—"

"Tell me, Lena. Or um gone. *Forever!*"

Tears ran down the sides of Lena's face. "I had her raped for messin' with my husband."

Thomas slowly slid away.

Lena didn't move. "She run away with him and left me to take care of my child, *alone*! She wasn't his, but he *owed* me . . . !" That part of the confession had slipped. Lena wanted to lie, but she didn't know what else to say.

Thomas was now breathing hard. He hadn't heard any of Lena's sympathy story. "You broke our family up like that?"

Lena could only cry.

Thomas crawled back on top of her. "You goin' pay for that, you old no-good hag!"

Lena tried to rise up and began hitting at Thomas open-handedly.

Thomas looked at Lena with a deep hatred; Lena could feel his wrath. He slapped Lena enough to make her feel his anger.

"Please don't hurt me, Thomas, please. I'm an old woman."

"You wadn't *too old* when you was teachin' me."

Chapter 7

To honor his aunt, Thomas vowed to stay away from Lena. His urges caused him to want her, but he refused to give in. He remembered Kerrissey and Gweneth's number, which he'd put in his jeans weeks ago, then he remembered that the jeans had been washed twice—they'd had so much paint on them. The numbers would no longer be legible, especially after the pants had gone through the wringer twice. He would be lucky if the paper was still intact.

Thomas went upstairs to his bedroom and began rifling through his jeans until he came up with the paint-stained pair. He searched the pockets. There it was—the ball of paper with the phone number. He gently unfolded it, but it did no good, the paper crumbled like old bread. Now he would have to go to Lena. In desperation he walked out into the late-night air that had began to turn a bit cool due to a fast-approaching autumn. He glanced up at Lena's window. She was there, but she quickly snatched her curtain shut to avoid him. Thomas grew angry. He walked over to Lena's house and pounded her back door. Lena was now walking in circles in her living room, wishing that she hadn't been so obvious when she'd snatched her curtain with such force. She headed for the phone, but by the time she'd gotten to it, Thomas was inside.

Lena screamed and backed away. "Go on back home, Thomas! I don't want no trouble—"

"You don't want me no more, Lena? We still mad?"

Lena wouldn't speak.

Thomas turned to walk away.

Lena ran up to him and grabbed his arm. "Wait, Thomas, wait!"

Thomas snatched away his arm. "For what, Lena? Wait for what?"

"Um sorry for what I did—"

"Um sorry for what you did, too, Lena. We had a good thing goin' here, and now—"

"You laid up with my granddaughter, and you tryin' to blame all this on me? You ain't goin' even say you sorry—"

"You got my aunt raped—"

"You tryin' tuh say that's why you laid up with my blood, Thomas, 'cause you didn't even know that until after—"

Thomas slapped Lena before she could continue.

Lena was now fed up with Thomas's irate actions. She ran into the kitchen and grabbed a large butcher knife out of her drawer. She returned to Thomas. *"Get. Out. Now!"*

Thomas's eyes grew large, but he wasn't going to run. A slight grin crossed his face. "So? You goin' kill me now?" Thomas grabbed himself indecently. "You tired of this . . . ? You know you liked what I done to you last time we was together—"

Lena had a flashback of Gweneth's real father, her ex-boss who had caught her off guard while she washed in his basement. Like most young black women during the Depression, she was a washer-woman who did laundry, to help contribute to her sharecropping parents' household. In order to supplement that little income, she also did domestic work for the boss's wife. The same white man who, after raping her, had made the same gesture Thomas had just done slapping her, humiliating her more because she had turned him down previously. How she wanted to abort the pregnancy, but she had been too ashamed and too afraid to leave her house until it was too late. Her blood boiled even hotter. She ran toward Thomas angry, crying, shaking her head wildly, and screaming with the knife over her head like a madwoman. She swung at his abdomen.

Thomas jumped back and tucked in his stomach. She ran at him again, trying to stab him in the head. Thomas ducked. The knife became lodged in the wall. While Lena tried pulling it out, he went under her, wrapped both arms around her thighs, lifted her up over his shoulders, and proceeded to carry her into the bedroom. Lena didn't struggle. She was too tired to struggle. Thomas slammed her down on the bed, somewhat knocking the wind out of her to make her come to her senses, then sat next to her. He had his motives and he wasn't about to be without what he wanted—even if it meant he had to find another way to get it from Lena. He stroked her hair. "So you don't love me no more?"

Lena almost went into shock. Thomas had never mentioned the word "love" before, nor had he been so affectionate. She knew what their relationship was about, didn't she?

Lena continued to sob.

Thomas swallowed and stared blankly at the wall. "Um sorry, Lena."

The apology sounded sincere. Lena began to nod her head as if to say okay.

Thomas stood up. "See what you do to me . . . ?"

Lena looked down at Thomas. She wanted to laugh through her tears. He looked as though he had a rolled-up sock wedged in his pants. She just stared.

"This is why I can't stay away. I wish that I'd never come here. What am I going to do now, Lena? What am I going to do now? I keep on sayin' to myself, 'She older than me. She hurt my family. Why do I still want her?' But it don't do no good, Lena. I can't stay away from you. I should hate you. . . ."

Thomas threw up his hands, then straightened himself up and began to walk away.

Lena sat up on the edge of the bed, tears streaming down her face. "Why did you have to do me the way you did, Thomas? I know I was wrong, but so was you. Why'd you do it? Why did you lay up with my grandchild? Why you hurt me and treat me the way you did that day?"

"I don't know, Lena. She was there. You wasn't. It was like I needed a fix—"

"You ain't never been that sweet with me, Thomas!"

Thomas put his head down and pretended to be sad to prevent himself from grinning as he thought, *And I never will be, witch!*

Lena continued. "And the way you abused me—"

"I swear, Lena. If you just take care of me this time, it won't never happen again—"

"Is that all I am to you, Thomas—"

"Look, Lena. Never mind, but you got me hooked. What am I supposed to do now?"

Lena shook her head in bewilderment. She was too confused.

Thomas slowly walked toward her.

Lena shook her head no.

Thomas gently took her hands. "Please, Lena. I need you. If we could have been together while your daughter was here, there wouldn'ta never been no me and Kerrissy."

Just hearing her granddaughter's name sent a wicked chill through Lena's body. She looked up at Thomas. "Do you love her?"

"Lena, that young girl don't mean nothin' to me. You seen what was going on. I hadn't really touched her. Do you think that I would have been with you later if I had? I lied to you that day—I lied. I never had no sex with her. I ain't goin' lie. It was leadin' up to that, but she still a virgin. What you seen is all that happened. I was just runnin' my mouth about her, tryin' to hurt you for what you said you did to my auntie. That's why I said I'd had her."

Truth be known, this was as close as Thomas would ever come to an apology. In his heart, he felt no remorse. In fact, he felt as if he had done nothing wrong to feel bad about, in the first place, so what was Lena griping about? Besides, in his mind, Lena deserved whatever he dealt her. Because she had approached him first and stolen his innocence, he considered her a forward woman. Forward women were thought to be as wanton as whores.

Lena's head dropped. She stared down in her lap. Thomas wouldn't let go of her hands.

Lena looked up. "You really don't love her?"

Thomas stepped between Lena's legs, wrapped her arms around his waist, and held her head close to him. "Baby, I don't even know that child. I told you what made me do what I did, and I wouldn't have ever hurt you if you hadn't told me that you were the reason why my auntie is gone."

His auntie, his auntie—that was all he'd ever talked about with Lena since she'd begun to train him. That's what had made it so easy for her to mess with this boy. He never shut up about that silly aunt of his, whom she hated, and he'd probably never see, or had he? Maybe that's why he talked about her so much. Maybe her ex-husband had quietly brought Chell back to visit without Lena's knowledge.

Until Thomas was caught with Kerrissy, he wasn't aware that his aged mistress's ex-husband was also his uncle. Nor had he even thought about why Gweneth and Kerrissy both looked half-white. They were both lighter than Kenneth, much lighter. But none of that stopped the lust he had for Lena's company, or her lust for his, and now he'd called her baby. He'd never called her that before. That one word dismissed all the negative feelings she was having for Thomas at that moment. Feelings that she wanted to dismiss—no matter what had happened between them—but she had to pretend. She needed to show some restraint, some dignity.

Thomas slid his pants down with one hand while Lena hugged him. His firm structure made her breathing intensify. Thomas guided her hands.

Chapter 8

The cold air touching Thomas's flesh made him realize what had just happened. The woman he thought he despised had just made him react in an emotional way, and he'd been begging her to prolong it. Why had he been so weak? Why couldn't he have just fought with her until he'd gotten what he thought he'd really come for? Now he'd have to spend more time with her to complete his mission. He slowly backed away from Lena, pulling up his pants in the process. He cleared his throat, "Do you want me to prove that your granddaughter didn't mean anything to me?"

Lena was too shocked to answer. She was sure he'd just conned her to get what he'd wanted, but she cared about him and was hoping he'd sleep with her.

Thomas lifted her chin. "Let's call her."

Lena shook her head feverishly. "No!"

"Yes, Lena, the only way that we can almost get back to where we were is for me to call and dismiss her. She done got the wrong idea. She at a age in her life where she could run away from her mama and believe that she can come back to me. Do you want to lose me, the way you lost your husband, to another young girl?"

Lena could feel the fear go through her heart. She thought deeply about what Thomas said. "What would you say to her?"

Thomas smacked his lips. "Just you let me worry about that. Are you goin' to call her or do you want me to do it?"

Lena stood up. "I don't want no part of it."

"What? You don't want to hear me let her down after what she's done to you—"

"You was there, too, Thomas. She didn't do it by herself!"

"Lena, I thought we'd gotten past that. Should I bring up what you did to my auntie—"

"Just call her, Thomas! Just call her!"

Lena shook her head in frustration and clutched the front of her collar with one hand.

"I need the number."

"Why can't we just forget about it, Thomas, and work things out from here?"

"Okay. We'll do it your way. Maybe she'll come back, maybe she won't. But if you want to make sure she stay where she is, I'll need the number." Thomas took Lena by the hand and led her into the living room. He picked up the phone. "What's the number?"

Lena couldn't bear to speak them out loud. She opened the drawer in the telephone stand, took out her pad and pencil, and wrote them down. She handed the number to Thomas. "Don't call her from here."

As soon as Lena said the words, she regretted them and her actions. He could call her from his house and she would never know what Thomas had in mind. Maybe he *was* just there to get to her granddaughter, and now he could leave at any moment if that was his intention. He'd gotten everything out of her that he could. But the one thing she knew was that her granddaughter wasn't giving him everything he wanted, or the situation would have been different the day she walked in on them.

Lena stared him straight in the eyes. "You goin' call her so that y'all can be together, ain't you?"

"Lena, here, take this number back." Thomas shoved the number back into her hand. "I don't need this. I thought we was gonna be okay, but I see that no matter what I do, your granddaughter is always goin' be between us."

Thomas turned to walk away.

Lena grabbed his arm."Wait! Um sorry. It's just that it would kill me if you went to my grandchild again. My own flesh and blood. I couldn't take it, Thomas. I just couldn't!"

"Why? What would you do? Have her raped like you did my auntie?"

"You said we was goin' git past that!"

"So did you. But you keep on accusing me of wanting your flesh and blood still. You keep throwin' that up in my face! Why I got to be different, Lena? Why I got to be different, huh?"

Lena looked at the crumpled paper in her hand.

Thomas's palms were sweaty from anticipation, but he didn't want to draw Lena's suspicion to his real feelings. He hadn't stared at the piece of paper for too long, only remembering a few digits.

He licked his lips, anxiously hoping to retrieve the numbers.

Lena stretched out her hand to give Thomas the numbers.

Instead of taking them, he took her hand and led her back to the bedroom, like the dog she'd trained him to be.

Chapter 9

Thomas stood and adjusted his clothing. Lena didn't feel old, and she wasn't hard on the eye, but Thomas had taken extra precaution and had sex with her from the rear so that he wouldn't have to see her face. All the other times the lights had been off and he'd imagined that he was with some young girl he'd made up in his mind. But he knew that wouldn't work this time. Kerrissy was real. Kerrissy was beautiful and eating away at his thoughts. The sooner he got to her, the quicker his mind would be put at ease, and so would his concealed lust for her.

Lena lay on her side, watching Thomas. He walked over to her bed. He held up the number. "I'm going home to fix this."

Lena slightly hoisted her body with her arm. "Tonight?"

"You mean this morning."

Lena threw him a wave. "You know what I mean."

"You know I ain't goin' call this child, now even if it's still early enough in L.A."

Lena looked at the clock. "It's midnight there."

"You still worried about me callin' her, Lena? 'Cause if you are, I can leave this number here."

Lena pushed herself up some more. "Thomas—"

"*Just forget it!*"

Thomas dropped the slip of paper on the floor and stormed out of Lena's, without looking back.

Thomas gently opened the door and entered his house. As soon as he got inside, he quickly, but quietly, found a piece of paper and something to write Kerrissy's number down with, before he forgot it. He could feel himself becoming excited at the thought of how she'd felt and the things they'd done. He stared at the number he'd swiftly scribbled down; he almost drooled. There was no way he'd get to sleep. He wanted Kerrissy then and there. His head was so full of her that he began to dial the number, then stopped. He had to be smarter than that. They might change the number if he called now. He couldn't let that happen. He placed the phone back on the cradle. He tiptoed to the front door and stared out at Lena's house. As usual, her kitchen light was still on, which meant she hadn't locked the back door yet. He eased out of his house again and headed for Lena's.

Lena stepped out of the shower, dried herself, and headed to lock her back door. She screamed when she saw Thomas sitting at the brand-new red-and-white metal kitchen table that her daughter had bought her. He was having a cup of her tea, and he hadn't even looked up to acknowledge her. She wanted to become angry but couldn't. She was also happy that he'd come back, that he wasn't angry with her for her earlier actions.

She pulled the towel, which she'd almost lost, tighter around her. "I thought you was gone."

Thomas wouldn't lift his head. "Do I look gone?"

Lena took a deep breath. "Is somethin' wrong?"

Thomas finally looked up. "Yeah. You knew what I wanted, and you acted like you was ready for me to leave."

Lena's face saddened. "I thought you was ready to go, Thomas. You left like you was mad again."

Thomas stood up and moved toward her. "I thought we had a relationship. You acted like you wanted me to take that number and call your grand-daughter. You acted like you didn't even care. You coulda stopped me. If you really cared, you woulda, Lena."

"I care."

"Then why you let me go?"

"'Cause I thought you was mad about me sayin' somethin' to you about that phone number."

"All you had to do was stop me, but you didn't. You know why? Because you either didn't trust me, or you was trying to get rid of me by putting me with your granddaughter."

Lena opened her mouth to speak.

Thomas put his hand up, then sat back down in the chair. "Don't worry about it. Just come over here and sit on my lap."

Now Lena was really puzzled. He'd never as much as gotten close to her on his own, until it was time for him to get what he wanted. Now he was acting like a schoolboy in love and she was frozen in place.

Thomas smiled at her. "Come on, baby. Sit on my lap."

Lena blushed like a schoolgirl as she slowly shuffled over to Thomas to do as he ordered.

Thomas pulled her onto his lap as soon as she was close enough, causing her to lose her towel. Lena tried to bend over to retrieve it. Thomas held her tightly around the waist. "You ain't got nothin' I ain't already seen. Why you tryin' to hide from me? You got another man? You cheatin' on me, Lena?"

Thomas quickly grabbed the back of her neck and squeezed it, pretending to be upset.

Lena had to catch her breath. "You know I ain't got nobody else!"

"You was goin' out too often with your daughter for me to believe that, Lena. And the way you let me just leave here, not less than an hour ago without tryin' to stop me, you got to be doin' somethin'. That's why I sneaked back in here. To see who else was goin' be here! Was you waitin' on another man, Lena? Was you?"

"No, Thomas, no! Ain't no other man! Me and my daughter only went shoppin'! You seen what we brought back!"

"That coulda been just a cover-up—"

"No, Thomas—"

"Then prove it."

"Thomas, we just got done layin' up. What else can I prove?"

Thomas undid his pants as he whispered in her ear.

Lena had wanted what Thomas was whispering to

her, but now she'd changed her mind. She'd just bathed, and depending on his mood, Thomas might be rough with her. Lena squirmed. "Thomas, not now. You know it's too soon. And not in the kitch—"

Thomas put his lips to her ear again. "Sh-sh. Let Daddy have his way."

Lena started to speak, wanted to speak, but she felt too insignificant to do anything. At one time, she was in control. She couldn't even look in Thomas's direction now, and she wondered if she would ever be able to do so again after this encounter.

Thomas hugged Lena's waist tightly. He needed Lena until he could get to Kerrissy.

Lena felt totally ashamed. To be dealt with like a nobody by a boy who could have been one of her grandchildren, especially the one she'd taught—and him making his grade in her *kitchen*—was almost unbearable to her. The boy had been temporary and naïve. His mother would know about them when the time was right. Lena had lost control.

It all seemed to excite Thomas. He was in control, and now Lena didn't want anyone to know what was happening between them—even if she died.

Thomas kissed the crease in Lena's back. A cold, dirty chill went through her. She closed her eyes, swallowed, and wished he'd release her, then leave.

Thomas whispered in her ear, "I wanna go again."

Lena's toes curled in fear; she clenched her fists tighter. Thomas wrapped his shoed feet around her bare ones. "I said, I wanna go again."

Lena could feel the roughness of his shoes on her

feet and felt more degraded. She wouldn't answer Thomas, hoping to discourage him—but it didn't.

The table rumbled as Lena used it to force herself away from him. "Please, Thomas, don't!"

Thomas looked up at her. "Did I hurt you?"

Lena lowered her head and played with her fingers. She didn't have the courage to tell Thomas how degraded she felt. She'd never admit to that.

Thomas put his hand out to her. Lena slowly took it. Thomas pulled her back down onto his lap.

Chapter 10

For the first time in his life, Thomas had stayed out all night until the following evening. He called his mother and lied, telling her that he was with the girl he thought he wanted to marry, and Venn accepted it.

Thomas stayed with Lena until nine o'clock the following night. He wanted to make sure that Kerrissy would be up and at home when he called. Having her on his mind while he was alone made it hard for him to sleep. Being at Lena's house wasn't much better. Each time he thought about Kerrissy, Lena had to be her. Lena was quickly tiring of Thomas's company. She had made up her mind to tell him to go and never come back after the last time he put in his order. When she turned over from another short nap, Thomas was gone.

When Thomas walked into his house, it was just the way he wanted it. Quiet and empty. He took out the number and dialed.

The phone rang four times. "Hello."

Thomas's breath almost left his body. He became dizzy with desire. "Kerrissy?"

"Yeah."

"This Thomas."

There was silence on the other end.

"Kerrissy? You still there?"

"Yeah. But why you callin' me?"

"All I could think about was you since you left me, girl."

"How you get our number way out here?"

"Why do you ask so many questions?"

"Look, Thomas. I gotta go."

"Oh. You done forgot all I did for you? You done used me now and don't want to be bothered?"

"What we did was bad. My mother just ain't the same. Things just ain't the same between us. She think that what happened pulled her and my grandmother apart forever."

"So that means that we can't love each other?"

Kerrissy's heart raced. Did he say "love"? None of the boys she knew had said they loved her, they'd only flirted. Thomas was her first sensual encounter. Kerrissy sat up straight on the sofa. "What if we could love each other? We live too far apart."

"I got some money. I could send for you."

"Boyeee! My mama ain't lettin' me come there! I can barely go to my friends' houses that live here without her knowing it!"

"Why she got to know, Kerrissy?"

"'Cause I ain't grown, Thomas!"

"Girl! You grown in the eyes of the law! Grown enough to get married without your mother's consent—at least here, anyway!"

"You asking me to marry you, Thomas?"

"That's exactly what um asking you. You coming if I send for you?"

Kerrissy thought for a second. It had been early May when she and her mother had visited her grandma Lena, and her mother was still being a witch about what had happened almost a month ago between her and Thomas. Reminding her of it every day. Kerrissy was tired of hearing about it. She had apologized to her mother so many times that it seemed like it was something she had to do each time she saw her. She was even avoiding her mother whenever she could.

Kerrissy took a deep breath. "Yeah. I'll come."

"You ain't gonna waste my money, are you? I work hard for this money."

"I thought you told me you only work four hours a day."

"So? I still work hard at the factory as a paper cutter. People pay me to cut they lawns and fix stuff, too. Wait. You sound like you goin' waste my money."

"No, Thomas. For real. Um comin' if you send for me."

"When you wanna get here?"

"As soon as you want me there."

"I'll send for you in a week."

Thomas hung up the phone before Kerrissy could say good-bye or change her mind.

Kerrissy leaned back on the sofa, looking at her ring finger, imagining what her wedding ring would look like on it. She smiled.

Thomas was smiling, too. Soon he wouldn't have any use for the old leather bag that had torn his family apart. Besides, she had taught him enough.

What she hadn't, he had already figured out on his own. His best friend, Jasper, had told him many things, which was why he'd been so bold with Kerrissy to try to get her to have sex with him. Still, he needed Lena until he could get with her granddaughter.

Chapter 11

Thomas had been going out into the yard and waiting for Lena to signal to him or be in the window, but that hadn't happened. The third day he'd gone up to her back door, but he couldn't get in. He tapped on the door lightly, and quietly called her name when he really wanted to yell and kick in the door, but he decided to just walk away. The fourth day he'd given up, but Lena was ready to give in. Trying to end the mismatched affair was as difficult as she had imagined. When she saw Thomas out in the yard, she appeared in her window. Thomas glanced up and saw her. He put his head down and pretended that she wasn't there. Lena tapped on the window and made a gesture that he knew too well. He'd already made up his mind to go over there, but not until she'd summoned him.

Lena was wrapped in a towel again when she walked into her kitchen to lock her back door. She squealed nervously when she saw Thomas sitting at her table again, not quite invited, having another cup of tea. She had given up on the rendezvous.

Lena took in a deep breath. She was still trying to figure out when things had changed. How did her prey become the predator, and get control over her? He even called the shots as to when and where they would have sex. Thomas generally initiated sex in the kitchen because this was his pattern. He liked kinky sex in an unconventional setting. Thomas wanted everything done his way, where he wanted it, and when he wanted it done. Not only did he like to degrade Lena, his desire for depraved sex was growing. Their encounters only left Lena feeling cheap, used.

Thomas looked up at her. "Why you playing all these games with me, Lena?"

"I wasn't gonna see you no more."

Thomas laughed short and wickedly. "Maybe you goin' git that request. Maybe soon."

The threat made Lena's body grow cold. She took a deep breath and let it out. "What that mean, Thomas?"

"You figure it out, Lena."

"You got somebody else?"

"Maybe."

"Then why you here?"

"You called me, didn't you?"

Lena put her head down.

Thomas went back to his tea. He lifted his head. "Come here. Sit on my lap."

Lena hated this. This wasn't why she'd called him. She wanted anything but this. It made her feel like nothing. Maybe she wouldn't feel so bad if she was still controlling the situation, but she wasn't, and she felt like a piece of trash that had to hold on to the new broom that was trying to sweep her out the door.

Thomas sipped his tea again and didn't bother to look up. "You comin' or should I leave?"

Lena held her towel tighter and stepped closer.

Thomas pulled her so hard she had no other recourse but to let go of the terry cloth that left her body flying.

Thomas gripped her wrists tightly and taunted her. "You want to fight with me, Lena? You like it better that way?"

Lena's voice trembled. "I don't want to fight with you, Thomas."

The fear made Thomas more aggressive. He grabbed the back of her neck and breathed hard as he spoke. "Then why you playin' with me, huh?"

Lena's voice was trembling. "I figured if we stayed away from each other, we would—I don't know—but I just couldn't—"

Lena was stumbling over her words.

Thomas slammed his fist down on the table. *"Don't play with me!"*

Lena jumped and closed her eyes tightly. Tears lay on her lashes.

Thomas pushed her, giving her the signal. Lena stood up. Thomas grabbed her roughly around the waist and slowly sat down again.

Lena threw her arms out to her sides. "Uh, uh, don't, Thomas. I ain't young no more—"

"You wasn't young when we got started, Lena. What's so different now?"

"You wasn't doin' me like this then."

Thomas clenched his teeth. "Like what? I ain't never did you no way. You was the one who showed me what to do."

Thomas laid his head on her back in frustration. "Um ruined, Lena. You ruined me. Ain't no other woman goin' treat me the way you do, and I don't know what else to do about it."

Thomas began to cry.

Lena soon figured it out. He'd been getting high. She could smell it on him. *What all has he been using?* She'd never known Thomas to touch as much as a beer. Now he was so high, she was terrified of him.

The intoxicants had worked like a truth serum. Thomas felt what he'd spoken, ruined and lost, and that Lena was the cause of it.

Lena leaned her elbows on the table and put her hands over her face. This was sick. She was over fifty, and being controlled by a man who could have been her son.

Thomas relaxed, breathed hard, and held on to her for a while then. He whispered in her ear, "I want to go again."

Thomas was in Lena's bed in a deep sleep. Lena wanted to hurt him while he was unconscious, but the feelings she'd acquired for him ran too deep.

Lena dozed off with angry thoughts in her head of Thomas. She was tired, although it was practically daylight. She had to get some rest. She needed the strength for the attacks. She didn't have the strength or nerve to fight back.

Lena's eyes fluttered, then opened. When she woke, Thomas was gone. She was both relieved and saddened. Something about him had changed— they had changed, and it was more than Thomas wanting control. Something just wasn't right. Lena wondered if she'd ever see Thomas again.

Chapter 12

"Speed up! Speed up! Pass him!"

Jasper had allowed Thomas to drive his car to pick up his soon-to-be wife so that he could look good doing so, as long as Thomas agreed that he could tag along. Jasper was in a big hurry to see what Kerrissy looked like. Thomas hadn't mentioned a woman to him since he'd known him. Jasper was getting suspiciously concerned that his best friend might be homosexual. He knew that he was a mama's boy.

Jasper was the only friend Thomas had. Jasper was ten years older than Thomas, and married to Cleonta Fable. He thought of Thomas as a little brother, but sometimes he tried to act like Thomas's father.

Jasper continued to backseat drive. "Come on, Thomas, man, speed up so that I can see this gal! I done told my wife that I was takin' you to your new job! She better be worth me lyin'!"

Thomas smacked his lips. "Man! Where is your

common sense? Why you keep on wantin' me to pass up all these people, you tryin' to kill us? One of them same people you tryin' to pass 'n' junk might be sleepin' with your wife when you gone!"

"Shoot! What I puts on my woman can't many men do, Thomas! You know what I taught you! She'll be celibate for a long time after um goan, my brother!"

Thomas grinned broadly and almost choked on his laughter. His light skin turned bright red. He never thought that Jasper would remember all the times he'd demonstrated the most private thing Thomas had already done to Kerrissy right in her grandmother's house to get her taken away from him so soon.

Jasper snickered. "What's the matter? You think old Jasper be too drunk to remember, don't you?"

Thomas pushed his head, but wouldn't take his eyes off the road. "Man. You ain't that old. You ain't but twenty-nine!"

"Not for another three months, Thomas. I won't be twenty-nine for another three months. And that's when I take me on a mistress."

Thomas just shook his head. Jasper always bragged about cheating. He even got women's phone numbers, but he was just too lazy to carry out any of what he preached. He was just too lazy to cheat, because Cleonta Fable took good care of her man, right down to whatever made him high and drunk. The same elixirs he'd shared with Thomas the last time Thomas had been with Lena. So why did he think that he could act like his father—Jasper wasn't mature. Not many mature fathers would assist their child in wrongdoings. But there was a double standard. It was cool for sons to sleep with women of any age, but their daughters were sluts if they did it without marriage. If his father knew that he was sleeping with Lena and going to get Kerrissy—his older mistress's granddaughter, he would probably pat him on the back. That was just the way it was, and he wondered if the perception would change in the future. If so, how would men feel? He also knew that women blamed men for problems they could walk away from, and never blamed a woman for any of the bad things that happened to her—whether it was her fault or not. He wondered how many women would feel sorry for him if they knew how Lena had ruined him. His thoughts went back to Jasper. Jasper was comfortable, very comfortable at home, but he had to brag about something in front of the guys or they'd think he was soft, and that, too, was a no-no. Thomas hated how men had to put on acts, lie about their conquests, and act on their lies. *Would things ever change?* The standards led him to drink.

Thomas and Jasper pulled up to the bus station at 2:30 A.M. Kerrissy was nowhere in sight. Thomas nervously rubbed his hands together. Maybe she had stood him up.

Jasper pretended to be cool and wait around with Thomas, but as soon as Thomas walked over to the information desk, he ran to the closest phone available to call his wife.

Kerrissy's bus didn't arrived until 3:17 A.M. They were running late as usual. When Jasper saw her, he was pleased, very pleased that his self-proclaimed little brother and friend had found himself such a pretty young thing.

As Kerrissy headed toward them, Jasper leaned over and whispered, "How old is that girl, Thomas?"

Thomas cleared his throat and moved his lips as little as possible. "She seventeen, why?"

"She look about twelve, that's why."

"Well, she ain't. She seventeen, Jasper, seventeen!"

Jasper stuck his bottom lip out, put his hands in his pockets, and nodded.

Kerrissy was now standing face-to-face with them.

Thomas had been admiring her full, bouncy Afro and perfect figure way before she'd reached them. He just didn't want Jasper to know how anxious he was. But the way her hip-hugger jeans molded to her body with the colorful leather braided belt, which looped through them that hung between her legs, along with the beautifully colored popcorn blouse that fit her so perfectly, made him want to lose his cool. He wanted to pick her up and kiss her until he was tired.

Thomas and Jasper immediately grabbed the three pieces of luggage that Kerrissy was struggling with. Thomas held one of the large suitcases in his hand, put her overnight case under his arm, grabbed her hand, and led Kerrissy to the car. The cross-country trip had taken her three days by bus to get from L.A. to New York. Meantime, there had been no word from Gweneth looking for Kerrisy probably because of her estranged relationship with Lena. Even if Kerrissy's mother had placed a police report, they would only have looked around town or contacted her friends. Moreover, the police did not see runaway or missing black females as a priority so Kerrissy felt free. Jasper followed, carrying the other large piece. They loaded the luggage into the trunk and piled in the car. Without hesitation Jasper quickly got in the back.

All the way home Jasper chatted away like he usually did.

Thomas truly loved Jasper like a brother. Jasper was very unselfish, friendly, and caring. Thomas had always believed his friend's nature was due to the good wife he'd married. He loved being around Jasper, but he did talk too much at times—mostly when he was excited or drunk. Right now he was excited for Thomas. He'd already agreed to stand up for Thomas when he was ready to marry Kerrissy.

Thomas dropped Jasper off at home. He was to go pick him up by 2:00 P.M. the next day, which was Saturday. Cleonta liked shopping on Saturdays and she wanted to be out of the house before the kids got back from all of their activities.

Thomas pulled the car up into the vacant area on the other side of his house, where no one would see them enter his side door. He and Kerrissy took the bags inside. Kerrissy cringed at the thought of living in another old dilapidated house like her grandmother's, but she took a deep breath and decided to accept it. They had fixed up her grandmother's house; they could do the same here. The outside was already done. She stepped inside and was very impressed with the cleanliness and physical upkeep of the house. There were no cracked walls with plaster missing or worn furniture. It had that unlived-in magazine look, nothing like her grandmother's had been. She quickly remembered how even the exterior was nicer than the rest of the houses in the circle. It had been the only one that didn't need cosmetic attention when she had first visited. Kerrissy continued to smile as she looked around. Yes, she was quite pleased.

Instead of going to his bedroom, Thomas took Kerrissy to the finished basement. He couldn't allow his mother to find out about her too soon. Thomas had his lies lined up. Kerrissy was eighteen. She'd left home because she wasn't getting along with her mother because her mother's boyfriend had tried to rape her. He'd called Kerrissy a liar, and her mother believed him and took his side. She could never go outside without Thomas for fear of her mother coming to look for her and bringing her no-good boyfriend along. He'd surely have succeeded in his plans if they were able to drag Kerrissy back home.

Kerrissy sat down on the sofa. Thomas turned on the small black-and-white set, then began to place Kerrissy's luggage against the far wall of the finished room. He knew just how to work his mother. If Venn saw Kerrissy or her luggage before Thomas could explain, Venn would fly off the handle. Although Venn had never gotten the chance to meet Kerrissy, she would be standing at Lena's fence and telling their business at the break of dawn. Lena would know about Kerrissy before he wanted it.

Thomas walked over to the sofa and straddled Kerrissy.

She playfully placed both hands on his firm chest. "What you doin', Thomas?"

Thomas laughed through his nose. "Um trying to get a kiss." He put his hand on the back of Kerrissy's head, pulled her face close to his, and gently kissed her. He parted her lips with his tongue and used it to pull hers into his mouth. Kerrissy began to breathe deeply. Thomas tried to remove Kerrissy's top.

Kerrissy spoke into their kiss as she took his hand and placed it on the zipper of her pants. "You gotta remove my jeans to get to the snaps on my top."

Thomas undid her jeans, then slid from over her onto the floor. He stared up into Kerrissy's eyes as he tightly cuffed the waist of her snug jeans with his fingers and pulled them off. He spread her legs to unsnap the top. Kerrissy wasn't wearing any underwear. Thomas became angry, but he resisted the urge to show his real emotions. Instead, he looped one hand around the crotch of the top and pulled Kerrissy into a lying position, ripping the snaps away from the material. As he did so, he knocked the wind out of her. Thomas looked up at her. "You been messing around on me, Kerrissy?"

Kerrissy's eyes and mouth flew open in surprise. She tried to sit up. Thomas put the flat of his hand on her stomach and pushed her back down. "Just answer the question."

"Thomas, I don't even know no other boys. Why you think that?"

"Where your draws, Kerrissy?"

"I don't need panties with this top—"

Thomas slightly raised his voice. "You do if you my woman!"

Kerrissy sank into the sofa and wouldn't speak.

That made Thomas even angrier. *What is she trying to prove? Has she been with another man?* Thomas thought about slapping her in a playful manner, just enough to make her feel good about him being jealous. But then he thought about something else Jasper had taught him—physical abuse that couldn't be traced. If it could, she'd be too ashamed to admit it in public. Jasper said that this was a sign that no other man would ever take control over his woman. You'd always have her love, and control her mind. And as long as she was never aware of the indirect abuse, he'd be able to control Kerrissy forever. *"Let them know that you are a little jealous, but never show too much anger to the one you believe that you're in love with."* Jasper's lesson repeated itself over and over in Thomas's head as he made Kerrissy tremble, squeal, and try to free herself from his hold. Thomas wouldn't let go until she squealed again, then a third time. Kerrissy curled into a fetal position. Thomas sat and watched to see if what he'd done would have the effect Jasper promised before he crawled up to her and massaged her stomach and thigh. His eyes roamed Kerrissy's body to see any resemblance in hers and her grandmother's. Her mother was superfine, but he'd been told by Jasper that some things skip a generation or two. He thought about how he'd almost tried talking to Gweneth because he'd noticed how beautiful she was—but she'd been to college, and with him barely graduating high school, she intimidated him. She would have been too much to deal with. He liked the idea of Kerrissy being young, pretty, naïve, and a virgin. Controlling her would be a lot easier and less troublesome. Having her would do things for him that he couldn't explain. He wouldn't give Lena a second thought with something like Kerrissy in his pocket.

* * *

Thomas continued to rub Kerrissy's thigh as he cleared his throat to say the words—the line that Jasper had taught him—"That's how much I love you, Kerrissy. I want you to be satisfied when I'm done. You don't need nobody but me, baby. Can you remember that?"

Kerrissy nodded her head, with her eyes closed, as she cried silently.

She still looked so beautiful to Thomas that he felt like he was living in a fantasy. He felt bad about what he was told he had to do to make Kerrissy understand who was in charge, but he couldn't be honest with her. Jasper said that a real man just didn't handle things that way or his woman would think that he was a punk.

Thomas lifted Kerrissy's body to his, hugged her tightly, and lied some more, like Jasper had taught him. "I'm sorry. I didn't know that was gonna be too much for you. I just wanted to satisfy you. That's all I'm concerned with. You know that, don't you, Kerrissy?"

Kerrissy nodded again.

Thomas let out a fake breath of defeat. "You mad because I did that?"

Kerrissy's tears were still flowing. She shook her head no, her voice was weak. "You didn't know."

The sorrow in Kerrissy's voice broke Thomas's heart, made him want to cry with her. He held himself together. "You want me to take you back to your mother?"

Kerrissy wiped her tears and shook her head no again.

Thomas put his face in his hands and smiled impishly. It hurt, but Jasper's lessons had paid off. Thomas wouldn't look up. "I guess you probably don't want to have sex with me now, huh?"

Kerrissy wouldn't answer.

Thomas sat up and moved closer to Kerrissy. He pushed her soft hair away from her ear and gently kissed it. He proceeded to plant kisses down her neck until he reached her breast. Kerrissy slowly rolled over onto her back and held Thomas's head. He wanted to massage her to make sure she'd be ready for him. He didn't want her too tender to support him. This was his first copulation with a female his age, and untouched. His head felt light. Kerrissy trembled and whined from the pain and discomfort, then allowed tears of desire to flow down the sides of her face as Thomas took his time satisfying both their bodies' yearnings.

Thomas was in love with Kerrissy. She wasn't going anywhere, as far as he was concerned, and he was going to make sure of it. She would soon be his wife.

Chapter 13

Thomas stood in front of Venn. "Ma, I love her. She ain't got no place else to go."

"Thomas. You are too young to be tied down to one girl like that! And she looks too young—"

"*Maaa!* She my age!"

"Well, she looks younger! And y'all both still too young!"

"Ma, please. This the only girl I ever had. If she go back home, her stepfather—mother's boyfriend or whatever—goin' take advantage of her. She might even end up on the streets or in a home where they won't treat her right. Ma, I ain't gonna let that happen. I love her too much for that. If she go, I gotta go with her—I mean, I love you, but you got someplace to stay and you safe. Kerrissy ain't got none of that and I'd be less than a man if I let her go on the streets by herself or back home, knowin' what I know!"

"Thomas, you probably don't even know that girl's last name."

Thomas bit his bottom lip so that he wouldn't

lie, then smiled when he remembered Kerrissy had her father's last name. "It's Frazier. Her last name Frazier."

Kerrissy sat in the basement and listened to the back-and-forth bantering. Picking at her thumbnail, she was glad that Thomas had introduced her to his mother, then told her to go back downstairs. This way he could talk to his mother about her and Thomas's situation. She would have been too embarrassed to sit through Thomas's lies without looking guilty.

Kerrissy could no longer hear what was being said; then there were footsteps coming down into the basement. She quickly jumped up off the sofa.

Thomas ran over to her and hugged her. "You can stay, baby! Mama say you can stay as long as we goan get married!"

"When we gonna get married?"

"Soon, baby, soon!"

Kerrissy wrapped her arms around Thomas's waist and leaned her head against his chest. They rocked in each other's arms and smiled. The thought of being one had them totally love-struck.

Chapter 14

Thomas was awakened by Kerrissy's whining cries. He touched her head. "What's wrong, baby?"

"It hurt when I try to pee."

Thomas bit his lip. He knew that he had gone too far with her. Jasper had warned him that intimacy could be overdone and become an irritant to a woman's body. Thomas knew that this was the case with Kerrissy—without the opinion of Jasper or a doctor. He stood up and turned on the light, ran downstairs, and got her a glass of water. He quickly brought it back up and put it to her lips. "Here. Drink this down. The water will help the discomfort until I get you to the hospital."

Kerrissy slowly drank until the glass was empty, then handed it back to Thomas.

Thomas set the glass on the floor. "You feel any better?"

Kerrissy nodded.

Thomas proceeded to dress them both for the hospital visit.

Chapter 15

"She pregnant now, Thomas! What are you going to do? You told me three months ago you were going to marry that girl, and now she's carrying your child!"

Thomas folded his arms across his chest. "Ma, um goin' marry her." His voice was high-pitched, but he spoke in a low tone. He knew how excited Venn could get.

Venn put her hand on her hip and leaned on one leg. "When, Thomas? When?"

"Ma, um goin' marry her soon. I just need some time. You know I only got a part-time job. . . ."

Kerrissy was now sitting upstairs on Thomas's bed, listening to the argument that was about her. She held her stomach and rocked. Although Kerrissy was three months pregnant, she hadn't given her mother Gweneth a thought. She didn't care about having her mother's blessings. She was in her own little world. Thomas was acting loving and attentive. And, best of all, no one was looking for her.

Thomas tried to hug his mother. "Ma, come here—"

Venn stepped back and slapped his hands. "Boy— you know better. Now I don't care what you got. You told me that you were gonna marry that girl. Now do like you say."

Kerrissy heard Thomas walking up the stairs. She quickly lay down, turned her back to the door, and pretended to be asleep. She wanted to see if Thomas was actually going to make a wedding date because of his mother's request.

Thomas eased down on the bed and gently shook Kerrissy. "Baby, baby, please. Wake up. We need to talk."

Kerrissy turned over, wiped her eyes, and pretended to yawn. She waited for Thomas to speak.

Thomas stood up. "It's about time we did it."

Kerrissy looked confused. "Did what?"

Thomas cleared his throat. "Got married. So we goin' to go get our blood tests tomorrow."

Kerrissy wanted to smile. She lowered her head. "Okay. What time?"

"Three o'clock. Jasper will let us use his car when he get home from work."

"Okay. I'll be ready."

Thomas went back downstairs and told his mother his plans. Venn was emotionless. She knew her son. She knew that if she showed any concern, he might change his mind. She knew that Thomas really felt love for Kerrissy, but she also knew that he didn't do much of anything that he didn't have to.

Venn smiled over Thomas's shoulder as he hugged her.

Chapter 16

Thomas walked out into the late-night autumn air. This was the first time in months he'd been on his own front lawn casually. The weather had been exceptionally mild for the area, but Thomas had been keeping his prize a secret. He'd paid Jasper's son, Jasper Jr., age ten, to cut the lawn. Lena had kept watch, but had been very disappointed each time she saw Jasper Jr. cutting the lawn instead of Thomas.

Thomas took a quick look at Lena's house. She was there, in her window, slyly watching him. She was happy to see Thomas, until she saw Kerrissy come waddling out behind him. She looked to be about five months pregnant. Lena's hand flew to her breast, her mouth fell open. Her heart was palpitating so fast, she could barely breathe. Lena thought the top of her head would pop off. She stared intently, making sure that she was seeing correctly. Kerrissy's Afro, the new look young colored people sported, was so long, it hung over her shoulders. Kerrissy was even more beautiful, but Lena had instantly recognized her. *That* was her granddaughter, and Lena was more than jealous. She was filled with rage and hatred. It flowed through her like a hot stream, but she wouldn't move away from her perch.

Thomas knew that she'd be nosey enough to watch, and that's exactly what he wanted. He'd thought over and over again about what she'd said about him and Kerrissy being together, and what it would do to her. He wanted Lena to die, he wanted to be the cause of it, and he wanted to watch it slowly happen. He took Kerrissy's hand and led her to the side of the shed. Lena's heart was still racing from her jealous anger. This was why she hadn't seen Thomas in so long. He was just after her granddaughter's phone number, like she'd argued. Because of her anger at Gweneth, Lena hadn't noticed Kerrissy living nearby. She hadn't spoken to or called her daughter, so she didn't even know that Kerrissy was missing. No police had called saying her granddaughter was missing and neither had any private eye come nosing around, so how was she to know? Lena's eyes slanted as she watched Thomas remove his jacket and put it on the ground for Kerrissy to sit on. Without an exchange of words, he helped her to sit, lie down, then began to massage her stomach. He pulled up her dress and began kissing her stomach. As usual, Kerrissy allowed Thomas to control her. She'd learned way back that Thomas had to be in control or he wasn't happy. Being discontent meant that he wasn't loving her enough and she hated going through that.

Lena snatched her curtain shut. Thomas snickered through his nostrils. He continuously glanced up at

Lena's window. He knew that she'd be too concerned
not to spy some more. She spied on everyone.

Lena rubbed her hands together and paced the
floor. She walked back and forth, then back over to
the window to see if Thomas was still there. She
knew that he did things—ugly things—to get to her.

As soon as Thomas saw Lena return, he quickly
lay down next to Kerrissy and began to kiss her passionately.

Lena gasped at the sight and threw her hand
over her mouth. She knew Thomas' Svengali effect
on women—that Kerrissy probably did whatever it
took to keep them happy. Even if the sex was con-
sensual, Kerrissy would have to endure Thomas's
eventful discontent.

Thomas took one last glance at Lena, then continued to kiss Kerrissy as he pulled her on top of him
for emphasis. Lena would see some of the lust she'd
missed the last time she'd seen him and Kerrissy
together. He wanted to give Lena a memory that
she'd take to her grave. He had been wishing—
and hoping—that Kerrissy's mother had called to let
her know that her granddaughter was missing. He
wanted Lena to suffer the way his mother suffered
for so many years because she couldn't see her twin
sister out in the open. He wanted her to suffer the
way he would whenever he thought about or saw his
mother's and aunt's grief.

His nostrils flared. No one really knew the whole
story. No one knew what Lena had done to his aunt.
Why his aunt was too afraid to be seen on Hussey
Place. Why his aunt didn't want to be seen with her

husband there. Why his aunt always had to sneak into town. No one knew—but him and Lena. But what Lena didn't know was that maybe, just maybe, her husband would still be with her or would have stayed with her a little longer until his eyes roved again—possibly in another direction, maybe away from the secluded loop. If he had fallen for someone outside of the circle, that would have eased some of her shame and pain.

Her little scheme had actually backfired and pushed Chell into the arms of her husband, a man more than twice her senior, and she'd run off with him because she'd felt worthless. He'd heard his aunt talking to his mother and telling her that no other man would have wanted her, but he hadn't heard why. Now that Thomas knew all the details, Lena would pay, and she'd pay big. How did she like watching the man she loved with her hidden granddaughter? How did she like being a part of a dirty threesome? She'd thought that it was over, but as far as Thomas was concerned, her troubles had just begun.

As Lena cried and watched, she realized how much she loved her granddaughter. Lena gently closed her curtain, sat back in her chair, and bawled.

Thomas slyly watched to see if Lena would open her curtain again. If she did, she was going to see exactly how her granddaughter had gotten her big belly. Lena never returned to the window.

Thomas straightened Kerrissy's clothes up on her,

like a father would his child, and helped her up off the ground. He put his arm around her shoulders. She wrapped an arm around his waist as they both walked toward the house and went inside. Kerrissy had gotten pregnant in June, as soon as she'd returned to Hussey Place. Kerrissy was five months pregnant. Her stomach protruded. Thomas knew Lena could see it from her window.

Kerrissy was still on cloud nine and clueless—Thomas loved her enough to display his affection for her in the beautiful autumn air. He made their love feel immortal. No one had ever shown her so much love or given her so much attention, and Kerrissy believed that no one else ever would.

Chapter 17

Sable Mae Tutor sat on the bench closest to the fence and the courts in the Bronson Street Playground and watched a group of boys play basketball. Thomas and Jasper were among them. Sable Mae liked eighteen-year-old Wesley Eastwell. Although she was exceptionally pretty, and would be seventeen in a few days, he'd never given her as much as a glance. She watched as Wesley's slim body leaped in the air and slammed the ball into the basket. This made her heart flutter more rapidly for Wesley. All the other guys were much older than him—they could play him like a juvenile if they wanted to, but he would keep them in check with his game. His aim was to be a professional athlete, and they were good practice dummies.

Sable stood up and paced along the fence to be seen. She turned a few heads, but Wesley's wasn't one of them. She leaned her back against the fence, placed her fingers through the links, and put her foot up so that her breasts would stand out. This made the players check her out more often, but the game proceeded. Wesley still hadn't looked her way.

Jasper had to go. It was six o'clock and his wife would have dinner waiting for him. She'd be upset if he was late. Thomas decided he'd quit, too. Everyone else stayed to play ball. Sable looked on intensely, waiting for Wesley to finish so that she could talk to him. If she had to make the first move, she just had to.

Thomas and Jasper walked toward the gate. Jasper looked over at Sable. He smiled, licked his lips, then nudged Thomas in the side. "How would you like to have one of them?"

Thomas grabbed his side and frowned. "One of what, man?"

Jasper nodded at Sable swinging back and forth, still trying to get Wesley's attention.

Thomas squinted. His heart jumped, he quickly became erect as he watched Sable swing on the fence. He'd seen that girl many times, but the last time he'd seen her, she didn't look like that.

Jasper tapped him lightly upside the head. "Man. You know that girl too young for either one of us."

"Man, I know that. She just look like somebody I know."

Jasper gave Thomas a questionable look. "You know that kid?"

"Yeah, Jasper, yeah. As a matter of fact, I do. I don't know her name, but I remember her being in the same grade as my little cousin Juniper Lee."

"Damn, Thomas. Somethin' like that can get a man in a lot of trouble."

Thomas continued to stare at Sable. She was

dark-skinned and looked like a young version of Lena—only her waist was small, she had firm, large breasts, and a behind that should have been on a twenty-one-year-old. Now this was what Lena must have actually looked like back in the day.

Thomas walked with Jasper to Jasper's car. Thomas sat in the car with Jasper and talked until he felt his condition ease up, then told him he had to get home. Getting out, he waited until Jasper pulled away, then walked up behind Sable, who was still swinging on the fence, trying to get Wesley's attention. "Boo!"

Sable squealed and turned around. "Don't do that!"

"I scare you?"

Sable smiled. "No."

"Yes, I did."

"What ever you say." Sable turned her back to Thomas again.

Thomas shook the fence. "Girl, you don't know me?"

Sable turned around and looked at him. "Am I supposed to?"

"Girl, I been watchin' you since you was about five or six, and you ain't never noticed me in the neighborhood before?"

"Yeah. I done seen you."

"Then why you tryin' to play like you don't know me?"

Sable glanced over at Wesley. "I don't know." Sable was beginning to get irritated.

"Um bothering you?"

Sable took a deep breath and let it out. "No."

"Then why you act like you don't wanna talk to me?"

"'Cause . . . you don't even know my name—"

Thomas cut her off. "Most people don't know each other by name when they first meet. . . . My name, Thomas—"

"I know your name."

"Then what's yours?"

"Sable . . ."

"Sable? What, you ain't got no last name?" Thomas tried to sound younger.

Sable huffed. "My name Sable Mae Tutor."

Thomas smiled as he spoke silently in his head. *Your name might be Sable Mae Tutor, but um gonna be doin' the teachin' if I get the slightest chance.*

Sable turned around, hoping that Thomas would leave her to her mission.

Thomas whispered in her ear, "You got a boyfriend?"

Sable kept her back to him. "No, not yet."

"Can I be your man?"

"I heard that you married."

Thomas was shocked. Now, how did that get out? Had his mother been running off at the mouth again? *Probably.* He knew then and there he'd lie about his age—he'd say he was only nineteen, instead of twenty-four.

Thomas stood up straight. "You ever seen me with anybody?"

"No."

"Then why you think um married?"

"I be hearin' people talk."

"Well, you hearin' wrong. Why would a nineteen-year-old boy like me want to be married? You ready to be married?"

"Naw. But um still sixteen. I don't know what um

gonna feel like when I turn nineteen. I might wanna get married then."

Thomas suddenly felt old. He was still young. *Wasn't he?* "So you don't wanna be my girl?"

"I don't even know you!"

"We just introduced ourselves—Oh, wait a minute. You lookin' at Wesley, huh?"

Sable snickered. "Yeah."

"Okay, but you wasting your time." Thomas turned to leave.

Sable turned her back to the court. She securely locked her fingers through the holes in the fence. "What you mean?"

"I mean he already spoken for."

"I ain't never seen him with a girl."

"That's because she don't live on this side of town, and you must go to a different school than him, Sable."

Sable was no longer smiling. "I do."

Thomas had gotten lucky. "Well, I don't. He be with this tall, light-skinned chick all the time. When he ain't playing ball, that's where he be. You know he plannin' to play pro-ball, right?"

Sable sadly nodded in agreement.

"Why you so sad about him? There's more than one man in the world. Why don't y'all girls just like who like y'all?"

Sable was almost in tears. She'd felt so much in love with Wesley that she'd thought about losing her virginity to him as soon as she could.

Thomas touched her chin through the fence. "You don't have to be sad about him. Meet me at the gate. I'll walk you home so we can talk."

Sable slowly headed toward the gate, feeling

like the whole world had come crashing down around her.

Thomas took her hand. "Don't worry about him. As good as you look, if he didn't notice you by now, something wrong with him, anyway."

Sable wouldn't allow Thomas to walk her all the way home. Her parents hadn't allowed her to date. She wouldn't get their permission for another year.

She and Thomas sat quietly on the rail in the empty parking lot at the corner behind the vacant church, where Sable played quite often with her cousins, baby sister, and flirted with boys. Before breaking the silence, Thomas looked around at all the big trees with large branches that practically hung to the ground. "You okay, Sable?"

"Yeah."

"Then um gonna git home. I know my mother looking for me." Thomas could see that Sable was still sad. He took her hand, urging her to stand with him. He looked her up and down. "Um sure gonna miss you . . . damn you fine!"

Sable began to grin and couldn't stop. She knew that she wasn't a picture-perfect petite—at five-four, 135 pounds—but she knew she had it going on, and loved to be complimented on her figure.

When Thomas realized that his words piqued her interest, the compliments kept coming. "Girl, if you was mine, couldn't nobody get close to you without a fight. Wish I was Wesley. He a fool. He don't know what he missin' out on. Not many females fine as you around here. Shoot. A brother almost got to get him one of these old women to get close to anything look as good as you." Thomas raised his voice. "Wesley gots tuh be crazy!" Thomas felt himself becoming excited again.

Feeling in control, and trying to impress Thomas further, Sable put her hand on the back of his head, pulled him to her, and kissed him.

Thomas grinned at the innocent kiss, then took over, holding Sable's head as he parted her lips with his tongue and took hers into his mouth. Sable tried to push away. Thomas held her a few seconds before allowing her to do so.

Sable wiped her lips. "Why you do that?"

"'Cause . . . I'm in love with you. You didn't like it?"

Sable wouldn't answer.

Thomas took her hand. "Can I kiss you like that again?"

Sable wouldn't answer. She just waited.

Thomas kissed her forehead. "I'll watch you until you get to your house and wait until your birthday to give you another *real* kiss." Thomas opened his hand slowly, allowing Sable's to slip away from his.

With hesitation she began to walk home. She looked back at Thomas. Thomas pretended to look sad until she was out of sight, then smiled at the thought of being with a teenage Lena.

Thomas walked in the house. He tiptoed up behind his mother and kissed her on the neck.

Venn fanned him away. "Boy, don't you see me trying to fry these pork chops? You trying to put us both in the hospital?"

"Sorry, Ma."

Kerrissy could hear the friendly bantering downstairs. She grinned from ear to ear; she was so happy to have her husband back home.

Venn turned around. "Boy, you musty. What you been doing? Wrestling a bear?"

"Just about. I was tryin' to beat Wesley at ball. That boy gonna make it, too."

"Yeah, well. You need to go make a bath and take it!"

"That's where um headed right now . . . and um hungry, too. So I hope you cooked enough to feed some bears."

Venn smiled and shook her head as she turned the pork chops.

Thomas headed upstairs. He peeped in at Kerrissy. "Hey, baby. Be in when um done bathin'. Okay?"

Kerrissy smiled and nodded her head.

Thomas stepped into the room with a towel wrapped around his waist, drying his hair with another. "Baby, Mama cookin' her famous pork chops again." He walked over to Kerrissy, sat on the bed, and began to kiss her as they reclined. He lifted his head. "But you gotta love me first, or you ain't goin' git none."

Kerrissy was happy to see Thomas in such a great mood. He always made her feel extra special whenever he was. As he gently massaged her stomach, she knew that tonight would be no different.

Chapter 18

Sable sat on the bench. This time she looked around for Thomas. When she saw him come out of the alley, she perked up even more.

Thomas saw the smile on Sable's face. He kept his hands in his pockets and his head lowered as he walked toward her so that she wouldn't see the smug look and pre-victory grin on his face as he thought about what he was getting away with so close to home.

Thomas stood by the fence directly in back of Sable. He didn't want the other guys to see him talking to her—some of them knew his secret. He leaned sideways on the fence. "You want me to walk you home?"

Sable's grin got broader. She jumped up. "Yeah. Last time we had a good talk."

Sable wasn't really interested in talking. She wanted Thomas to kiss her again. He'd quickly turned her head with the short, strange kiss they'd shared just the night before.

* * *

It was hard for Thomas not to shake his head and display his usual sneaky grin. Another one had fallen so quickly. Lena had been an excellent teacher. Even if Sable would only be his second conquest since Sable, he knew that he could now get any young girl he wanted. This time he would be the aggressor. He felt invincible.

Sable ran around the fence, grabbed Thomas's hand, and began to swing it as they walked. Thomas allowed her to do so as they walked slowly toward her house. Again they sat in the parking lot and talked until dark. Thomas pulled Sable up from the railing. He wouldn't kiss her again, but his brain was racing a mile a minute. He pecked her cheek. "You still want Wesley?"

Sable didn't want to answer, but she did . . . slowly. "Not really."

Thomas playfully dropped to one knee. He looked up at her with his praying hands. "Please, Sable, please. Say that you don't love him no more. What about us?" Thomas wrapped his arms around her legs.

Sable laughed. "I gotta go, Thomas. You know um supposed to be home when it get dark."

"Just answer my questions, Sable."

"Thomas, I don't know yet."

Thomas pulled her closer, placed his face in her pelvic area, and allowed her to feel his breath through her clothing. Sable's knees became weak.

Thomas looked up at her. "Me"—Thomas kissed her through her clothing—"or him?"

Sable removed his arms from around her legs. "I—I—I—I—I'll tell you tomorrow." Sable hugged herself and tried to calm her breathing, but there was no way for her to hide her nervousness.

Thomas rose. Sable backed away from him and walked away on shaky legs. She slowly turned her head to see if Thomas was watching her. He was gone.

Thomas slid into bed with his wife. Sable had him so wound up that he didn't bother waking Kerrissy. He eased his way into Kerrissy while she slept; he moved slowly so that he wouldn't wake her. He wanted to fantasize about Sable and Lena. A conscious Kerrissy would take that away from him. A conscious one could argue and destroy his illusion. Thomas wanted it to last as long as possible.

Chapter 19

Kerrissy thought her water had broken. She hurried downstairs to phone Thomas at the plant. She waited impatiently while his boss called him to the phone. As soon as she heard Thomas's voice on the telephone, tears came to her eyes. "Thomas! I think the baby coming!"

Thomas's voice shook. "You having cramps? You hurtin'?"

"No. I think my water broke!"

Thomas turned red. He looked around the factory to see if anyone else could see his guilt. He was alone. He cleared his throat. "Oh, that. I saw that on you this morning. That ain't your water. That just happened 'cause you so far along. It happens to a lot of pregnant women. Mama told me that."

Kerrissy took a deep breath. "You sure, Thomas?"

"Yeah, baby. Don't you know that if I thought anything was wrong with you, I'd be home in a flash?"

Kerrissy whined. "Yeah . . ."

"Then stop worrying so much and trust me, okay?"

"Okay, Thomas."

"Did you eat the breakfast I left on the tray for you next to the bed?"

"No. I got too scared when I saw what had happened."

"Then hang up the phone and go on back upstairs and have your breakfast, Kerrissy. I'll be home in a few hours. Me and you gonna go out. We gonna spend some time together. Okay?"

Kerrissy dropped her head and smiled. "Okay."

Thomas kissed her through the phone, then hung up.

Kerrissy slowly waddled back up to the room. She couldn't wait for Thomas to take her out. She ate her breakfast and smiled as she imagined their time together.

Chapter 20

Thomas had been with Kerrissy for two days, taking her places and treating her extra nice. She was getting closer to six months now and it was late fall. Friday night he told her he wanted some time to himself. He and Jasper wanted to go out, and that if he got too drunk, he'd probably be spending the night at Jasper's. Kerrissy agreed that he should have some time to himself.

Thomas put on his dark blue knit shirt, navy blue pants, and white sneakers to look a bit juvenile. Although the weather was still somewhat warm, he threw on his fall jacket to protect himself from the night chill and headed for his destination. He had purposely left home later than usual to see if Sable would wait for him. He also knew that he had to work fast. He'd deliberately made Sable wait more than two and a half days after teasing her, and now that her birthday had passed, they could get to know each other better. He stepped outside. Earlier, he'd stashed his cologne and gin bottle in his jacket pocket. Once he hit the yard, he splashed on the expensive cologne he'd bought for this special occasion. He didn't want Kerrissy becoming suspicious if she smelled it, and Venn was home, too. Her mouth spun fiery yarns that only a mind like hers could develop, and could only be subdued with a fire extinguisher, to say the least. He took a drink from his gin bottle to kill his conscience, then another, as he walked toward his mark. He slipped the gin bottle back into the inside pocket of his coat and wiped his mouth.

As he reached the sidewalk across the street from the playground, Thomas could see Sable twisting around on the bench, looking for him. This was a good sign. She'd forgotten about Wesley, and her mind was on him.

Thomas approached the fence just as Sable had turned her back to him. He leaned over. "Where you been, girl?"

Sable quickly turned her head. "What you mean, where I been? I been right here!"

"Here watching Wesley, Sable?"

"No! I been comin' here—"

"Meet me at the gate." Thomas stood up straight.

Sable walked so fast to meet Thomas, she was almost running.

Thomas was surprised to see that Sable looked even sexier than before. She was wearing a beige mohair sweater, what he thought was a dark brown skirt, and beige suede boots. This stopped his smile on his face. He took Sable's hand, shook his head, stepped back, and took a good look at her. "You sho do look good, girl!"

Sable jerked her neck. She thought she smelled alcohol, then got a whiff of Thomas's cologne. She tugged on his hand, urging him along.

Sable tried to walk fast. Thomas had shown up later than usual, and it would be getting dark soon.

Thomas jerked her hand. "Where's the fire, Sable?"

Sable reluctantly slowed down.

Thomas tightened his hand around hers and walked with his head up high, like he owned her. He was anxious, but he wasn't going to reveal himself to Sable. Kerrissy was big, and Sable had to be controlled for his purposes only. There wouldn't be any love involved, at least not on his end. He would slowly leave her alone once his baby arrived and his wife was okay.

He let go of Sable's hand, walked into the parking lot, and sat on the rail. Sable followed. Thomas looked at her. "How old do you think a person should be before they got married?"

Sable grinned and put her head down. "Twenty?"

Thomas smiled. "You askin' me or tellin' me?"

"I'on know. I thought twenty was a good age."

Thomas knew that most girls Sable's age thought twenty was old. He took her hand. "You wouldn't marry me if I asked you to? You'd make me wait three more years for you?"

Sable hunched her shoulders.

Thomas stood up.

Sable became nervous. "You leaving already?"

Thomas looked at her. "Naw. I'm waitin' for my

good-night kiss. I know you got to be home in a few minutes."

Sable stood. Thomas took her hand and led her to the corner of the railing behind the large branches he'd checked out during their first meeting.

Sable giggled. "Where we goin'?"

"Just over here."

As soon as they were behind the trees, Thomas leaned her against the building and kissed her the way he knew she wanted. He wanted to touch her breasts, but he figured that might turn her off before he could really turn her out. Instead, he slid down and let her feel his warm breath again. He ran his hands up and down the sides of her smooth thighs. He tried to put one of his hands under the front of her skirt and discovered that it was really some sort of pleated shorts with wide legs. Thomas pulled one leg open and touched Sable's underwear.

Sable became nervous. This wasn't part of the routine.

Thomas slowly let Sable slip away, then looked up at her to see her reaction.

Sable kept her eyes closed and breathed intensely as she leaned against the building, trembling, trying to support herself with her upper arms and elbows, then suddenly burst into tears.

Thomas stood up, pulled her away from the wall, and held her in his arms. "Sh-sh-sh. Why you crying?"

Sable was trembling and crying so hard, she couldn't answer. Thomas continued to comfort her. "Now, come on. I can't let you go home like this. Um sorry, okay?"

Sable nodded. A few minutes later she'd contained herself. Thomas walked her as close to home as he could, kissed her good night, and headed home.

Fooling around with Sable had given him the feeling that he thought it would. He'd hoped he could relax shortly after so that he could go home, but he was unable to. For backup he had told Kerrissy he would be spending the night with Jasper. He knew that Kerrissy and his mother would be up waiting for him if he went home now, and they'd know that something was wrong. Thomas had to use his alternate plan.

Chapter 21

Thomas quietly twisted the knob to the back door and tiptoed inside. He didn't stop until he got to the bedroom. He rubbed his eyes. Someone had taken his place. He began to back away until he realized who it was. Thomas squinted. "Jasper?"

Jasper's head sprang up. His eyes widened when he saw his best friend standing in the doorway, actually watching him put on the show he'd only illustrated for him.

Jasper stood up, his voice trembled. "T-Thomas? What you doing here, man?"

"That's what I come to ask you. Saw your car outside, thought it was a mistake." Thomas folded his arms. "Thought it was a big, fat mistake."

Jasper closed the bedroom door behind him and walked over to Thomas. He put his hand on his shoulder. "Listen, man. This ain't nothin'. Just a little somethin' to celebrate muh birthday—"

Thomas could tell that Jasper was high. He pushed his hand away. "This was what you was talkin' about? You'd do this to your wife, man?"

"Come on, Thomas, man. She ain't bad. Shoot, Lena pretty and a good cook. She just need to fix herself up more often, like she be doin' for me—"

"You mean it's been more than once?"

Jasper looked at the floor. He was speechless.

Thomas shook his head from side to side. "You need to get yourself together, man."

Jasper looked up. "What about her?"

"You just think about your wife. I'll take care of her."

Jasper went back into the room. He tried to finish. Thomas could hear the female voice saying, "No, no. Just go ahead. I don't want you to get into any trouble."

Jasper came back out with his shoes in his hands and his T-shirt on backward. Thomas talked to him as he dressed, then sent him on his way.

Thomas went back into the bedroom and slammed the door behind him so hard that the house shook. "What the hell you tryin' to prove, Lena?"

"Thomas, go on now. I don't want to fight with you."

"What make you think you have a choice, Lena?"

Lena moved closer to the headboard. "Thomas, you know you got my granddaughter—"

"What the hell that's supposed to change! You ain't never made no commitment like that to me—oh, so you trying to be smart! You trying to say that you messed with my friend because of me and Kerrissy!"

Lena put up the flat of her hands. "Thomas, um not going to mess with you no more. It's over."

"Lena, as close as we been, how can you say that?"

Lena wrapped the sheet around her lower body as tight as she could get it and tried sliding off the bed.

Thomas ran and stepped in front of her. "Where you goin'?"

"To talk to Jasper, Thomas. Now, will you please leave my house?"

"Lena, Jasper gone."

Lena rolled her eyes at Thomas.

Thomas grabbed her hand. "Come on, if you don't believe me."

When they entered the kitchen, Lena yelled out to Jasper. When he didn't answer, Lena gave Thomas a dirty look. "What you tell him, Thomas?"

"That he had a wife he needed to be with—"

"And you got my granddaughter!" Lena became furious.

Thomas remained cool. "Um gonna keep her, too. But you ain't gonna mess with Jasper no more. You know why? 'Cause if you do, he gonna know everything about us. Um gonna tell him everything."

Lena wanted to charge at Thomas like a bull, but she could only stand staring at him evilly, with the sheet wrapped around her.

Thomas sat down at her kitchen table and summoned her. Lena thought about running back into the bedroom and locking the door, but she knew he'd kick the door in. He liked being with her after their fights, and she didn't have the strength to fight with Thomas after being with Jasper. Jasper enjoyed what he was doing with Lena when Thomas walked in, and she didn't have to pay him back. Sex was good enough for Jasper, and it didn't have to be the kinky kind that Thomas loved. Lena stood in a daze, thinking.

Thomas slammed his fist on the table. *"Um callin' you, Lena!"*

Lena jumped and trotted over to Thomas.

Thomas was ready. He thought that he was going to explode any minute, especially after witnessing Lena and Jasper together.

Thomas pulled Lena to the floor.

Lena knew that Thomas meant business.

Thomas sat back in the chair, pleased. He looked down at Lena. "You let him have you?"

Lena shook her head from side to side, then stood up.

Thomas pulled her back down on his lap. "Watchoo think you doin', Lena?"

Lena squirmed from the pain of the gin bottle, which Thomas had concealed under his coat, hitting her in the back. "I thought we was done, Thomas."

"When we ever got finished this quick, huh?"

Lena sat with her hands in her lap.

"I wanna go again," Thomas whispered in her ear.

Chapter 22

"Thomas, how in the world did you get dirt and grass stains on these pants? It ain't even summer! Was you playin' ball in your good stuff?"

Thomas was already angry with Jasper and Lena. Kerrissy's question irritated him further, but he couldn't show it. He sat up on the bed. He really couldn't believe how Kerrissy was so nosey. How could she know that he had been making out behind the trees with Sable? To throw her off the scent, he said, "Come here, Kerrissy."

Kerrissy walked over to Thomas and stood in front of him. Thomas began to rub her stomach. He looked up into her eyes. "Why you asking me about those pants?"

Kerrissy became nervous. "I was just kidding—"

"No, you weren't. You think I don't love you, Kerrissy? I do."

"I don't think that, Thom—"

Thomas put his hand behind Kerrissy and pulled her toward him. "I don't believe you."

Kerrissy wanted to fight him off. Didn't he realize

that she was too far along for this, for his special love treatment—his overzealous oral inquisitions? Kerrissy closed her eyes as Thomas helped her to slowly recline onto the bed.

Thomas released Kerrissy. She trembled, then turned on her side. Thomas gently massaged her stomach. "I don't ever want you to think that I don't love you, Kerrissy. That I'd cheat on you."

Kerrissy remained quiet and tried to breathe normally. Thomas lay silent, flexing his jaw as he thought, *Maybe that will keep her quiet, confused, and from questioning me.*

Chapter 23

Thomas looked for Sable on Monday. He couldn't find her in her regular place, and that infuriated him. He took a sip of the courage that he now carried around with him regularly. No woman stood him up, and Sable wouldn't be any different. His long-term relationship with Lena and his six-month experience of living with his wife, Kerrissy, had made him used to having his way. He controlled women, mentally, physically, and sexually. He assumed that Sable knew this was something she should do automatically because he already felt he was in control of her body and mind.

He walked past Sable's house and stood next to the house on the corner, watching for her. He ducked beside it when he saw her front door open, then peeped around the strangers' house. An older man with a woman, who looked like Sable, walked out onto the front porch. They had to be her parents. The woman turned toward the door. "You be good for Mommy and Daddy till we get back, Sable, and watch your sister! We'll bring you your favorite Chinese food! We won't be gone but two hours!"

He could hear voices. "Y'all eatin' there?"

A woman answered, "Yeah. You know we haven't been out in a while, baby. You afraid to stay home alone?"

Sable hesitated. "No."

Her mother took a deep breath. "Then what's wrong? You've never wanted us home before."

Sable giggled. "I ain't trying to make y'all stay home. Um just askin', that's all."

Thomas leaned against the structure, drinking his old courage, and smoking his menthol. He was thinking of his next move, allowing the alcohol and nicotine to flow through him and the conversation to fade. Both highs caused his heart to race extra fast with anticipation for Sable as he watched the couple pull out of the driveway in the brand-new Cadillac. He wanted to see Sable. He had to see her. It was dark enough. No one would see him now. He put his hands in his pockets and walked up to Sable's house. He started to keep moving but couldn't. He slowly walked up the steps and rang the bell. He could hear Sable talking as she approached the door. "What y'all forget?" She flung the door open and screamed. Thomas held the door open with his right hand as he gazed down at Sable wearing only her nightshirt. He licked his lips at the shapely sight of her breasts, the tips of them protruding through her clothing—the firm bounce they did. He quickly stepped inside. Sable began to tremble from the wicked and demeaning look in his eyes. She tried to shield with her arms what she thought he could see.

"You gotta go, Thomas! You can't stay here! My

parents gonna see you here! I'll get a beatin' if they do—"

Thomas grabbed her around the waist and kissed her as he closed the door. He lifted his head. "I ain't gonna be that long, baby." He slowly walked Sable backward as he held on to her. He slid his hand under her shirt. She had nothing on underneath. Thomas smiled. He let his hand travel as he spoke. "Why you ain't been at the playground, Sable?" His voice was deep, low, and lecherous.

Sable grabbed his hand. "Please, Thomas, you gotta go—"

Thomas's breathing became heavier as he thought of Lena and put her in Sable's place. He quickly looped his arm through Sable's legs and lifted her up, forcing her to grab ahold of his head with both arms as he quickly carried her over to the sofa. He gently lay her down and swiftly made his move before Sable could rise.

Sable screamed.

Thomas whispered, "Did you miss me, Sable? Did you miss me?"

Sable wouldn't answer.

Thomas jerked her closer. "Tell me that you missed me, or I'll stop, Sable. And you know that you don't want me to."

"I missed you, Thomas. I missed you," Sable whined through her sobs.

Thomas continued to talk into her body. "You gonna meet me like you suppose to?"

"Um gonna meet you," she agreed.

"If you don't, there ain't nobody else who gonna make you feel like this, and if you don't, you might not even have *me*. I can't keep on loving you, if you ain't gonna love me back."

Sable held on to Thomas as she squealed, cried, and tried to breathe, allowing Thomas to dominate and addict her body even more.

Thomas stood up. "Wear something just for me tomorrow, Sable."

Sable lay on the sofa, nodding her head.

Thomas walked to the door and put his hand on the knob. "Be there for me, or I won't come looking for you again." Thomas continued out the door.

Sable burst into tears. The dampness on her shirt and thighs made her feel dirty. She could smell Thomas on her, and it made her remember too well what she couldn't resist. She slowly straightened out her leg, pulled her shirt down, then lay on the sofa for a while before going to take another bath. Maybe water would remove what she was feeling. It had done so before, at least temporarily— the last time Thomas had been with her.

Thomas walked inside his house, smiling and feeling victorious. He'd gotten to Sable. She was hooked.

After bathing, he slid in bed with his wife and put his arm around her, feeling his first-to-be-born as it moved around. Kerrissy could feel him against her. She waited for him to travel farther. Thomas was suddenly snoring.

Chapter 24

Thomas quickly finished his dinner and made his excuses to leave the house. Kerrissy was so disappointed she yelled at him, hoping that he'd at least prove to her that he still loved her. He hadn't. He'd continued out the bedroom door like a dazed man, and hadn't as much as looked back at her, and practically ran down the alley once his feet were off the porch. He drank his courage as he approached the playground, his eyes fixed toward his destination. She was there. Waiting as promised, and wearing what he'd asked, *something just for him*.

Sable sat in her usual place without looking around for Thomas. She wasn't as happy as before. The game had gotten a little too serious, making her feel old for her age. She wanted to get out of it, but she didn't know how. Thinking about the feelings made her want Thomas; his giving them to her made her believe that she wouldn't need them again—that each time would be the last. Sable couldn't understand this addiction. She was confused on how it all had gotten started so quickly. She had been in love with Wesley.

Thomas approached the fence. "You ready to go?"

Sable stood up and went to him.

Thomas took her hand. "You mad at me?"

Sable's eyes watered. She shook her head.

"Then why you crying, Sable? You don't want me to bother you no more?"

Sable hunched her shoulders.

"Look, Sable. We don't have to do this at all, if you don't want. Why did you show up if you don't want me? I told you that I could just leave you alone. I told you the truth. Look, why don't I just go on back home." Thomas walked off.

Sable stood still, embarrassed.

Thomas walked back over to her. "Come on, girl. Let me just take you on home."

Thomas stopped at the parking lot again.

Sable's heart pounded heavily.

Thomas sat down on the rail.

Sable sat next to him.

Thomas could see the tears in her eyes and took her chin in his hand. "Sable, I love you so much. You gotta know that. I love you enough to leave you alone, if you want me to."

Sable wiped the tears from her eyes. Her voice trembled. "I just don't feel right."

"Then why you here, Sable?"

"'Cause . . . I just wanna be with you sometime, Thomas."

"You don't like the way your man make you feel?"

Sable couldn't deny the addiction. She lowered her head. "Yes."

"Then why you trippin', Sable?"

"I'on know."

"Look, Sable. Me and you got a real good thing going on. You want us to lose that? You wanna break up with me?"

Sable shook her head.

Thomas cleared his throat. "Then you gonna have to grow up and act like you suppose to. You just had your seventeenth birthday. You're almost grown." Thomas stood up and took Sable's hand. "Come on." He led her to the rear of the abandoned building. He took off his jacket and placed it on the ground. Sable sat without being coaxed. Thomas sat down beside her and began kissing her. She could taste the gin on his tongue, but she'd always loved the way it mixed with his cologne. Just the scent of him had aroused her on their second meeting. It had become familiar, made her feel safe—too safe. Safe enough that the thought of letting him be the first had crossed her mind. She'd tried to get away, break it off. But the day he forced his way into her parents' house, Thomas had recaptured the small piece of her heart that had almost forgotten about him.

Thomas lay back, pulled Sable on top of him, wrapped his arm around her waist, and began unbuttoning her blouse with his free hand. Sable grabbed his hand again. Thomas sat up, causing Sable to have to open her legs and straddle him. Her knees touched the ground; her hands landed flat against his chest.

Thomas looked into her eyes. "What's wrong . . . now?"

"Why you gotta do that?"

"I thought you was my woman, Sable."

"I am, but—"

Thomas snatched her bra up and lowered his head to her, touching the caps of her breasts with his teeth and tongue. Sable could feel the current-like feelings flowing through her body and couldn't stop him.

Thomas reclined, pulling Sable along with him, while removing her underwear with one hand. He slipped his hands under her thighs and hoisted her upward. This was the night he'd make her more in love with him than ever. She'd never hide from him again—even if she was told to do so by her parents.

Chapter 25

Kerrissy lay on the bed, feeling tired. They had gone to the hospital, but it was a false alarm. They were only a week or so into December, but God how she wanted the baby to come in her sixth month. Thomas was upset. He'd missed his time with Sable. As soon as he got Kerrissy settled in and off to sleep he walked down to Sable's house.

Thomas rang the bell. Sable's mother answered the door. Thomas stood back. "Good evening, ma'am. I met your daughter the other day. Me and my wife were asking her about babysitting for us. We live in the neighborhood. Do you think it would be okay for her to watch our niece? You see, we're raising my sister's child."

"How old is your niece, sir?"

"Oh, she's six, going on seven. It would only be on weekends when we go out. Me or my wife would make sure she got home in one piece."

Sable's mother smiled. "You know, it would be good for her to get a little job like that. But she'll have to talk to you about it—*Sable! Somebody's at the door for you!*" Sable's mother turned back to Thomas. "She'll be right down."

Sable quickly came to the door. When she saw Thomas, she almost fainted.

Sable's mother turned to her. "This man said that he was talking to you about babysitting. I told him you'd have to decide that."

Sable's mother walked away and went back into the kitchen.

Sable opened her mouth to speak. Thomas stepped up to her, slid his hands around her waist, and whispered as he looked into her eyes, "I missed you today. I had an emergency, but it won't happen tomorrow, baby."

Sable grabbed his wrists with her trembling hands and whispered, "Don't do that, Thomas."

Thomas wouldn't remove his hands.

Sable looked over her shoulder to see if her mother had returned.

Thomas looked at her. "Do you think I'd do this in front of your people and risk not seeing you again?"

"Thomas, please, just leave. I'll see you tomorrow."

"Okay, Sable, but don't try what you did before, or I won't be back."

"I'll be there, Thomas. I promise."

Thomas left the house.

Sable told her mother that she didn't want to babysit, that she didn't even like kids. She went back to her room.

Chapter 26

Thomas ended up at the hospital again with Kerrissy. The doctor concluded that her being tired of carrying the baby was her real labor pains.

Kerrissy was fuming. She was tired of carrying the baby and being fat. She was ready to hang out more with her husband. His uncle and aunt were visiting more often, and she was tired of the way Thomas's old crazy-looking uncle was looking at her. Thomas wasn't touching her much, and his uncle was looking at her like a plate of crisp, golden brown fried chicken—it made her feel dirty and emptier than the times Thomas was supposedly showing her how much he loved her. Now she wished for that—but Thomas had stated that the way he wanted her might harm their baby, if he lost his head and got started and forgot about her condition. Kerrissy had cried herself to sleep because of his comments; Thomas had comforted her, but he hadn't given in. The truth was, Thomas had stopped having sex with his wife altogether. He just wasn't attracted to her in her present condition and was saving himself for

Sable. He'd have to work extra hard now that he'd stood Sable up again after making a personal appearance at her house.

As he left for work, he looked at his naked pregnant wife as she slept and wondered again about her body. It was still beautiful—even her protruding stomach. But would it remain deformed *after* she had his child, like her grandmother's had after she'd had Kerrissy's mother? He'd seen pictures of Lena when she was younger, and she was shaped like Kerrissy. She was even prettier. Her face wasn't bad now—she actually looked good for her age, just older.

Kerrissy was still asleep when Thomas came home from work. He felt sad as he prepared to walk out the bedroom door and go look for Sable. He thought about how Kerrissy had cried herself to sleep again. How she'd wanted him, but he hadn't touched her in weeks. How he'd made up another story about her being too far along in her pregnancy and he hadn't given her any affection other than hugs, kisses, and a night of passion that only he knew about, instead of letting her in on his fantasy. He kissed her on the forehead. She stirred but didn't wake up. Thomas smiled as he continued out the door.

Thomas held his head down as he walked slowly and sadly down the alley, drank from his fresh bottle, and smoked his menthol. He was later than usual. Maybe Sable wouldn't be there. He felt so low, he almost turned around, until he saw Sable leaning on the fence. Wesley had his arm over her head, grasping the holes in the fence, and she was grinning like he'd never seen before. He was standing in back of Sable so quickly that he hadn't realized it, until he heard himself say her name. Sable had a frightened look on her face when she turned and saw how close Thomas was to her, plus the unpleasant look on his face.

Wesley let go of the fence and stepped away from her.

Sable played it off as she walked away from Wesley, talking to Thomas like he was an old friend from school, and nothing else.

Sable came around the fence and reached for Thomas's hand. He kept them both in his pockets. Sable tried to talk. Thomas wouldn't say a word. When they got near the parking lot, Thomas took her hand and led her to the back of the old abandoned building. He spun her around. "What the hell did you think you was provin'?"

Sable's brows wrinkled. Her mouth flew open. *"Um goin' home!"*

Thomas snatched her back. He put his hand around her throat. "Who you think you talkin' to like that, Sable?"

Tears formed in Sable's eyes as she held on to Thomas's hand.

Thomas shook her. "You think um gonna just let you walk all over me, don't you, Sable?"

Sable had began to plead. "No, no."

"Then how you goin' try tuh play me like that? That nigga did any of the stuff I done for you?"

Sable shook her head.

"Then you need to keep that nigga out your face!"

"But he was talking to me, Thomas—"

Thomas slapped her. *"Do you think I give a damn about that? Do you know what I'm givin' up for you? Do you know what'll happen to my reputation if people found out about how much I love you?"*

Sable held her face and cried. "Um sorry. It wasn't nothing."

"You call what I been doing for you nothin'?"

"I wasn't talking about that!"

Thomas slapped her again. "Don't talk to me that way!"

Sable held on to her face and put her head down.

"You know what, Sable? All that time I was trying to prove how much I love you—-then you go and make me do this to you! Didn't I love you enough?"

Sable nodded.

"Maybe I didn't, Sable. Maybe you need to know just how much I love you, how much you mean to me—and look at me when um talkin' to you!"

Sable lifted her head.

"And look at what you wearing!"

Sable looked down and gave herself the once-over.

Thomas led Sable to the rear wall of the structure and began tugging at her jeans. "These. Are. Not. Acceptable!"

Thomas finished loosening Sable's jeans and proceeded with his plan.

Sable was hysterical. Thomas had made it all happen so quickly. She couldn't understand why he was treating her the way he had. The only boy she had looked at up until she met Thomas was Wesley, and now . . . Thomas had forced her body to find new yearnings. Yearnings that she never knew existed.

Thomas pretended to console Sable as she cried. "I love you too much to see you talking to some old bum that ain't gonna do nothing but ruin you, Sable." Thomas held her face in his hands. "Don't you see how much I love you?"

Sable nodded.

"You gonna make me have to do this again, Sable?"

Sable shook her head.

Thomas took her in his arms. "Girl, I love you so much, I might just kill that nigga tomorrow!"

Sable wrapped her arms around Thomas and cried some more. "No, we was just talking. He don't mean nothing to me."

"Then meet me here tomorrow. I don't want you back at that playground. You hear?"

Sable sniffled. She shook her head up and down as she leaned on Thomas's chest.

Thomas smiled. She was hooked. He'd made her weak, or she would have left after he sent her through his torture test. Mission accomplished. . . .

Thomas sat on the railing, thinking about Sable and drinking his gin, until it was all gone, then headed home. He needed more than what he could get from her right now. He would have to be with Kerrissy again without her knowledge. As he approached his house, he looked up and saw Lena's light and stumbled toward their secret way to her house. He turned the knob, entered, and began loudly calling out her name. Lena scurried out of the bedroom. When she saw how drunk Thomas was, she wanted to break down in tears. Not out of pity for him, but for herself. This wasn't going to be a good night.

Chapter 27

Sable was where Thomas had told her to be. He'd been watching her from down the street to see if she'd go to the playground where Wesley was before obeying him, but she hadn't. She was waiting for him in the parking lot and wearing the type of clothes he liked to see her in.

Sable looked Thomas up and down as he walked toward her. He was dusty, wearing a T-shirt with rolled-up sleeves, and he was carrying an old coat over his arm. She looked at his body again and began to admire it. He was nicely built and bowlegged. She'd heard her mother and her friends talking about this—so this must be good. If only she could let her mother know about her fine catch, she'd be so proud of her daughter. The closer Thomas got to Sable, the stronger her feelings for him became. She wanted to jump up, hug, and kiss him—like the husband whom she knew she would have someday, who would come home from work, and she would greet him at the door.

Thomas walked up to her and stood in front of her.

Sable rose without him having to say a word.

He took her hand. "You ready?"

Sable nodded.

Thomas led her to the rear of the structure, up the brick steps, and pulled the board back that kept the door closed.

Sable jerked his hand.

He looked back at her and smiled. "It's okay. I've been working on it."

He held the board for Sable to step inside. She put her hand over her mouth when she saw what he had done. The wooden floor had been cleaned; the fireplace was lit. He even had wine, food, and blankets.

Thomas looked into Sable's eyes. "I did this all for you, baby. That's why I look like this. Now we can be alone until you can tell your parents about me the right way. You see. I stayed home from work—just for you."

Tears were in Sable's eyes. He hadn't said it, but she knew that he'd also done it because he had hit her the night before.

They sat down on the blankets and ate. The food was really good, and Thomas had told her he'd used the fireplace to cook it. His resourcefulness added to the stars he had already put in her eyes.

Thomas handed Sable a glass of wine. She put her head down. "I ain't old enough to drink that, Thomas."

Thomas took her hand and put the glass in it. "You old enough as long as you with me. Now try it. It ain't gonna hurt you. Besides, it's Friday night, time to have some fun."

Sable put the glass to her nose. It smelled okay, sort of like juice. She tasted it. It was sweet, but somewhat strong; it made her swallow hard. She wanted to put the glass down.

Thomas smacked his lips. "You ain't even tried it, Sable. Drink some more. It ain't that bad, once you get past the little bit of alcohol they put in it."

Sable took a few more sips, then the rest. Thomas was right. It wasn't that bad. Actually, it tasted good because it was so cold and sweet. She drank another glass. Thomas watched her, then took the glass from her. While she sat on the blanket, he pulled her closer to him, near the fireplace where he was seated. Sable giggled. Thomas moved over and sat down on the blanket with Sable, then pulled her to him until she was straddling his lap. He pulled her legs straight out and wrapped them around his waist. Sable giggled until Thomas kissed her. She put her arms around his neck and kissed him back. Thomas began unbuttoning her blouse and removing her bra. He pulled his shirt over his head, then held and kissed Sable so that he could feel their naked upper bodies touch. He ran his lips down her shoulder, around to her chest, until he found her breasts. Her legs shot straight out. Thomas unzipped her skirt and slid away from her, removing it and her underwear with one motion. He stared at Sable's deep-chocolate body. The body he'd been longing to see for weeks in its entirety. The body that kept him awake nights. The body that made him go to another woman and take from his wife while she slept, because he knew that it would take time for him to get to Sable the way he wanted.

Thomas kissed Sable's thigh. "God, you beautiful, baby. I better not catch you talkin' to no other man, Sable. You got me half-crazy."

"I love you, Thomas. I don't love nobody else."

"Not even Wesley?"

"I been over him, Thomas."

"You sure, Sable?"

"Um positive, Thomas!"

Thomas smiled as he lowered his head to her. Sable moaned passionately as she felt the soft flesh enter her. Thomas looked up at her. "This our anniversary. Um glad you let me see how beautiful you are and let me make you feel that way, too, Sable." Although it wasn't their anniversary, Thomas was a smooth talker. He knew a way to a woman's heart was often through her ears. He just wanted to look at the girl's body and use her up.

Sable could only moan and repeat herself. "I love you, Thomas. I love you."

Sable walked home in a daze. Each step she took felt light and airy. She stared down every once in a while at the ring Thomas had given her at the last minute of their night together. He loved her. He really loved her. He'd been extra intimate with her and hadn't had genital sex with her at all. He was waiting for her to be his wife—the way he was supposed to—and he treated her like a queen. If only she had someone to brag to, then the feeling she was carrying around wouldn't have her so overwhelmed.

Sable removed the ring and put it in her pocket before entering the house.

Thomas didn't feel like being bothered with Lena. If Kerrissy was asleep, he would just take what he

wanted again. Having her awake made him feel
married and old—especially with the baby inside
her—and after being with Sable. He would have to
face reality, which he didn't want. He wanted the fantasy. Sable made him feel sixteen again, and even
more hot-blooded than he already was. The fantasy
made his sexual appetite more insatiable than any
of the other things he was involved in. As he climbed
the stairs, he could feel himself become alive from his
thoughts. He tried massaging the excitement away,
but he was too far gone. He removed his dirty clothes
and slid into bed without bathing or turning off the
light. He put his arm around Kerrissy. She was snoring. He slightly lifted her thigh. She continued to
snore. Thomas again made love to his wife while she
slept, then cautiously moved away from her when he
felt himself ready. He eased out of bed and tried
making it to the bathroom, but he found himself
wiping the floor with his dirty clothing. Thomas
laughed at his asinine behavior as he threw the soiled
garments in the hamper and went to bathe. He was
proud of himself. He'd become as slick as Jasper—
no, slicker. He'd become the master. He'd fooled
Jasper out of Lena's house so that he could get what
he wanted there, too. And Jasper had never been
slick enough to fool his wife about having to work
overtime, and not go in at all, so that he could get a
roost ready, where he would be alone with another
woman. He leaned back in the tub and let the warm
water flow over his body as he shook his head and
thought about his last accomplishment. He'd had his
wife again as she slept, and she was too naïve to ever
discover it. He had earned a cigar—baby or not.

Chapter 28

Thomas was lying on the bed again, his hands under his head, pretending to watch television as Kerrissy took the clothes out of the hamper preparing to wash. She saw the T-shirt he'd thrown in the hamper the night before and glanced up at him. Thomas stared straight ahead at the television.

Kerrissy began examining the shirt.

Thomas looked over at her. "Something wrong, Kerrissy?"

"Your shirt? What happened to your shirt?"

Thomas sat straight up. "Just soak it!"

Kerrissy's mouth flew open. Why was Thomas talking to her like she meant nothing to him? She began to cry silently.

Thomas became irritated. "You crying . . . *again*!"

"Um sorry, Thomas I just wanted to know what—"

"Look, Kerrissy, I'll be back when you feel better, okay?"

Thomas put on his coat and walked out of the house. He went to Jasper's to see if he was still messing around with Lena. When he discovered that he wasn't, he went looking for Sable. Wesley was in the playground, alone, playing ball. He called out to Thomas as he went by.

"Hey, Thomas, you seen Sable?"

Thomas half-grinned. "Naw. I ain't seen her. Why?"

"Hey, she cute. I like her. She my age. I know y'all friends . . ." Wesley hesitated. "Y'all ain't got nothin' going, do you?"

Thomas laughed nervously. "Man! Is you crazy? You think I'd go to jail for that? She jailbait!"

"Sorry, Thomas, but she seventeen now, like me—anyway, my bag. But if you see her, tell her um looking for her."

Thomas slightly squinted and nodded. "Will do, man, will do."

He continued over to the parking lot. Sable sat there, waiting. Thomas jerked her by the hand so hard, she almost fell to the ground. He jerked her again so that she would be walking ahead of him as he talked to her back.

"Why that nigga looking for you, Sable?"

"Who, Thomas? I don't know—"

"Wesley! That's who!"

"Thomas, please—"

"Shut up!"

Thomas held the board back so that Sable could enter. When she stepped inside, he immediately walked up on her. "What I tell you last time we had this problem, Sable?"

"Thomas, I didn't do nothing—"

"You *had to do somethin'* for him to be asking about you! You been back over there to that playground, screwin' around with that nigga, aintchoo?"

"No, Thomas, no—"

Thomas slapped Sable so hard, she got dizzy. She balled up her fists when she became coherent.

Thomas stepped back, narrowed his eyes, and laughed. "You wanna hit me, Sable? You wanna fight me?" He took her hands and made her hit him.

Sable pushed him away.

Thomas grabbed her throat. "This what you want, ain't it, Sable? You like this, don't you?"

Tears streamed down Sable's face as she shook her head from side to side.

Thomas pushed Sable against the wall.

Sable became hysterical. She wasn't going to allow Thomas to drain her the way he had the last time they fought over Wesley. She began to swing wildly, hitting Thomas in the mouth, causing it to bleed. Thomas restrained her, then slapped her some more.

Sable dropped her head and cried.

Thomas continued to chastise her as she cried in anguish. He finished removing her clothes and pushed her on the mat.

Sable lay on the covers, whimpering, after the attack. Thomas rubbed her curves. "Did you think that you could stop me from seeing what's mine, Sable—what my woman looks like? I have a right to see my woman's body anytime I want to. So why do you keep on fighting me, Sable? Why do you keep on making me do this? You know how much I love you— how jealous I get when I think about you and another man. And I hope you don't think this is over with."

"Please, Thomas, don't hurt me no more. I ain't talking to that boy, I swear. . . ."

Thomas removed his belt. "You just lay there and

it'll be over after this. Maybe then you'll know who
the man is."

Thomas stared at Sable's smooth dark skin before
striking her five times on her curves, just enough
for her to feel it. Sable broke down again. Thomas
kneeled down beside her and rubbed her back.
"Please forgive me, Sable." Thomas rolled Sable onto
her back. She was still crying as he kissed her forehead, then her lips and breasts. He ran his tongue
down her stomach.

Sable tried to cover herself with her hand. "Please,
Thomas, no more, no more."

"Baby, I know when you done had enough. All I
want is for us to get an understanding, okay?"

Sable shook her head up and down.

Thomas continued. "I want you to go down to
that playground and tell that nigga you got a man,
and that you don't want him askin' nobody about
you no more, do you understand that?"

Sable sniffled. "Yeah."

"And don't mention my name to him. He'll put
our business out there, if he want you bad enough.
I'll go to jail and we won't never get married.
Monday, instead of me comin' here, meet me at my
house. I live in the alley. I'll be out in the yard about
four forty-five. I got some money for you, okay?
About four hundred dollars." Since he lived with his
mother, Thomas had not been paying rent, and he
had saved up his money. He only planned to be
sweet and generous until he had Sable hooked.

Sable nodded. Her tears dried up. Thomas stuck
his tongue in her navel. She moved her hand.

Thomas smiled as he thought about how far he
had pulled Sable in, in such a short time.

Chapter 29

Mondays were always the weariest for Kerrissy. She sat at the foot of the bed, staring at the television screen. She was feeling so depressed about her and Thomas's relationship. She hadn't bathed or dressed, and it seemed to take all the strength she had to move around. She put the palm of her hand on the mattress to stand. She needed to at least get dressed. She turned to rise, then screamed when she saw that the figure standing in the doorway wasn't Thomas.

"I didn't mean to scare you, baby. . . ."

Kerrissy quickly pulled the corner of the blanket over her. Her thighs and bottom stomach were still exposed.

"Here, Kerrissy. Take this."

Kerrissy looked confused. She held on to the blanket.

"Please take the money, baby. You and your husband can use it."

With each step the intruder took, Kerrissy backed farther away.

Kenneth walked over to her, kneeled on the bed, and crawled toward her.

Kerrissy folded one leg and covered herself with the pillow. "Git out of here before Thomas git back!"

"He ain't gonna be back for another two hours."

"Just leave me alone!"

Kenneth crawled closer. He took Kerrissy's hand, put the money in it, and held it shut. "We family, Kerrissy." He stroked her stomach through the pillow. "Ain't no reason for you to be afraid of me."

Kerrissy brushed his hand away. "You gotta get outta here, *now, please!*"

Kenneth backed away.

Kerrissy felt relieved, until Kenneth's hand slipped and he fell on the bed. She pulled the pillow away to see if he was okay.

Kenneth moaned, then held up his head, looking around to make sure that they were still alone. "Um okay. You ain't goin' tell nobody 'bout this, is you? I just made a mistake."

"I won't tell—not if you leave right now."

Kenneth continued to lean on his right arm. He reached out with his left hand. "Can I have my money back?"

Kerrissy unfolded her leg and leaned forward to give Kenneth the money. He quickly grabbed her ankle, causing Kerrissy to fall backward, giving him the chance he needed to get a good firm grip on both of her legs. Kerrissy tried to sit up, but Kenneth was already making his move. Kerrissy tried fighting him, but she could only gasp. She had to hold her stomach, once Kenneth embraced her flesh with his lips. Kerrissy let out a sound that Thomas had never gotten from her. She hated that this happened. She hated what was happening to her. This man was raping her—how could he make her body react so freely? Kerrissy suddenly recalled the conversations she and her mother had about telling stories, and how the story she and Thomas had cooked up had come true. But it was her husband's uncle, and this was even worse than a stepfather, if you could compare the two. Her husband's uncle was raping her with his great-niece or great-nephew inside her. He and his wife had made three unusual fall visits, this being their third, and now she knew why—and why he'd been watching her. Why he'd told Chell that she only had one sister and she should visit her as much as possible and not lose touch. He'd wanted Kerrissy the first day he'd laid eyes on her.

Kenneth mumbled, "Your husband ain't doin' nothin' but cheatin' on you, as pretty as you is. I know he ain't givin' you nothin', 'cause we be man talkin' all the time. All I want to do is be here for you when he ain't. You'll get used to it. The money goin' help y'all, too."

Kerrissy still tried to free her legs, but she couldn't. Almost out of breath, she struggled to sit up partially. "Please, Uncle Kenneth, please. Don't do this to me and my baby, please."

Kenneth continued.

Kerrissy wouldn't allow herself to touch Kenneth. He was determined that she would, and get used to it. He'd wanted Kerrissy the same way he'd wanted Chell. He massaged Kerrissy's lower body with his lips and sensual kisses until she was so weak she had no other recourse but to hold on to him. He had to make her get used to it—he had to have her. He definitely loved him some young woman.

Kerrissy cried in fear of losing her baby and from the disgust of being raped by her uncle. What she didn't know was he'd been her step-grandfather first.

Kerrissy was asleep when Thomas came into the room. He sat down on the bed and shook her. She jumped so hard, she scared him. When she saw that it was Thomas, and not Kenneth, she crawled over to him, hugged him, and began to cry. "He hurt me!"

Thomas pulled away from her, anger spread across his face. "Who hurt you?"

"The baby, the baby! I thought I was gonna have it early!"

Thomas put his hand on the back of her head and snuggled her face in his chest. "I keep telling you to call me at work when you feel like that."

"But it always be a false alarm. I don't want to get you into no trouble. We need that money."

"Kerrissy, we need our baby more. Now, don't let me have to tell you that again. Okay?"

Kerrissy nodded.

Thomas got up off the bed. "Did you eat?"

"No."

"Kerrissy, you gotta eat. Look, um goin' down-stairs to get us both a plate. Have you even been out this room today?"

Kerrissy put her head down. "No."

"You wanna come downstairs—"

"No! I mean, I don't feel that good. Can you just bring me something?"

Thomas went back downstairs. His uncle had been secretly watching him since he'd come through the door. He barely looked up from the television when Thomas came to the living-room door and asked if he and his aunt had eaten.

Kenneth thought for sure that Kerrissy would break, although he sensed her somewhat enjoying his touch. Maybe she had told Thomas how his lust for her had taken over and he'd raped her, but perhaps she hadn't told. Kenneth relaxed. If she hadn't told, she probably never would.

Thomas picked up the two plates after he and Kerrissy finished eating and headed back downstairs. "Um goin' out to do the yard. I'll be back in a hot minute."

Kerrissy became afraid, until she remembered that Thomas's aunt was downstairs with his uncle. He'd purposely taken her to one of her friend's houses on the other side of town earlier that day so that he could get to Kerrissy without any disturbances, but she'd figured that out too late. She swung her legs off the side of the bed and walked over to the window to watch Thomas in the yard. He was standing at the fence talking to a girl who looked younger than her. He handed the girl something, then felt her behind as she walked away.

Thomas looked up at their window and saw Kerrissy watching them. Kerrissy quickly moved away from the window. She leaned against the wall next to it, covering her mouth with her hand, but she refused to cry. She wouldn't even acknowledge what she'd seen—if Thomas asked her about it.

Thomas was cool about his game. He stayed outside for almost two hours, purposely allowing Kerrissy to hear him working. When he entered their bedroom, she pretended to be asleep. Thomas showered, slid in beside her, and wrapped his arm around her. Kerrissy wanted to remove it; she was angry enough to bite his hand, but she didn't want him trying to prove how much he loved her. She lay with her eyes wide open, feeling her tears dampening the sheet, thinking furiously. *Is this why he pretends to show me how much he loves me? Is it all a game? Is he messing with another girl? Has he done it before? Is she the reason for him walking out on me?* She wiped her eyes, then closed them. She was no longer ashamed for liking what Thomas's uncle had done to her.

Chapter 30

Kerrissy could hear the creaking on the steps. She knew he'd be back, but she didn't care. Her world had come to an end the day before.

Kenneth entered the room. Kenneth did not know that Kerrissy was his step-granddaughter and he never found out. However, just as he had no qualms about being with his nephew's wife, he probably would not have cared, even if he'd known. He didn't view his actions as being incestuous because, technically, Thomas was only his nephew through marriage. And, if he'd known that Kerrissy was Lena's granddaughter, he would have rationalized his actions by saying she wasn't his blood.

Kerrissy sat zombielike, waiting for him to make his move. As before, he put the money in Kerrissy's hand and folded his hand around hers. He massaged her stomach. Kerrissy didn't stop him. He touched her, urging her to recline. Kerrissy wouldn't. He tugged on her legs. Kerrissy sat motionless, then closed her eyes as she thought about their previous encounter. She thought of how much she would

have enjoyed the closeness if Kenneth hadn't been
Thomas's uncle. Kenneth had done something
that Thomas hadn't, but she didn't know what it
was. As Kenneth massaged her stomach, she slowly
reclined.

Chapter 31

Kenneth was right. As time went on, she did get used to him. He was all she had. Thomas was home very little, constantly making up lies so that he could go see Sable. Kerrissy knew it, but she refused to show her feelings, nor did she try to find out who his other woman was. She'd pay Thomas back in the worst way possible, with his own flesh and blood.

Kerrissy was in her eighth month when things became more serious than she'd anticipated. Kenneth had been having his way with her for a couple of months by this time. It was now Kenneth's turn to really feel her. He drooled at the thought of being with another young woman after so many years. He could always be faithful to his wife, until he found one he really wanted. It was just unfortunate that the one he wanted now was the one married to his nephew, and, although unbeknownst to him, was his step-granddaughter.

Kerrissy thought Kenneth was too old and didn't

put up a struggle. When she realized she was wrong, and tried to fight him off again, it was too late. His hands were strong. What Kerrissy wouldn't do, he forced on her.

Kerrissy's head spun. She felt filthy, disgusting.

Kenneth couldn't maintain himself. Kerrissy could feel him flowing inside her. She held the bottom of her stomach. "My baby, my baby! You contaminating my baby!"

Kenneth continued until he was exhausted. Kerrissy was so enraged, she sat up and threw the pillow at him so hard that it hit him in the face, knocking him backward.

Kenneth was confused and nervous. "What's wrong with you, girl?"

Kerrissy became hysterical. "I'm going to tell my husband! I'm going to tell—"

"Tell him what? That you let me have you, then changed your mind?"

Kerrissy finally began to cry, releasing months of pain and frustration. Kenneth tried to console her. He put his hand up to touch her hair. She pushed his hand away. He sat on the bed with her. "I love you, Kerrissy. I know that you ain't goin' believe this, but all the years I been with my wife, I ain't never cheated on her. Dat little nigger ain't been with you but a few months, and he can't keep his stuff in his pants. Now um gonna tell you this for your own good, Kerrissy. When you finally see just how trifling he is, let me know so that me and you can leave together."

Kerrissy looked up at him, her face red and full of tears. "What about your wife?"

"She ain't been havin' nothin' to do with me for

months. She only married me because some men raped her and she thought I didn't know, and nobody else would want her but me. . . ."

"You raped me, Kenneth. You raped me!"

"Kerrissy—uh-uh. What I did wasn't no rape. I was falling in love with you and did what I had to, 'cause I wanted you so bad, and you gave in. I wanted you to love me back, Kerrissy. I wanted you to love me back. But the way I see it now, it seems to me that neither one of us don't have much to hold on to. Will you think about what I said, baby? Just think about it?"

Kerrissy turned her head. "Thomas loves me and this baby. I shouldn't have done nothing with you— no matter what he doin'. And you his uncle. Don't you even care?"

"Hell no! That little knucklehead been spoiled since I know'd him! All he do is go around trying to get what he want from people—any way he can! When he don't get it, he got ways of makin' them feel bad without them even realizing it!"

Kerrissy caught her breath. Kenneth had hit a nerve. He'd made her think about the times Thomas didn't want her questioning him, claimed she didn't think he loved her—and he had to prove he did. Although she hadn't done anything, he'd turn things around so much that she'd feel guilty.

Kenneth brushed her hair with his finger. "What's the matter?"

Kerrissy jerked her head away. Her voice was deep and cold, almost unrecognizable. "Just get out, Kenneth, and don't come back to this room. If you do, I might do something to you that we'll both regret."

Kenneth slowly rose and quietly left the room.

Chapter 32

Thomas and Sable sat in the abandoned structure near the fire he'd made for them to stay warm. They were looking at all the intoxicants Thomas had lined up on the blanket. He gave Sable a glass of wine, while he smoked some weed and snorted cocaine. When she was done, he told her to hit the joint. She did as ordered and choked. Thomas ordered her to drink some more wine to soothe her throat and try it again. She did. He showed her how to snort cocaine. She lowered her nose to the spoon and inhaled. That was okay. She took in some more, then finished off her third glass of wine. Thomas turned on the portable radio, then took Sable's hand and pulled her to her feet. "Dance with me, baby. This my favorite song."

Sable stood. She leaned on Thomas's chest and staggered back and forth to the sound of the slow tune. Thomas kissed her, pulling on her tongue much harder than before. Sable didn't argue. He moved it down her neck. Sable moaned. He unbuttoned her coat dress and continued taunting her smooth skin, tracing it with his tongue. Sable was becoming weaker and weaker.

Undressing on his way down, Thomas pulled her back to the floor. She followed his direction and waited for his action. He removed her underwear, then crawled on top of her.

Sable tried pushing him away, until she felt the hand she'd almost become accustomed to. Her voice trembled. "Please, Thomas, don't! Um gonna git pregnant! Don't!"

Thomas slapped her again. "What? I can give you my money and everything else, but I ain't good enough to have you?"

"I ain't say that, Thomas—"

"Then shut up"—Thomas saw Lena's face— "*bitch!*"

Sable cringed and squealed as Thomas continued. He pulled her legs around his waist and moved like a man starving for affection. As he stuttered in Sable's ear. "I—I—I knew that it would be like this, baby. I—I—I knew it would be like this. I—I—I got some more money for you, baby. I—I—I got some more money for you. J-j-just let me finish without a problem—been waiting a long time for this, Sable. I—I—I been waiting too long."

Thomas flooded Sable. He held her so tight, she almost passed out. She wondered how she was going to get herself cleaned up before she got home. Then she felt a cold, moist rag touching her flesh. Thomas was cleaning her thoroughly. He'd planned it all.

Sable sat up but kept her head lowered. She wrapped her arms around herself to stop shaking. She waited awhile, then reached for her clothes. Thomas grabbed her hand. "Wait a minute, baby, wait a minute." Sable's heart began to race. She looked up. She hadn't seen it all the other times, but she could actually see how high Thomas was. What Thomas had done to her had removed the veil from her eyes.

Thomas made Sable ready again, explored more of her, until he was content, then rolled away.

Sable lay on her stomach, still in a daze, wondering what had happened. How had Thomas taken her virginity, and in that other, unnatural way so quickly? She did not expect him to penetrate her rectum.

Thomas massaged the back of Sable's head. "Girl, you something else with your young ass."

Sable remained quiet.

Thomas leaned up on one elbow. "What's wrong?"

Sable still wouldn't answer him.

Thomas snatched her arm. "Do you hear me talking to you?"

Sable nodded, then burst into tears again.

Thomas smacked his lips. "Oh, it's gonna be like that, huh?"

Sable wouldn't answer him.

Thomas sat up. "Just get your shit on and leave then."

Sable turned over and began slowly dressing. The tears were still running down her face like a waterfall.

Thomas put his hand on her shoulder. "I ain't gonna mess with you no more, Sable. I should have known better. But I thought you knew what a relationship between two people was about. I guess not. I just won't bother you no more. You too young and silly."

Sable finished dressing, then left. As she walked home, she thought about what had happened, and if her parents would see how she was walking differently. She could surely feel where Thomas had been, like he'd left himself inside her. She thought about the events that led up to what had happened to her in that vacant building, and she wished she could turn back time. She'd been ruined, and Thomas had done it to her. Hadn't he told her he loved her? Hadn't he said that he wanted her to be his wife? Good girls didn't do that stuff, and definitely not the ones who wanted to be someone's wife. Her mother had told her so. And now she was ruined, *ruined*! And now Thomas didn't even want her anymore.

Thomas quickly finished putting on his clothes and caught up to Sable. She was somewhat relieved to see him walking beside her, but she was still speechless.

Thomas spoke gently. "You and me one, Sable, that's all that meant. That me and you one. Um the only one had you, and, from now on, you the only one who gonna have me—that's if you still love me after me lovin' you so hard. Um gonna go on home now and give you some time to think about us. Then you'll see me again—that's if you ever come back to the parking lot."

Sable kept walking. Thomas turned around and headed home.

Chapter 33

Thomas headed upstairs to his room early, forgetting that he'd told Kerrissy he'd be working late. He could hear Kerrissy moaning. He hurried up the steps, thinking that she was having labor pains. He stood in the doorway, looking puzzled. He must have been so drunk that he went into the wrong room. Kenneth lifted his head from Thomas's wife's lips and allowed his kisses to travel her neck to her bosom. Something Thomas hadn't done since his wife's pregnancy.

Thomas didn't remember going across the room—all he remembered was having the back of his uncle's collar, slamming him to the floor, and hearing himself shouting. "What the hell you think you doing with my wife, you old-ass bastard!" Thomas walked up to Kenneth and stood over him. "Um gonna kill your old ass tonight!" Thomas kicked Kenneth in the side. "What kind of dog-eat-dog shit is this!"

Kenneth rolled away from Thomas, staggered to his feet, and quickly ran out the door. Kenneth had been seeing Kerrissy on a regular basis, and he had taken Thomas's absence for granted. Unfortunately, he'd become careless.

Meantime, Thomas headed after him, then changed his mind. He was going to find out what was happening. He must have been raping her. He turned toward Kerrissy, who had jumped up and backed away from them as soon as Thomas grabbed Kenneth.

Thomas's eyes narrowed. "What the hell goin' on here, Kerrissy?"

Kerrissy was trembling. She couldn't answer.

Thomas fed her what he wanted to hear. "Was that old nigga makin' you do that? I saw him watching you, but I thought it was just a man thing. Did he rape you?"

Kerrissy nodded nervously and cleared her throat. "At first." She threw her hand over her mouth. That had slipped out. She'd weakened and allowed Kenneth back into her room after telling him to never return.

Thomas looked at his wife inquisitively. His voice raised a few octaves and squeaked. "You mean—you had something going on with my old-ass uncle?"

Kerrissy began to breathe hard, then erupted. "You been messin' around with that young black girl that look like Grandma! *You even gave her ten weeks of your pay!* I seen you, Thomas, and you know I seen you!"

"So that's what made you let my blood touch all over you and my baby? Now tell me that he done been inside of you to shoot sperm on my child, Kerrissy. Just tell me that so that I can kill you." Thomas's voice was calm.

Kerrissy stared at him. "Everything you did to that black whore—he did to me." She jumped up off the bed.

Thomas lunged at Kerrissy and put his hands around her throat. She didn't move. Just like her grandmother, she took his hands. "Go ahead. Kill me. Kill this baby. I ain't got nothin' left, no way."

Thomas raised his fist. Kerrissy didn't flinch.

Thomas backed away. He couldn't hit her. That's what Sable was for. Kerrissy was his main woman. The one Jasper told him should be treated gently.

Thomas backed away. "I shoulda married a white girl."

Kerrissy's eyes and nose were running. "Maybe you still should! Maybe I should just kill myself for letting you talk me into ruining my life! Maybe I should just get all my stuff and leave—go back home! It don't make no difference now what happen to me! 'Cause my life over now!"

"You ain't leavin' me, and you ain't takin' my baby no place!" Thomas backed farther away from her to prove that he was still in charge. *"Now, come here, Kerrissy!"*

Kerrissy fell on the bed and continued crying.

Thomas stood looking at her, thinking how he couldn't let his mother know about all that had happened. If he told on his uncle, then Venn would find out about Sable, the other seventeen-year-old to whom he'd been teaching everything sexual under the sun. He had been committing adultery with that young girl so that he could remain pleased while Kerrissy got so big. He walked over to the bed and sat beside Kerrissy. He began running his fingers through her soft hair. "Baby, you know um sorry.

That girl just like a little prostitute to me. I didn't wanna hurt our baby, so I used her for stuff. I don't love her—she too dark for me, anyway. Me and you light with good hair. We gonna have one pretty baby. She could never give me that."

Kerrissy still wouldn't look up; she continued to cry. "Then why you give her your money—*our* money? Why you come in here trying to choke me?"

"Just to scare you, baby. I was scared, and I wanted you scared, too. That girl threatened to tell on me. I had to pay her." Thomas thought about what Kerrissy had seen the night he'd told Sable to come to the house so that he could further suck her into his game. "Since she was bold enough to come to my house for it, I tagged her ass while she was leaving, Kerrissy. I'd stopped seeing her—that made her mad, too. I ain't goin' see her no more. . . . We even now?"

Kerrissy wouldn't answer, but that lightened her heart.

Thomas massaged her back, then her rear, then gently helped her to recline. He began kissing his wife passionately to keep her quiet.

Kerrissy could feel herself weakening for Thomas again. She couldn't help but hold him tightly and believe that he would never cheat on her again . . . and they would remain happy forever.

Thomas couldn't afford to have Kerrissy leave him under the present circumstances. His mother's mouth was too big, although she had always told Thomas that it was her morals that were big—not her mouth. Thomas had still deduced it to be her mouth.

Thomas crawled up behind Kerrissy and gave her the attention he had only been giving her while she slept. Kerrissy held his hand as he massaged her stomach and took his time.

Kerrissy lay on her side, feeling somewhat relieved. Thomas brushed her hair back. "We even now, right? We even, and now you know how much I love you, Kerrissy. Um beggin' you. Please, please, please, don't leave me, and don't let my uncle touch what's mine no more."

Kerrissy wouldn't answer. She wasn't sure that she was able to stop herself. In Thomas's absence Kenneth had done something to her, something that she had craved as soon as Kenneth had left her side the very first time.

Thomas laid his head on her back. "Please, Kerrissy, talk to me. Say you won't let him touch you no more. That you won't leave me, baby. I'd die without you!" Thomas began to cry. "I wouldn't want to live! Um sorry for what I done, Kerrissy! Um sorry!"

Although Kerrissy allowed her husband to make love to her again, she just couldn't commit to his words.

Thomas rolled her over to face him. "Kerrissy? You don't love me no more?"

Kerrissy could smell the liquor on his breath. She looked in his eyes. "Do you love and want me 'cause you drunk, Thomas? 'Cause you think um gonna leave you, or because you trying to have two women without us knowing it?"

Thomas blinked the tears out of his eyes and stared back at her. "I whipped her ass for you—"

"You ain't do it for me, Thomas. She don't even know me."

"I swear I did, baby. She was all up on me, and I told that girl I had a wife. She said to 'F' you, and that's when I whipped her—"

"But you still slept with her, didn't you?"

"Naw, baby. She—she—she—she just, you know."

"No, Thomas. I don't know."

"You want me to say it, Kerrissy?"

Kerrissy knew he was referring to fellatio, which was something that Sable performed on Thomas as the outside woman, but Kerrissy was not expected to do because she was the wife.

"No. But is that what you need, Thomas? A woman who can do that because I don't?"

"No, baby, I just thought that was what I needed until I came close to losing you. Now I know it won't hurt our baby to touch you if I do it right. I ain't gonna never see that girl no more."

Kerrissy turned her back to Thomas. "*Hmpf.* We'll just see about that, Thomas. We'll just wait and see."

"So you ain't gonna leave me, Kerrissy, and take my baby from me?"

Kerrissy lay on her forearm and shook her head from side to side.

Chapter 34

Thomas had stayed close by Kerrissy until she went into labor. He'd taken her to the hospital and worried until the nurse came out and announced that he had a seven-pound six-ounce daughter, nineteen inches long. He had wished that they would change the rules and let the fathers into delivery, but the regulations did not permit it.

Thomas gazed up at the ceiling and smiled at the thought of having a wife and child. He closed his eyes so that the sweat that was being generated from the activity below him wouldn't pour into them. He looked down and opened them and smiled. He loved seeing Sable on her knees, like a dog, in any way. Her sleek, dark body made him forget all of his worries, including that he was almost four years older than her and could go to jail if anyone told what he'd been doing to her, what he'd taught her— the drinking, the drugs, the sex. He opened his fingers and firmly palmed her head and whispered in a raspy voice, "Do like I told you. Go slow, or you won't see me again at all."

Sable had been sitting in the parking lot, waiting for Thomas every day at the regular time since he'd seized her innocence. She'd thought she'd hate him, but she couldn't. Instead, it was like she'd become a part of him after their last encounter. Her body began to crave him even more, and she'd waited and prayed until he returned to their spot. There was no way she could live without Thomas.

Thomas had broken his promise to Kerrissy almost as soon as baby Thessia had come out of her. He had gone looking for Sable, believing that she'd never want to see him again after what had happened, and having not seen him for so long. However, she did come back. Sable had daydreamed about her and Thomas, the things they enjoyed. Believing the lies he'd filled her head with. That he'd helped her to grow up. No one else would want her or treat her as good. The same lies he'd put in his wife's head. After the second week of their reunion, Thomas had squatted across Sable's body, giving her the pleasure he'd trained her to love, then coaxed her to please him too. Sable had been apprehensive, but she had slowly tried what he'd requested. And quite frankly, she enjoyed pleasing Thomas. It had made him weak for her, the way he'd made her weak for him, and now she was doing all she could to keep him. She wanted to do things for him without his direction so that he'd love her more than ever, and never leave her again.

* * *

Sable stood up. Thomas gave her more money. Unlike the other times, the amount was menial: *only twenty dollars*. She was his ready whore, and the only one in the relationship who didn't know it was Sable. She looked down at the bill with her mouth open, but she was afraid to look up at Thomas afterward or question him about it.

Thomas grabbed her wrist. "What? That ain't enough?"

Sable swallowed. "Yeah. Yeah. You been giving me too much money, anyway."

"Glad you said that, Sable, 'cause from now on, I ain't gonna have that much to give you. I got to start doing things for my mother. We need a lot of things—my mother just had a baby girl."

Sable smiled. "Wow. You must be happy to have a little sister. I was happy when my little sister came, only we four years apart. We was lucky that day you came by. She was sleep. She got a big old mouth. Tell everything she see."

"Lucky for you, Sable. 'Cause the first time I hear about us on the streets, or anybody ask me anything about you again, me and you through, Sable. I mean it, we through. I can't afford to go to jail for you. Sometimes I wish that you hadn't let me kiss you. Now I can't get enough of you. But if I hear about us, then um gone. Now come on. Let's finish."

Sable felt hurt and empty after the way Thomas reacted, but she wouldn't show it. Thomas pulled her to him. Sable tried to kiss him. He turned his head. Something about him needing her, and not being able to stay away from her and keep the promise he'd made to his wife, angered him.

The way Thomas used Sable made her feel like

a rag doll, and still somewhat empty, but she was happy that she could please him. At least no one would take him from her—she knew it all. No other woman could come close to doing what she and Thomas did together. It took nerve, Thomas had told her so, and that no other female could ever please him because of that—unless it was an older woman. No one would ever come between them.

Thomas got up and began buttoning his shirt.

Sable sat on their pallet, nude, staring up at him. "Do you still love me, Thomas?"

Thomas grinned. "What do you think, Sable?"

Sable smiled. "You gotta go already?"

"Yeah, Sable. I gotta go already, and so do you."

"But it's still early."

Thomas kneeled down and took her chin in his hand. "You wanna spend the night here with me?"

Sable swallowed hard.

Thomas stood up. "I didn't think so. Now get dressed and get home."

Sable slowly stood and began to dress with her back to Thomas and her head lowered. He'd embarrassed her. As she pulled the strap of her bra over her shoulder, she slightly lifted her head. "Thomas, I gotta tell you something."

Thomas sucked his teeth. "What, Sable?"

"We need to get married."

Thomas snatched her around by her forearm to face him. "What the hell are you talking about, Sable? You trying to threaten me?"

"No, no. I just think um pregnant."

Thomas frowned hard. *"What!"*

Sable put up her hands. "Please, Thomas. Don't git mad and hit me. I didn't do it on purpose. I told you I could get pregnant. Remember?"

"Look, Sable—how many weeks—when was your last period?"

"Two months ago."

"Why didn't you tell me sooner?"

"'Cause you told me we would get married if that happened."

"Well, we can't! You gotta get rid of it!"

"But I don't wanna get rid of my baby, Thomas!"

Thomas slapped Sable, then grabbed both of her arms. "You'll either get rid of it or me, Sable. Make your choice!"

Sable lowered her head and mumbled, "Um keepin' my baby."

"Good. Then you find another father for it, because um leaving tonight. We both knew this was a wrong relationship. I ain't going to jail for you or no baby that neither one of us can take care of right now, and might *not* be mine, anyway!"

Thomas walked toward the exit. Sable chased him, fell down, and grabbed his leg. "Please, Thomas, don't! Don't leave me like this by myself! This is your baby, I swear it is!"

"Then make a choice, Sable. Me or that bastard you carrying?"

Sable cried uncontrollably. "But it's yours, Thomas!"

"Me or it, Sable. Me or it, or I'm walkin'."

Thomas tried pulling away from Sable so that he could pretend to walk away.

Sable held on tightly. "I'll get rid of it, Thomas. Just don't leave me, please!"

Thomas looked down at her with no compassion. "Then meet me here Saturday morning so that we can take care of that so that we can continue seeing each other. You got that, Sable?"

Sable continued to hold on to Thomas's leg and cry.

Thomas pried her away from him. *"Did you hear what I said?"*

Sable nodded.

"Then get up and get your things on. I told you that I needed to be home with my mother and my new baby sister. How um gonna take care of another baby, anyway? If you can't respect that, maybe we shouldn't see each other anymore—no matter what happens."

"Please, Thomas, no. I'll do whatever you want! Whatever you want!"

"Then get up, Sable, and take your ass home until Saturday morning!"

As soon as Thomas walked into his house, the phone rang. It was Jasper. Thomas was still angry with Jasper, but he made his voice sound pleasant. "Hey, Jasp, what's up?"

"Man, thought I'd take you to the strip club to celebrate your new baby and as a bachelor party gift, since you didn't have one."

Thomas's excitement turned genuine. "Yeah, man. Let me go check on Kerrissy and the baby first. I gotta ask her permission. She kinda mad at me—"

"Man, what? You gonna tell her where you going?"

"Naw, Jasper. Um just gonna ask her if it's okay for me to go to the club."

"What she mad at you for, anyway, Thomas?"

"She saw me from our window that night when we had that little run-in with Lena."

Jasper became instantly embarrassed over his best friend's story, which he didn't know was a lie. "Um sorry I put you in that position, man."

"Wasn't a problem, man. I got just what I deserved." Thomas chuckled. "That probably won't be the last time, either."

Jasper shook his head and laughed, not catching on to Thomas's innuendo. "Man, you all right, you know that."

"It ain't nothin', man. Let's just forget about it. As soon as I talk to Kerrissy, I'll call you back."

Thomas hung up the phone and ran upstairs. Kerrissy and the baby were asleep. He shook Kerrissy. "Baby, baby . . ."

Kerrissy slowly turned over. "Hmm . . . ?"

"Jasper wanna take me to the club to celebrate the baby and because he didn't give me a bachelor party or nothin'. Can I go?"

Kerrissy stroked the side of his face with the backs of her fingers, "Yeah, baby. Go ahead. Have a good time. Okay?"

Thomas felt a little guilty. "You sure, baby? 'Cause I really need to be home with you and our daughter—"

"No, Thomas, go ahead. Celebrate. Me and you can celebrate when I'm better. Okay?"

Thomas kissed her forehead. "Okay, baby. Later." He stood up, feeling a little sad and guilty as he went to bathe and get ready to go out, but he did as he'd promised Jasper.

* * *

Thomas sat on the side of the bed, talking to Kerrissy and stroking her hair. She felt so comfortable to him, so comfortable that he was wondering why he needed to leave home at all. She'd fallen asleep again when Jasper pulled up, but he felt like telling Jasper to go ahead without him. Something felt different about his and Kerrissy's relationship, something that he had never noticed before—bonding. Kerrissy wasn't only pretty, she was smart and sweet. He loved her, but, out of hatefulness and lust, he'd pushed his wife into the clutches of another man—his uncle's. He couldn't stop feeling guilty or responsible for it. He wanted to do right by his wife, but something about women and sex kept him dishonest. Thomas knew that his uncle Kenneth was once married to Lena, but he'd kept it a secret. For one, he wanted to retaliate against Lena for how she'd set up his aunt to get raped. He also didn't want to divulge this family secret to Kerrissy because it would bring up his aunt's rape and her real reason for marrying Kenneth. His aunt's feelings were important to him, and he didn't want to see her hurt anymore.

Jasper blew the horn again. Thomas slowly stood up and reluctantly headed out the door, looking back at his wife, who looked like a sleeping angel.

Thomas was unusually quiet as he and Jasper rode along. He sat hunched down in the seat with his hands in his lap. Jasper flipped his radio dial until he found a soul station. He carelessly crooned along with the singer, making Thomas laugh out loud. Jasper knew that would work. Thomas could sing.

Thomas looked over at Jasper. "That mess is worse than that ugly mark on Lena's behind. Let me show you how it's done, man."

Thomas began to sing while Jasper drove along, smiling. The comment Thomas intentionally made about Lena went completely over Jasper's head. His concentration was on Thomas. He'd brought his buddy out of his deep funk.

Thomas and Jasper stepped out of the car and headed for the club, chatting all the way. Once inside, Thomas grinned from ear to ear. He'd forgotten all about the pressure he was carrying around with him. The topless waitresses and girls in G-strings went straight to his libido. He glanced down as he followed Jasper in the dim light to a vacant table. He hoped that no one but himself would know what was going on beneath his clothing. They sat at a front table and watched the girl that was already performing. Thomas didn't know if he would be able to make it through the show if all the girls looked like the one on stage. As she bent over and shook her rear at the audience, Thomas swallowed his drink so hard that he almost choked. Jasper patted him on the back and laughed hysterically.

Thomas actually made it through the shows, but the night wasn't over. He couldn't go home to Kerrissy in his present condition. She wasn't well enough to be intimate. He was craving Sable, but he knew that the late hour made a meeting for them impossible. He took the secret way to Lena's house. If her light was off, she'd better get out of bed and answer the door.

* * *

After he pounded on her door for a while, Lena finally let Thomas in. He lunged at her as soon as she opened the door. "What the hell you trying to prove, Lena! You heard me out there knockin'!"

"Thomas, I ain't seen you in, I don't know how long. Why you doing this to me? Why don't you just be with my granddaughter and leave me alone? Please! You just being greedy. . . ."

Thomas's eyes narrowed.

Lena swallowed.

Thomas came closer to her face. Close enough for spit to fly in it. "*Bitch!* I'll *kill you* if you so much as mention my wife to me again! You *don't tell me* what I should do—or *ask me* or *tell me* what *I am!*" Thomas jabbed his chest firmly with his finger as he spoke. "Um in control when I come up in here! Um in control!"

Lena backed down. Her shoulders slumped. Her head went down. "I just don't want no more uh this, Thomas. It ain't right. I just can't take the hurt no more."

Thomas's nostrils flared. "You won't git hurt if you just do like I say and, keep your big mouth *closed* until I tell you it's okay to say somethin' to me!"

"I don't mean that kind of hurt—"

"Lena? Since when this been about you, huh? You think I really care about you, what you think, what you feel? At one time I kinda cared, kinda liked you. But when you told me how you done my auntie, that did it for anything I felt for you. You think I didn't figure out why you was really messin' with me after that? You think I didn't figure out that you was just usin' me to git at my mother? You'd probably planned on tellin' her about us to hurt her some more when you was ready. Probably would have if I hadn't turned things around! Now you too ashamed! You don't want nobody knowin' what really be going on between me and you, in your house. Do you, Lena? That the boy you scarred is now scarring you!"

Lena lowered her head.

Thomas punched the inside of his hand. *"Do you, Lena?"*

Lena's head popped up. She quickly shook it from side to side.

"I want you naked, Lena, and I want you to do it right now! Me and Jasper been out to the strip club just now. You gonna strip for me, since all they could do for me was show me what I could look at but couldn't touch—*what you waitin' on!*"

Lena began to pull her gown down over her shoulder.

Thomas backed up until he was at Lena's little metal red-and-white table, then sat crossways in his usual kitchen chair as he watched Lena remove her nightgown.

Thomas stood up when he realized that Lena was wearing a brand-new baby blue sheer gown. Her hair was up extra pretty, she looked younger, and she didn't look as tired as she once did. Before she could totally remove the gown, he hooked his fingers beneath the front elastic. "Where the hell you get this from, Lena?"

Lena cleared her throat. "Jasper." Lena's voice was raspy.

Thomas's look became more evil. "You can barely talk 'cause you know you due. Don't you, Lena?"

"Please, Thomas, I ain't seen you—"

Thomas slapped Lena. "Go gitcha knife now, Lena! Go git it!"

"Thomas, please. Don't. Let me explain—"

"I don't give a damn about your explanation! You know better than to come to the door wearin' this!" Thomas flicked her hair. "And why your hair up! You was waitin' for that nigga, wadn't you?"

Thomas ripped the gown straight down the front, exposing Lena. She tried to cover up with her arms.

Thomas smiled. "Now you really strippin' for me, whore—and move your arms, whore!"

Lena slowly allowed her arms to drop to her sides, then hung her head.

Thomas could feel himself finish expanding. He still couldn't understand why Lena had such a strange effect on him—it was a powerful effect. His wife and Sable should have been enough, but he'd think about Lena, even when he'd been with them. Staying away from Lena so long had really been hard. The pretending with Sable had worked only so long. If Lena only knew—if she *really knew*.

He moved his chair back and turned his body around so that his back would be against it. "Come here."

As Lena slowly walked over to him, Thomas noticed her shuffle was gone. Thomas could feel jealousy and insecurity saturate his nerves.

Lena began to lower herself onto his lap. Thomas put his hand on her butt to halt her. She wanted to look back at him to see what he was doing, but she was too afraid. Thomas stared between her legs and thought about what he'd seen Jasper doing to Lena.

He wondered how hard it would be for him to do the same. He'd been firm about her and Jasper, but maybe she'd gone back to Jasper because of it, and would suffer the consequences of him catching them again. He knew how he craved certain things. He was taking chances, big chances. He stared at Lena indecently for a long time before making up his mind. He would make her more addicted to him than ever. He couldn't afford to lose Lena—for some strange reason she had more of his heart than his two younger women.

Thomas was determined to be better to Lena than Jasper. He had to keep Lena waiting for him. Maybe he loved her, maybe he didn't, but he wanted her, and Lena was right about him being greedy. She was one of his women that gave him what he needed, and she'd better get used to being with him—and only him.

The uniqueness made him enjoy Lena far better than his younger women. He would do Lena like he'd done his wife and Sable before Jasper got to her again.

The second time he touched Lena, she trembled so hard she slid away from the table and began falling to the floor. Thomas put his arm around her waist, helping her to ascend, but continued his mission on their way down. He'd thought about not doing it the third time. Lena might have a heart attack. But as soon as he felt her hands on his head, he proceeded to exhaust her again.

Thomas lay beside Lena on the kitchen floor, massaging her stomach, and comforting her as he whispered seductively in her ear: "Don't make me compete with that nigga, 'cause y'all will lose every time. Next time um gonna give you something I know will make you leave him alone."

Lena lay without talking or moving. She feared whatever Thomas was warning her about. Lena's thoughts diminished when Thomas snuggled up closer to her. She tensed some more as Thomas planted firm moist kisses on the back of her neck. She closed her eyes, relaxed, and let her mind believe what was easiest. *At least I have a man who wants me—he was mine first. My granddaughter had no business messing with a man as old as Thomas. She wasn't ready for a man as advanced as Thomas. Everything will be okay as long as she never find out.* She could feel Thomas massaging her in a familiar way. Her last thought flowed quickly. *Oh, God, I ain't goin' never git outta this!*

Thomas lifted Lena up off the floor, carried her to the bedroom, lay her down, then sat with her. Lena tried pulling the cover over her naked body.

Thomas snatched it. "Don't play with me, Lena! I brought you in here to make sure you was gonna be okay, but that can change!"

Lena lay quietly, trying to avoid eye contact with Thomas.

"Lena, you know we got a bond. Look at me, Lena! Look at me when um talkin' to you!" Thomas clasped her chin with his fingers. "If I catch you with Jasper or any other man, or wearing something one bought you, um gonna have to show you what I was talking about. I'll use whatever it take to make you stay with me—and, believe me, I got more to use!"

Lena nodded through Thomas's entire speech. She was too weak and afraid to take any more. She was hoping that he would leave. Instead, Thomas crawled up in the bed with her and lay down, pulling the covers over her as he did, to show her just how much control he had over her. Once she fell asleep, Thomas went home.

Chapter 35

The baby was aborted in secret at Lady Salena's house. Salena was also a midwife. She'd delivered babies for many of the people who couldn't afford to go to the hospital. She'd delivered Sable, but Salena didn't know that, nor did Sable. Salena also sold drugs, booze, numbers, and held card games in her basement. Everything about Salena was illegal, right down to the birth control pills she gave out. She ordered the pills for herself but didn't need them, because she'd never been able to have children. She was old enough to take the pill and the doctors couldn't refuse her. Salena stashed them for her patients. Thomas was oblivious to any other services Salena offered other than abortions. Getting rid of his problem was his only concern. It hung over his head like a large concrete slab.

Sable wanted to hang out with Thomas right after she left Salena's, but Thomas made her go home and lie down as Salena had ordered. He didn't want to take a chance on her hemorrhaging or something. This would definitely cause suspicion. Sable would have to tell it all, and Thomas couldn't afford the scandal. His mother and Jasper always believed that he was a golden child—and he didn't want to mar his reputation.

Thomas whistled as he walked home. He was relieved until he realized that both Sable and Kerrissy were out of commission for at least three more weeks. Suddenly he couldn't breathe. What would he do about his male urges? Thomas felt heavy as he walked along, thinking about what he deemed the most important thing in the world, *having a woman to fulfill his needs.* Lena suddenly popped into his thoughts. He'd forgotten that quickly about the seed he'd planted with her. She wouldn't turn him down now—no matter what he did, and she'd wait for him as long as he wanted her to.

Chapter 36

Lena lay in bed thinking about Thomas and their last encounter—the same as she had the first morning she'd awakened after it had happened. She'd watched and waited for him, hoping that he would return. She closed her eyes and massaged her stomach. Chills ran through her entire body. She shivered and lost her breath. Her husband had been good to her—he'd always made her feel something that no other man had—and Jasper had been better. But Thomas sent her to a place that she didn't want to return from, although he'd exhausted her. Maybe she loved him, totally loved him. She became angry at the thought of him and Kerrissy. No wonder her granddaughter was so in love with the man she'd had first, the one Lena had trained. But where did he learn what he'd done to them, and how did he become so good at it? Feelings of years past came over her. She wanted to get rid of Kerrissy. She wanted to run her out of town. Looking at Thomas with her caused jealousy to rage within her.

* * *

The light rapping on her door broke Lena's daydreaming. She hurriedly jumped out of bed, hoping that it was Thomas. She had gotten one foot in the blue satin slippers that were partially hidden under her bed, but remembered what Thomas had told her. She kicked them farther back. Jasper had bought them and she didn't want a big scene if Thomas was the impatient visitor. She walked to the door as fast as she could to avoid his brazen tongue. She didn't want to give Thomas any indication that she didn't want to see him. The wrong behavior might cause him to hit her, or worse, leave her for too long, like he had done so many times before. He'd gotten under her skin again, and she wasn't so willing to let go, the way she had been in the past. Lena instantly flung her kitchen door open without looking out. There stood Jasper, with his head slightly bowed, his hands folded. Lena threw her hand over her open mouth and began to tremble.

Jasper looked up. "Can I come in?"

Lena couldn't speak.

"Can I come in, Lena?"

Lena wanted to say no, but Jasper was always so polite and sweet. She thought a minute. It was too early for Thomas to catch him there. Lena stepped aside, pulling the door farther open as she did. She quickly closed it, once Jasper was inside and took off his hat.

Jasper licked his dry lips. "Lena, I know that boy know about us, but I love what we got—"

"Jasper! You gotta make it quick. Just speak your piece and go—"

"What's wrong with you, Lena? Somebody hurt you? Your husband back?"

"No, no. He ain't back. Um scared that boy gonna tell your wife, and—"

Jasper put his hat on Lena's head. "You my woman, too."

Lena let out a defeated breath. Thomas had never said anything like that to her, nor had he ever treated her kindly. The shameful thought made her put her head down. Tears ran down her face.

Jasper walked up to her and wrapped his arms around her curvy bottom. "Let me make them tears go away, baby."

Lena pried his arms from around her and began to back away. Jasper continued to walk up on her until her back hit the kitchen wall. He wrapped his arms around her bottom again and buried his head between her breasts. "Lena, I missed you. Just let me be quick and leave, baby. You done got me hooked on you. I'll be quick, so Thomas won't catch us. Okay?"

Lena continued to cry.

Jasper slowly moved his hands over her body. He pulled her robe open. He almost attacked her when he saw that she had lost weight, and how curvaceous she had gotten.

Lena accidentally screamed out, "No! Don't, Thomas!" She quickly put her hand over her mouth and allowed Jasper to explore her body with his tongue and soft kisses as he spoke. "Thomas ain't gonna catch us again. This gonna be quick, baby. This gonna be quick."

Lena closed her eyes and allowed Jasper to make her groan with desire and shiver. She'd forgotten how Jasper filled her. She lost all resistance and allowed him his time with her.

Jasper moaned, indicating that round two of their contact had been completed. He slowly stood up straight; his pants and underwear still around his ankles. "Lena, I can't stay away from you. Not the way you make me feel."

Lena closed her robe and tied it together. "Please, Jasper, just leave. I don't want that boy catching you here again—"

"Why, Lena? You got somethin' goin' with him?"

"No, no. He just so mean. He come back and threatened me last time we was together. He think of you like his father or something—"

"I'll take care of him—"

"*No! Don't!* I been knowin' that boy all his life! All his life, Jasper! He nice around people, but when he don't like somethin', he got his ways of getting what he want, Jasper! What we doing wrong, anyway, and you know it, 'cause you got a wife! Just please, please, please! Don't come back! Um too old for this! I don't need no trouble!"

"I'll leave if you have me again before I go. I need you to last me if I ain't gonna see you no more."

Lena let out an irritated breath through her nose.

Jasper grabbed the belt on Lena's robe, causing it to fly open before she could answer. He stared at Lena's body, making her feel uneasy. Lena mindlessly reached around, trying to grasp the sides of her robe so that she could close it. Jasper pushed her against the wall and forced her to submit. He spoke to Lena as he took her again. "I don't know how you can let that silly boy come between us, after all I done did for you. I don't know how you

could do it, Lena. I just don't know how. But if you
that concerned and scared, I won't come back
here. I care too much about you to keep comin'
here, and you don't want me. . . ."

Jasper left Lena's house angry, but he would
allow Lena her request for now. But what he did
behind his wife's back, or in front of her, was his
business, nobody's but his. Jasper fumed a little
more. Being with a woman like Lena—who did so
many things right, and almost undetectable to a
wife's suspicion—was hard to come by. He wanted
to deal with Thomas; instead, he headed home.
He'd wait until things settled down.

Lena was devastated. She ran and jumped in the
tub as soon as Jasper let the door close. Why didn't
she just stop Jasper? If Jasper decided to confront
Thomas about him being at her house and their relationship, Thomas would come back to her with a
vengeance she'd regret. Lena thoroughly scrubbed
her body, trying to wash away all traces of Jasper.

Thomas changed his baby while Kerrissy watched.
His hands trembled as a vision of Lena popped into
his head. He dropped the baby pins he held in his
mouth and almost drooled.
    Kerrissy picked up the pins and pushed him with
her hip. "Move over before you stick my baby girl."
    Thomas laughed inwardly, then wiped his mouth
with the back of his hand. "Girl, I wasn't gonna hurt

that baby. I had just thought about somethin' stupid and funny."

Kerrissy looked up at him. "That's okay. I'll do it. Go get her bottle, okay."

Thomas headed downstairs and took the warm bottle out of the pan of water. As he brought it back to Kerrissy, he wondered if there would be instant everything in the future—after all, they had come out with the disposable paper diaper, but his wife felt cloth was better for Thessia.

Thomas handed Kerrissy the bottle. "How do you know it ain't too hot?"

Kerrissy took the bottle from him and sprinkled a little of the milk on her wrist. "Like this."

Thomas wrinkled his brow. "So what that tell you?"

"Well, the skin on the inside of your arm is sensitive. If it was to sting me, I know it's too hot for Thessia. It's just warm, so I know it's okay." Kerrissy picked the baby up, put the bottle in her mouth, and sat down on the bed with the baby in her arms.

Thomas loved the sight of this. It caused him to grin from ear to ear.

Kerrissy rocked the baby back and forth as she smilingly stared down at her. "Thomas, do you think that I could go see my mom?"

Thomas felt a fearful chill go through him. His nerves in his stomach cramped. "Baby, why? She'll make us get our marriage annulled. You want that?"

"We got a baby now. Ain't nothing she can do, Thomas. She'll be so glad to see me, she won't think about doing nothing like that.

"She'll probably put me in jail and try to get me on kidnapping charges. But if you want, I'll let you and the baby go—ain't no way um goin' around that woman. She told me before she left, she'd kill me if I as much looked at you again. And from the way her eyes bugged when she said it, I believe her. Now don't tell me you forgot that."

Kerrissy put her head down and continued feeding the baby. "I didn't forget. I just thought that by now she'd be over it. Just wanted to see her. I miss her, Thomas. She's still my mom."

"Then go ahead and see her. I won't be mad, but I can't chance going to jail way out in California somewhere. Then my mama won't never see me again. I know you don't want that, Kerrissy."

"No, I don't."

Thomas let out a sigh of relief, then kissed Kerrissy on her forehead. He wrapped his arms around Kerrissy and the baby. "Um glad you love me."

Kerrissy slightly squirmed. "I still wanna go by myself and take the baby, though."

Thomas was uncomfortable again. Had he lost the hold he had on his wife, whom he'd always considered his property?

"So, you sayin' you don't care about leaving me or my feelings? You just wanna leave?"

"Yeah, I care, Thomas. But I need to see my mother. I miss her. You here with yours."

"I'll tell you what. Leave if you want. Maybe I won't be here, either, if you decide to come back."

"Thomas! I only wanna go for, like, a weekend or something! Mommy will send for me—"

"Go! And don't talk to me about it again. Okay?"

Thomas jumped up, grabbed his coat, and went straight over to Jasper's.

* * *

Jasper saw Thomas as he headed up his walkway.
He could see the unhappy look on Thomas's face.
Remembering his talk with Lena, he met Thomas
outside—just in case the entire ordeal would turn
into a shouting match. Jasper never wanted his wife
to learn about him *and* Lena. She'd whip him and
Lena if she ever found out.

Jasper threw on his coat and rushed up to Thomas
with his hands in his pockets before Thomas could
reach his house. He extended one of his nervous
hands to him. "Hey, Thomas, man, what's up with
you? Why you come by here so early?" Jasper's voice
was shaky.

Thomas looked down at the sidewalk. "She wanna
leave me, man. Kerrissy wanna go to her mother's,
take my baby, and leave me."

Jasper exhaled silently with relief. "Leave you?
For good?"

"Naw, Jasper, naw. To visit."

"What's wrong with that, man?"

Thomas lied. "Her mother ain't never met me,
Jasper. Shoot. Kerrissy been gone since way before
she got pregnant. She ain't seen her mother since we
picked her up."

Jasper put his hand on Thomas's shoulder. "Damn,
Thomas. I didn't know. Look, try to talk her out of it,
then treat her like you know I taught you."

Thomas smiled. He knew just what to do, but it was
too early for intimacy with his wife. He looked up at
Jasper again. "Man, you know she just had that baby."

Jasper massaged the sparse hair on, his chin. "Oh,
yeah, right. Then you gotta make her jealous. Tell her
we goin' down to the strip bar. That maybe you can
find a woman down there that will understand you."

"What if she don't believe me, Jasper?"

"Then leave and come back down here. We'll go for real."

Without another word Thomas turned to walk away. Jasper touched his shoulder. "Man, we need to talk about something else."

"What, Jasper?"

"Lena. Man, I know you don't approve of what me and Lena had, but she really help me out when my wife actin' stupid. She okay, Thomas. Please try to understand."

Thomas was now grinding his teeth and clenching his fists. "You been back over there, man?"

Jasper became a little intimidated, but suspicious. He thought about his answer. "Naw, man. Why you so dead set on me not talking to that old-ass woman? You want her?" Jasper was now taking a defensive stance and glaring at Thomas.

Thomas loosened up. The question had caught him off guard. Jasper's stance made him back off. "Naw, I don't want no old-ass Lena—"

"Then why you so worried about what me and her do? You ain't even that close to my wife, man. Maybe you done seen Lena naked or something, though. I thought about that comment you made about her ass in the car that night—"

Thomas threw up his hand and pretended to laugh. "Man! You crazy! What I want with that, huh? No offense, but my wife the prettiest thing around here!"

"Then you won't give me or Lena a hard time if I go 'round to her house every now and then, will you?"

"Naw, Jasper. You can go over there whenever

you want. I just don't like that broad—she the reason why my auntie left." Thomas made his eyes water, then wiped at the fake tears. "She just ain't right. And I just couldn't take you being with her 'cause me and you tight. I don't know if we can stay friends if you goin' be sleeping with my enemy."

"She the one run your aunt out of town, Thomas?"

"Yeah. She told me she did it. Her husband wanted my auntie. She had my auntie raped. She was trying to mess with me for revenge so that she could shock my mother, so I raped her, made her do things. I don't want her to have nobody! Nothin'!"

Jasper became a little disgusted. "I ain't goin' back over there then. I didn't know she was so low, so foul. . . . Damn, Thomas, why you didn't tell me a long time ago, man?"

Thomas hunched his shoulders.

Jasper patted him on the back. "Go on home and deal with Kerrissy. If you come back, we'll head down to the club later, okay?"

Thomas nodded, then walked off, smiling, with his head down.

Thomas jogged up the steps to the bedroom. Kerrissy was folding the baby's clean clothes and putting them away. He walked over to her and took the tiny T-shirt out of her hand. He took her wrist and guided her downward onto the bed next to him.

"Kerrissy, I don't want you to go, baby."

"But, Thomas, I need to see my mom."

"Then I might as well go out and look for me another woman tonight, because I know that once you leave here, you ain't coming back."

Kerrissy tried to hug Thomas.

He pushed her arms away. "No, Kerrissy, no. That ain't gonna work this time. You go ahead and do what you need to do, and I'll do what I need to do. Okay?"

Tears filled Kerrissy's eyes.

Thomas stared in her face. "Those ain't gonna work, either. I'll tell you what, Kerrissy. I'm going out to the club. If I find another woman, I'll let you know—"

Kerrissy put up her hand to touch Thomas. "No, Thomas, don't—"

Thomas pushed her away again. "Don't what?"

Kerrissy dropped her head and cried.

Thomas stood up. "I'm going out. Don't wait up for me. And you can go wherever you want, but you ain't taking my baby from me, Kerrissy. I'll fight tooth and nail for my child."

Chapter 37

Thomas stood in the dark hallway that separated the men's room and dancers' dressing rooms and the stairs that led to other vacant quarters. He had gotten as drunk as possible so that he could stop thinking about Kerrissy leaving him. Then snatched by a stripper as soon as he'd left the men's room, he quickly paid for her services, and he was more than ready to have his fantasy fulfilled. He would also take the frustration he felt for Kerrissy out on her.

The stripper dropped to the floor on her knees as soon as she was free. Thomas hadn't been at all kind.

In pain she looked up at Thomas in disbelief.

Thomas squinted evilly. "So what did you think, Miss Bunders?"

The woman's mouth flew open in astonishment.

Thomas smiled, "I'm drunk, but I know them big boobs and that mole on your face anywhere—even if your hair is blond now and you still look young. How old you now, forty—fifty?"

The woman tried to crawl away.

Thomas put his foot on her back and pushed her to the floor. "Answer me or I'll tell everybody we know that you an after-hours stripper and whore. That sure won't be good—even if you ain't still no principal."

She slowly crawled back up on her knees and stared up at him. Her eyes begging for sympathy. "I'm forty-seven."

Thomas stared back at her blankly. "It's people like you who cause people like me to hate so deeply."

Miss Bunders lowered her head.

Thomas grabbed her hair tightly. "I could kill you back here and no one would know—wouldn't even care—you considered white trash! You already know that, though, or you wouldn't be back here with me!"

Thomas pulled Miss Bunders up off the floor by her forearm into a standing position. He grinned broadly as he thought of just how he would torture her. Maybe he would find out where she lived and give her visits the way he did Lena. This was his favorite thing to do to a woman whom he wanted to get back at, and Miss Bunders was one of them. She had been his grade school principal, and when he was in kindergarten, she had slapped him and called him "little nigger" just because he'd been sent to the office for protecting himself from another student who just so happened to be white. Many children of color had told stories about her, but Thomas had never believed them. . . . *Wouldn't no adult treat a child that way just because they black or somethin'.* He had cried his eyes out at the time from the let-down, and his unjust punishment, and now it was her turn.

Through clenched teeth he whispered, "How you like 'little nigger' now, huh?" Her eyes stretched so wide, Thomas thought they would pop out of her head.

Thomas shook Miss Bunders up a bit and gave her a few slight taps on the face to scare her as he laughed. Who else could be this lucky? Not many people got the chance at this type of revenge, and he'd gotten it for many of his classmates.

Thomas let go of Miss Bunders and began straightening out his clothes as he looked down at his appearance. "You still the principal?"

Miss Bunders wouldn't comment.

Thomas snickered. "I can come down to the school and find out. Now, is you still the principal?"

Miss Bunders nodded.

Thomas snorted, then stuck his pointed finger on her nose. "Tell, and we'll both be in trouble. . . . You got another show?"

Miss Bunders shook her head no.

"Then stay back here until I'm outta here or I'll make this a routine for you. Do you hear me?"

Miss Bunders nodded. Fear was making her stomach churn. She held her throat as she vomited.

Thomas slipped back to his table.

Jasper looked at him. "Man, where you been so long?"

"Had too much to drink, man. It wouldn't stay down."

Jasper laughed and went back to the show.

Thomas continued to think about his encounter with his grade school principal. He couldn't admit it to himself, or to others, but he loved being with an older woman—like how many men loved what they called the healthy ones, the ones with some meat on their bones. He was going to find Miss Bunders again before he went home. She'd be just what he needed to keep him satisfied until he was ready for Lena again.

Thomas looked around the club for Miss Bunders as Jasper walked ahead of him, but he couldn't find her.

Chapter 38

Thomas looked at his watch before exiting Jasper's car. It was 4:00 A.M. He entered the bedroom loudly and plopped down on the bed. He wanted to wake Kerrissy. He wanted her to see the time.

Kerrissy turned over to see that Thomas was still dressed. "You going to work, Thomas?"

"Work? I just got in. I told you where I was going." Thomas's voice was harsh. "And that's where I'll be permanently if you leave here."

Kerrissy sat straight up. "But I only wanna go for a few days—"

"*I don't give a damn if it's for a few hours, Kerrissy!* If you leave here, stay gone, and don't come back for my baby. Don't even come back to visit your child! You know what, Kerrissy. I shouldn't have risked my freedom for somebody like you. You don't care about nothing or nobody but yourself."

Kerrissy crawled over to Thomas. "That's not true, Thomas. I love you and my baby so much. But I miss my mom—"

"Then go to her. See if I'm still here when you decide to come back."

"But, Thomas—"

"Kerrissy, you know just as well as I do that you were too young for me. What do you think your mom is going to do when she finds out about all this shit, huh?"

Kerrissy thought.

Thomas went in for the kill. "Yeah. Now you understand. Even a short visit with your mother can get me a long term in prison." He held Kerrissy in his arms. "Baby, I know that I can't show you how much I love you right now, because you ain't ready, but in a few weeks, um gonna make sure you know how much I care. All I thought about while I was at that club was you."

"Then why it took you so long to get home after it closed, Thomas? You gonna leave me for somebody else, like you said?"

"No, baby, no. I planned it that way just to get back at you—just to scare you. I was hoping it would make you change your mind if you thought I wanted somebody else. Me and Jasper sat in the car and talked about me and you. That's all we did."

Kerrissy sighed. "I won't go."

Thomas hugged her tighter. "Thanks, baby. There's no way I'd make it in prison."

Chapter 39

Sable stood by her mirror and examined her profile, clothing, hair, and how much prettier she had gotten since the abortion. She had been lying around, reading comic books, going through her teen magazines for a week and a half. Her only other activity was school. Sable hadn't missed a beat there; she'd actually raised the bar for herself. Her grades had gotten even better. She was a B, or C student, now she was getting mostly A's. Her parents praised her constantly. They were so proud, they bought Sable all sorts of new clothes, footwear, and much more. Sable got almost anything she wanted. On occasion she thought about the baby she didn't want to get rid of, but she couldn't feel happier. She and Thomas would be together again real soon, would get married, and have children later.

She grinned from ear to ear as she thought about Thomas—the one who'd imprisoned her in her own home. He'd threatened her about being around the playground, where other males would want to look at her or—even worse—touch her. This was her day, the day he'd set up for her to meet him at the playground. He wanted to make sure that she was healing okay, and Sable could barely suppress her anxiousness.

Sable walked down to the playground and stood with her back to the fence with her fingers latched onto the openings of it. She stared in the direction where Thomas usually came from. As soon as she saw Thomas at the end of the alley, her heart pounded fiercely.

Thomas slowly approached Sable. He felt a lightness fill him as he got closer to where she stood. Instead of his nonchalant stride, Thomas walked with his head up, taking all of Sable in. The red leather coat with white fur collar and cuffs, red boots, and the winter-white miniskirt she wore made him look even closer. Sable had definitely gotten thinner, her hair had grown even longer, and her skin was prettier, smoother, and had gotten a little lighter.

Sable's attractiveness caused Thomas to feel somewhat shy, a little inferior. He'd just noticed from the way she was dressed that her family must have money. They weren't just any ordinary black folk. Not many people could afford what Sable was wearing—young or old—or the car her parents drove. He hid his discomfort from Sable and looked directly at her as he walked up to her. "Hey, you miss me?"

The smile Sable displayed made Thomas want to melt. The new perfume she wore hypnotized him. Sable released the fence and rubbed her red-leather-gloved hands together. "Yeah. I missed you. I missed you a lot."

Thomas wrapped his arm around Sable's shoulders and walked toward the parking lot. He looked up at Sable's diamond-studded ear and the baby hair that delicately surrounded it, then gazed in her eyes. "You know why I wanted you to meet me at the playground?"

"No."

"I wanted to make sure that you was gonna be faithful to me. That you wouldn't let some other guy talk to you after I told you I didn't like it."

"I wouldn't talk to anybody else. I love you too much."

"Good, Sable. I wouldn't want to have to teach you a lesson on our first day back together."

Sable dropped her head.

Thomas's confidence was back. He was sweet again. "Baby, you know how crazy you make me. We don't need nobody spoiling what we got."

Sable wiped a tear from her eye. "I keep telling you, Thomas. Can't nobody but you tell me nothing."

Thomas and Sable reached the parking lot. He pulled her closer. "Good, baby, good—that's what I like to hear. Now tell me. You been doin' okay?"

Sable whined. "Yes."

"Your parents ask any questions?"

"No. I been getting better grades and they just thought that I was staying home and studying."

Thomas's head jerked up. "Better grades?"

"Yeah, I been getting mostly A's. That's how I got this new outfit."

"Don't they think you too young to be wearing all this stuff?"

"No. A lot of the kids at my school be wearing this kind of stuff, Thomas."

"Where do you go to school, Sable? Beverly Hills?"

Sable began to think. Thomas had never asked her where she went to school. He really hadn't asked her too much about her personal life. Sable looked down at her outfit, then up at Thomas. "I go to school in the suburbs."

"Your people got money or something?"

"What do you mean by that, Thomas?"

"I mean, where your folks work?"

"My dad own a car dealership. My mom's a professor at the college—MCC—Monroe Community College."

Thomas became a little frightened. If these uppity Negroes found out about him and their daughter, wasn't no telling what they might do. If he backed out now, maybe all would remain well. "Uh, Sable, see, I didn't know your parents were like that. Do you know what would happen to me if they found out about us? Why didn't you tell me?"

"'Cause that's why none of the other boys would mess with me. That's what Wesley was telling me the day you got mad because I was talking to him."

The mention of Wesley's name made Thomas clench his fists. "Look! I don't want you talking to that—never mind. Maybe we should end this. I mean, I can't afford to get into trouble. Maybe I should let Wesley have you."

Sable became angry and began hitting Thomas in his chest with both her fists as she cried. "Why you trying to give me to somebody else? I don't want nobody else, Thomas! Um tired of you always trying to get rid of me! I do everything you want me to do—"

Thomas grabbed both her hands and kissed her as they slowly inched their way to the back of the vacant building. He continued to kiss Sable long and hard as she leaned against the structure. He released her. "Baby, I need to get you home. It's too cold for you to be out here after what you just went through."

Sable was still crying. "But we ain't even been together yet!"

"Baby, you know it's too early. Besides, I ain't too sure that we should continue seeing each other. Sable, you a high risk."

Sable grabbed the front of Thomas's coat and slammed him against the building, reversing their positions. "I ain't too big of a risk to do this!" She slowly slid downward.

Thomas tried to stop her by grabbing her arm. She just looked too pretty and her status had changed things.

Sable jerked away and continued.

Sable stared at Thomas while he tried to adjust. "I probably should be getting home now."

Thomas straightened his clothes. "Yeah. Okay."

Sable had embarrassed him. He tried not to show it, but his attempt to hide it made him feel more like a buffoon.

As he and Sable walked toward her house, Thomas didn't say a word. He could only think. *Was*

Sable this good before? Or has she been practicing? She just seemed to be so different. So much more mature than before. So mature that he felt like the one who was being taken advantage of. This was a feeling he hated—especially with women. He was the one who was supposed to be overpowering—controlling the situation. When the time came, Sable would have to be taught a lesson for trying to act so big, and making him feel so small.

Thomas thought about ways to get back at Sable but couldn't. By the time he hit the door, he was seething.

Kerrissy ran to Thomas and threw her arms around his neck.

Thomas grabbed her forearms and removed them.

Kerrissy stood back on one leg, looking at him, wide-eyed and openmouthed. She crossed her arms, then rolled her eyes.

Thomas walked up on her. "What the hell you lookin' at me like that for?"

Kerrissy's heart began to pound. She dropped her arms and backed up.

Thomas grabbed her by the throat. "I asked you a question, Kerrissy!"

Kerrissy held on to Thomas's wrist with her hands. "I was just wondering what was wrong with you." Kerrissy began to cry. "What did I do now, Thomas?"

Thomas calmed down and let go of Kerrissy, realizing that he had just violated Jasper's number one rule. But what else could he have done at a time like this? She needed to be put in her place. Thomas was still breathing hard. "You know what, Kerrissy. Um sick and tired of you acting like a baby—a little girl. Why don't you just pack your stuff up and go see your mother like you wanna do, anyway. And you know what else? You can take the baby with you. Maybe you need to get away."

Kerrissy kept her head down and let the tears flow. "But I thought we had settled all that, Thomas. All I did was hug you when you came through the door and you wanted to fight me. I don't understand—"

Thomas turned his back to her. "Um sorry. But all I could think about while I was out was how you wanted to see your mom and I knew you was right. You need to go see her. Maybe if you explain to her, she won't bother what we have. Just tell her how much we love each other. She'll probably just be glad to see you and not care that we married with a baby."

Kerrissy looked up. "You really want me to go?"

Thomas pulled Kerrissy over to the bed with him. "Yeah, baby. It's the only way we gonna feel free. I don't think your mother evil enough to put your husband and baby's father in prison."

"She ain't, Thomas. She just was upset about what she caught us doing. And we both know it wasn't right."

Thomas smiled, and apologized as he gently brushed Kerrissy's hair back. "It wasn't."

Kerrissy took a long breath. "When you want us to leave?"

"Not until after we can . . . ," Thomas whispered in Kerrissy's ear.

Kerrissy smiled broadly.

Chapter 40

Thomas was frantic. He'd smoked almost a pack of cigarettes before he reached the parking lot to meet Sable. He put his head down. When he looked up, Sable was headed toward him. She was smiling her usual lovesick smile. Thomas stood up quickly and nervously. "We gotta take care of something, Sable."

Sable looked confused. "What?"

"Baby, I think I got something. We need to go to the clinic."

"What you got? You real sick?"

"Sable, I gotta tell you something. You know that we couldn't see each other, right?"

"Yeah, but—"

"Just listen, Sable. I got horny, real horny, and messed up. I messed with a stripper down at a club. I used—I mean *she* used a rubber, but it must have had a hole in it or something—"

Sable threw her hand over her mouth and turned her back to Thomas. She was horrified. She hadn't had her eighteenth birthday and she had already been pregnant, and now this. She turned back to

Thomas with the same fearful expression. "What you got, Thomas?"

Thomas looked down at the ground. "I think it's gonorrhea."

"*What?*" Sable became hysterical and began to back away from Thomas. She knew that he'd contracted something, but she never thought that it would be so bad. She just didn't know what to think when he alerted her. She'd heard enough about VD to know that it could turn into syphilis if gone untreated, that it was supposed to be a dirty person's disease for only hookers and whores. How did this happen to her?

Thomas grabbed her arms and shook her. "Sable! Listen to me! You gotta get in control—"

"*How do you know you got it?* I mean, we didn't have sex—"

"*Sable!* I was burning when I went to the bathroom—"

"So you done had it before, Thomas? *We ain't had sex! I shouldn't have nothin'!*"

"Sable, come on now, you gotta control yourself. Look, um sorry, but I had got with that lady a little before me and you saw each other the last time—"

"You shouldn't have done it, Thomas—"

"Oh! So you turnin' your back on me now! You leaving me just bcause I got hot and messed up one time! You know what, Sable! You the one to blame, anyway! You went and got pregnant, then you did what you did to me to show me how much you care, and now you mad at me? I was willing to wait until you was better, Sable, but you ran up on me. Don't you see that?"

Sable began to sniffle.

Thomas turned and pretended to leave. "Let's just forget about us, okay? I ain't got time for this. Besides, I don't want no woman to be my wife that can't understand and trust me—who don't care about me. . . ."

"Wait, Thomas, wait!"

"For what, Sable? You done let me know where you stand. What you wanna do, huh? Make me feel worse?"

"No, um sorry, I just been through so much—I ain't never been through none of this stuff before. I just don't know what to do."

Thomas pulled Sable to him so that she could lay her head on his chest. "Baby, we goin' git through this together. We gonna go to that clinic. It's out of town, just a few hours. Nobody but me, you, and the doctor have to know."

Sable looked up at him. "How we gonna do that without my parents knowing, Thomas? They open on Saturday?"

"No. You got different classes, don't you?"

"Yeah, Thomas, but—"

"Okay. Listen. Go to your class. About nine A.M., I'll pick you up from school. We'll ride down. I'll get you back to school for your afternoon classes. If your parents find out, tell them that you got sick and had to go to the bathroom."

Sable thought about it. Yes, if she were caught, that would be a good excuse. This allowed her mind to temporarily elude the real problem. "You don't love that lady, do you?"

"Hell no! She just a whore! How could you ask me something like that about a whore!"

Sable hunched her shoulders.

"Let me walk you home so that you can tell me where your school is and where I should look for you. I'll see you in the morning." Thomas lifted Sable's chin with his fingers. "Nine A.M. sharp, okay? Be outside of that school waiting for me!"

Sable nodded.

Thomas took her hand in his. "This will be behind us soon, baby. I promise you."

Chapter 41

The clinic visit with Thomas and Sable had gone like clockwork. The only mishap was Mr. Harrison the neighborhood whoremonger being there. But he'd pretended not to know Thomas or Sable. Then there was the white lady that Thomas referred to as "Old Lady Bunders." When Thomas spoke to her, she pretended not to know who Thomas was.

When Thomas dropped Sable back off at school, she'd only missed fifteen minutes of her class, but everyone was outside. Someone had pulled the fire alarm.

As the students filed into the building, Sable couldn't help but look at the crowd she had slipped into and feel different. At age seventeen she'd had an abortion and a disease that many considered was for older women who were loose. She and Thomas had been sexual in so many ways, and so many times—even she had lost count. She shook her head and closed her eyes to clear the thoughts of lust she had for Thomas even now. She couldn't figure out why she still wanted him so bad—after

she'd just come from the clinic. And what was it
that made her smile each time she thought about
how she liked pleasing him. She strolled into the
building with the other students, but it was apparent to her that she was so much more mature.

The timing was great for Thomas. He couldn't
believe how everything worked out to his advantage. He and Kerrissy had been able to reestablish
their feelings, without him exposing or sharing his
secret. Four weeks later, Kerrissy and the baby were
on the plane and off to visit Gweneth without warning her.

Chapter 42

"Thomas, please, please! Um tellin' the truth!"

Thomas ignored the pleas of Lena as he sat on her bed, verbally disciplining her, threatening to make it physical. He knew by the way Jasper had talked about her that she'd seen him and had lied. She had to be punished for disobeying him.

Thomas stood up. "When um done, it won't happen again, Lena. I told you last time I was here that I didn't want no other man here. Me and you got a relationship till I say it's done, and I ain't gonna be going behind no other man, especially one I call my friend."

Tears flowed down Lena's face. "Why you doin' this?"

Thomas cut his eyes at her evilly. He sat down on the bed next to Lena. He clenched his teeth. "Why you lie?"

"About what, Thomas?"

Thomas jumped up and balled up his fists. He staggered backward. *"Stop playing stupid, Lena!"*

Lena cringed and rolled into a fetal position.

Thomas stood looking down at her. "Jasper already told me everything!"

Lena became frightened. Her eyes stretched wide. She knew that Thomas was full of his courage. She'd smelled it almost before she'd opened her door for him. She hadn't been afraid at first, but when Thomas began to instantly tear at her clothing, completely ripping them off her until they were unrecognizable, she had a change of heart, she hadn't tried to fight him off, like she wanted, as he dragged her to the bedroom.

Thomas scratched his head drunkenly. His eyes batted slowly. He looked at Lena's body. He hadn't seen her in a while. "You done lost weight, didn't you?"

Lena was afraid to answer Thomas. She nodded her head in agreement with quick movements.

"You do it for Jasper?"

"No-o-o-o-o!"

"Then why?"

Lena hunched her shoulders.

Thomas's body jerked as he grunted out his laughter. He sat back down on the bed and rolled Lena over onto her back so that he could get a good look at her. "This for me or Jasper?"

"I just lost some weight, Thomas. I was getting too heavy."

Thomas squinted. Lena's protruding stomach was almost gone. "You been exercising, too?"

Lena nodded.

Thomas squeezed her butt. "I don't want you losin' too much of this. You hear?"

Lena nodded timidly again.

"Come on. I need you,"

Lena slowly rolled over toward Thomas.

Thomas gripped her tightly. He hadn't touched Sable for more than two weeks. He had wanted her, but he was still planning her punishment for trying to belittle him. Lena could satisfy him just as good—better until he decided what Sable's fate would be.

Thomas let out a drunken wail. Lena knew that sound. Thomas would either go home quickly or be knocked out for a while.

Thomas was still angry with Lena. His plans were totally different. He was going to embarrass Lena again for being with Jasper, lying about it, and believing that he was too ignorant to know. As he reached his peak, he tried pulling away from her. Lena held tightly. Thomas was still too full of energy. Her original thoughts were wrong. Thomas had a different plan and Lena knew that it would be a dirty one. As Thomas tried pushing her away so that he could splatter her in shame, he felt himself nearly falling off the edge of the bed. He wished he'd moved closer to the middle. He reached for Lena and held on to her head as he slid to the floor. Lena was breathing hard with fear. Her heart pounded. Maybe she should have just let him do his dirt.

Thomas put his elbow up on the bed and pulled himself to his feet. "You think you done did something smart 'n' funny, don't you, Lena?"

Lena's eyes were teary. She shook her head.

Her voice screeched. "I was just tryin' tuh please you, Thomas."

Thomas grinned nastily. "Well, you will, Lena." He finished removing his pants and crawled upon the bed. Lena tried to get away, but Thomas, as usual, grabbed her ankle and pulled her to him. He dove on Lena to stop her. He clenched his teeth. "Um tired of you trying to be in control."

Lena continued to struggle. Thomas pinned her to the mattress. She let out a loud sigh and then collapsed her upper body. She reminded herself, *Relax, relax. You only make him mad when you try to fight him.*

Thomas whispered in her ear, "That's right, that's right. Act like you got some sense."

Thomas was still with Lena. She gripped her covers in confusion. What was taking him so long, and why was he being so gentle?

Thomas whispered in her ear again. "Jasper taught me a lot, but you the best teacher. Outta everything you done taught me, I like this best, Lena. You feel even better than you did before. That exercising must've tightened you up some more. If I had to choose who to lay with, I'd take you every time, Lena, every time. I just can't git enough of you for some reason. It's like I wanna leave you alone, but I just can't—I can't. I try not to do this, not to want you, 'cause um a young man. Sometimes I feel outta place being with you, but I can't stop myself. Ain't no way um gonna let you go, Lena. No way um gonna let you go to Jasper or nobody else right now—couldn't make it without you, just couldn't."

Thomas's arm muscles accentuated. He kept his eyes closed tightly and trembled as his desire was fulfilled.

Lena cringed and held back the nauseous feeling that his words and drunken breath caused. Her stomach did flip-flops, but she wouldn't—she couldn't—let Thomas know. It would surely anger him; he'd become savage. She was doing all she could to handle him, as it was.

She'd taught him, and taught him well, but it seemed much more forceful now that Thomas was in control. She couldn't get used to the pressure. She never dreamed that Thomas would get so addicted to this ritual. It was something extra to keep him. Something that they would do every once in a while.

Lena could only lie and wait and clutch the covers.

Thomas laid his exhausted body on hers. Lena continued to clutch the covers. If Thomas didn't pass out when he was this drunk, she never knew what to expect when he was like this. She breathed short, shallow breaths, hoping that Thomas was done. She flinched when he began caressing her.

Thomas could hear her breathing accelerate, and he smiled. He was good at what he did for her, for all of his women. Why was she trying to pretend to not like it—to not want him? Why did she always pretend each time he took her? Why didn't she just admit that she liked all of what he did to her? He could see her watching him on a daily basis, waiting and hoping that he'd come by. Sometimes she'd purposely let him see her; other times she'd snatch her curtains shut, hoping to anger him and make him come to her, stomping. Thomas laughed to himself. He knew all the games—all the cues that said she was ready for him, but he'd make her wait . . . suffer. But when Jasper approached him so viciously, he knew that something more had gone on between them. He was ready to put all thoughts of Jasper out of her head. No matter what he did—how long it took him to get to her—a woman was still his until he said it was over.

Thomas began to make love to Lena. She trembled and closed her eyes as Thomas moved slowly and rhythmically. He gently bit the back of her neck and whispered as he continued to stroke her. "You don't love me no more, Lena?"

Lena's breathing was now hard and out of control. She wouldn't answer.

Thomas made firmer contact while continuing to nibble Lena's neck. "You don't love me no more?"

Lena squealed, became dizzy from the feelings, but she refused to answer.

Thomas smiled. Why did women always do this when they know they like it? He continued to nibble Lena's neck. "Do you love me, Lena?"

Lena squealed again and trembled.

Thomas stopped. "You want me to stop? I'll stop if you don't answer me—"

"I love you, Thomas! I love you!" Lena let the tears from her weakness and lust for Thomas flow as Thomas continued his sex pattern.

Thomas whispered in her ear, "You gonna make Jasper stay away from here?"

Lena tried to talk. "He—"

"*Don't lie, Lena. I know he been 'round here!* But as

long as he don't come back, we won't have no more problems, okay?"

Lena nodded her head against the mattress, relaxed, and allowed Thomas to use her.

Lena ran her hand up and down her stomach, trying to stop her body from reacting to the feelings Thomas had just given her.

Thomas rubbed her thigh. "Go git your bath."

Lena was reluctant. She let out an exasperated breath. Thomas grabbed her hand and pulled, indicating that he meant *immediately.*

Lena rose slowly. Thomas finished pulling her to her feet, then sat on her bed, waiting for her return.

Lena took her time returning to Thomas, hoping—praying—that he would be asleep or gone. He was still sitting on the bed, naked, gazing at the bedroom door. The familiar leer he wore made her uneasy. Thomas opened his arms and legs, summoning Lena to enter them. As she stepped inside Thomas's human vise, a tear slid down her cheek.

Thomas took her chin in his hand. "What's wrong? You think um gonna hurt you?"

Lena could no longer hold in her emotions. Thomas grabbed her around the waist and lowered her onto his knee. Lena jumped. She couldn't take any more of the sex she knew he loved so well. Thomas ran his fingers through her long, stringy, wavy hair, which she had inherited from her Native Indian grandfather. "I ain't gonna hurt you. You just need to be punished sometime. You don't seem to

understand that I really mean business. . . . Do you
know how hurt I was to see Jasper here?"

"You didn't want me, Thomas—I figured you
never did. I hadn't seen you in so long, I figured
you didn't want me no more at all!"

"Lena, how many times I got to tell you how you
make me feel, huh? Ain't no way um goin' willingly
give you up to nobody. We got something special.
But you know I can't be here as much as before. It
may be wrong, but I got Kerrissy now, and she my
wife, and we got a baby."

"And that's another thing, Thomas. Why you
have to go marry my flesh and blood, then make
me do all this?"

"At first, I was just trying to get back at you, Lena.
Then I sorta fell in love with Kerrissy, but she ain't
enough for me, and I still need you. If I could find
an easy way to get rid of her, I'd do it, Lena. Too
many nights and days I be wantin' to be with you,
and it be killin' me—just killin' me, Lena." Thomas
buried his face in Lena's stomach and cried, "Tell
me you don't like what I do, and I won't be back.
Jasper kin have you."

Lena stroked his curly head. "I really never
wanted Jasper. But he treated me kind," Lena whispered. "Kind."

Thomas continued to cry, but not only for Lena.
He'd made a mess of his life, and the woman sitting
on his lap had helped ruin him. He was frustrated,
confused, and felt as if he couldn't go without a
woman for more than a few hours, unless he was ill.
He held on to Lena tightly and continued to cry. She
lifted her breast and offered it to him. Thomas felt
strange. Thoughts entered his head like a dirty flood.

He wanted to be understood, not oversexed. Surely, Lena understood this, didn't she? She was older. Why didn't she just wait? All he wanted to do was talk to her for a moment—just a little while, clear his head, his heart. Maybe get a real relationship with her— let Sable and Kerrissy go. Lena had been his first woman. She was more capable of helping him than either one of the others, in more ways than they could, and he hadn't missed Kerrissy or his child the way he thought he would. He had actually realized that he felt more comfortable being with Lena. He and Lena could move away. No one, absolutely no one, would know that he'd chosen this older woman over two beautiful young girls. But Lena had spoiled the moment. How did she expect for him to treat her any way but sexual when this was the only thing she gave, the only way she ever comforted him?

He pulled on Lena's long breasts as she held his head. Then it was time. Time to make sure that her confession about Jasper wouldn't be repeated. He slid Lena off his lap. "Lay down." His voice was low and raspy from crying. Lena lay on her back and waited. Thomas rolled her onto her stomach, then pulled her to her knees. She would get the treatment that was sure to make her stay with him. Thomas began planting kisses on Lena, then stopped at her curves, giving them extra attention. Lena suddenly let out the loudest cry Thomas had ever heard come from her, but he was familiar with it. He touched Lena's vagina to validate his prediction of satisfaction, then released her, allowing her somewhat full body to slowly descend into the mattress. He rubbed and stared at her buttocks. "If you let Jasper touch you again, after all I just gave you, I'll beat you, Lena. Maybe just kill me and you." Thomas stood up and got dressed. He stood in Lena's doorway. "Just remember what I said, Lena. I done went all the way with you now. You mine. I'll kill you if I have to."

Lena remained silent, confused, and filled with so many feelings she was light-headed.

As Thomas walked toward his house, a cloud of sadness covered him, which he recognized. He had never been able to comprehend it in the past, but it was now apparent. He did want to die, and he'd felt the urge for a long time. He wanted to kill the feelings that taunted him so strongly, almost daily, all day long, which he couldn't control. He couldn't understand his strong cravings, his desire for what he once read in a book was called "sexual deviant behavior." In his community, many of the practices he lusted for were frowned upon and even considered taboo. He felt like a junky—except his addiction was for sex. Anal sex. Oral sex. The things black people didn't talk about, but, which some secretly did in the dark. But all he knew was that his life was out of control. He strolled home with his hands in his pockets, close to tears, as he thought about taking Lena to the grave with him. He had done something for her and Sable—just to hold on to them for the sex—things that he would very seldom do for his own wife. Kerrissy was already his. There was no need to impress his wife—at least that was what he had heard in conversation from various men since he was a male child, and he believed it would always be that way. Besides,

Kerrissy was different. At times she made him feel somewhat uneasy with some of the things they *were* doing. Like she only participated because he wanted them. What he did for Sable and Lena on a constant to keep them *might* drive Kerrissy away permanently. She had already gone to her mother's and he wasn't sure if he would ever see her again—as it was. He needed something to hold her, to keep her tied to him. But trying something like that with her too often would probably cause him to lose her forever, and he wasn't ready to lose any of his women. However, he had never dreamed he would be doing things with Lena that he was doing, either. Was he still in control, or did Sable and Lena have the upper hand on him again?

Chapter 43

Thomas awakened out of his drunken stupor to the light tapping on the pane of the front door. He sat up on the sofa and looked around to see where he was, then at the wall clock to see what time it was. When he realized that he was at home, and had fallen asleep on the sofa, he panicked until he remembered that his mother would be working late. She had absolutely no tolerance for sofa snoozing. Thomas slowly stood and staggered to the door, pulled the curtain back, and peeped out. He ran his hand over his face and shook his head to clear his vision, to make sure that he was seeing correctly, then opened the door.

"What are you doing here?"

"I missed you, Thomas—"

"You know what. You have been taking just too many liberties with me lately." Thomas grasped the front of Sable's jacket and pulled her inside. "Come on. We need to talk." He led Sable down to the basement without letting go, until they reached the last step.

Sable looked around. She couldn't believe that it was just as clean and nice as the upstairs. Before she could make the compliment audible, Thomas grabbed her face. "Who the hell do you think you are, Sable?"

"I missed you—"

Thomas's eyes bulged. He put his hand around Sable's neck. "I didn't ask you that!"

Sable held on to his hands with hers. "You're choking me."

"Sable, if you don't answer me, and let go of my hands, I'll kill you."

"What do you want me to say, Thomas?"

"I wanna know what make you think you can keep on taking all sorts of liberties with me like you're *my man* or something. You think um a *faggot*, Sable, huh? You think um soft?"

"No, Thomas! No! You told me to come over here before. I haven't seen you in almost three weeks, Thomas."

"Sable, when I get ready to see you, I know how to find you. But you know what it is? You think that you can do whatever you want because your family got a little money. But I'll tell you what. If you ever, ever come here again, unless I'm the one to bring you here, you will never see me again. I told you already. I ain't willing to go to jail just because we laid up together, Sable."

Sable's mouth flew open in embarrassment. How could he talk to her that way—after all she had sacrificed to be with him and done for him?

"You got somethin' to say?"

"No."

Thomas pulled Sable to his chest. "I've been doing

a lot of thinking. Maybe we should call it quits. I'm really too old for you. I'll be twenty-one—"

Sable snatched her head upward. *"You got somebody else, Thomas! You got somebody else!"*

Thomas wouldn't answer.

Sable pushed away from him. "Who is it?"

That angered Thomas. He didn't answer to any woman, and Sable knew better. He slapped her so hard, she had to catch the banister so that she wouldn't fall on the floor. She grabbed her face, then charged at Thomas. Thomas grabbed her by the throat again, led her over to the sofa, and slammed her down on it. He straddled her and began slapping her continuously with the fronts and backs of both hands. Sable put up her arms to block him. Thomas grabbed her hair and pulled her head back. He gritted his teeth. "I. Will. Break. Your. Neck!"

Sable was crying streams of tears. "Please, Thomas, please. Don't! I won't do this again! I won't! I won't!"

"Come on. I'm taking you home. Maybe I'll tell your parents how you came to my house, looking for me, and you only a child."

"No, Thomas! Don't do that! I'll do whatever you want!"

"Okay. Then get your ass up from there, um taking you home! And don't come back here, Sable, unless I bring you or tell you to come by here. Do you understand me?"

Sable wrapped her arms around herself tightly and nodded. Thomas grabbed her by the arm and dragged her back upstairs. When he reached the porch, he lit a cigarette. He and Sable walked in silence until they reached the parking lot. Under the streetlight he could see that Sable's face was swelling.

He took her chin in his hand. "Tell your parents you had a fight with some girl who thought you was cuter than she is. Your face is swelling."

Sable touched her face and cried some more.

Thomas hugged her. "Um sorry, Sable, but um under a lot of pressure right now and you keep on pushing me. I don't know how it is at your house with your parents, but I'm *the man,* the leader in this relationship. Do you understand that?"

Sable nodded as she continued to cry.

Chapter 44

"Venn. How are you this morning?"

Venn's face contorted. "I'm fine. How are you?"

"Oh, I'm okay. You got any sugar, Venn?"

"Sure. Come on in—"

"No, no, no. I'll stay here until you come back with it. Here's my bowl."

"Okay, give me a minute."

Thomas ran downstairs in his underwear when he heard the familiar voice talking to his mother at the door. He could see the visitor peeking around, trying to spy inside. He dashed to the front door. *"What the hell are you doing here, Lena?"*

Venn quickly walked back to the front of the house with the bowl of sugar in her hand. "Thomas! Why are you talking to Lena like that, boy?"

"She ain't got no business here!"

"Thomas, I've taught you better. Now move out the way."

Thomas stood back and crossed his arms.

Lena looked up and down his toned body and slightly licked her lips.

Thomas stared at Lena in the sleek gray sweater-dress, her hair rolled neatly in a bun, her face made up. He could smell her perfume and felt himself come alive.

Lena took the sugar and looked at Thomas slyly. "Venn, don't be hard on Thomas. He knows that I very seldom speak to anyone. So why should I be here borrowing sugar?"

"Lena, that's me and your business. Thomas don't have a thing to do with this." Venn stopped. "Did you lose some weight?"

Lena smiled. "Yeah, a little."

Venn crossed her arms. "You lost more than a little. You look young enough to be my sister. You are so pretty."

Thomas wanted to stay and stare at Lena, but he turned and began to walk away.

Lena quickly cleared her throat and raised her voice. "Oh, I'm just made up to go to the store. Jasper said he'd give me a ride! I need this here sugar for my coffee! I done plumb run out!" Lena could see Thomas stop abruptly. She smiled even broader. "I'll see you later. He should be here in a little while." Lena walked back to her house.

Thomas continued up to his room with his fists clenched. Anger raged within him. Hadn't he and Lena just had a talk about Jasper? Did she believe that he was a joke? She'd find out as soon as he got the chance to get to her.

Venn called up to Thomas on her way out the door. "See you later, baby! Um going in early,

Thomas! They asked me if I could come in to the center tonight!"

"Okay, Ma! I'll see you when you get in!"

Thomas got up off the bed, went into the bathroom, brushed his teeth, quickly bathed, threw on cologne, dressed, and headed out the door, as if he was going to work.

Lena sat on her bed in a daze, still holding the sugar, waiting. She knew that it was only a matter of time before Thomas would come bursting into her house. She continued to wait patiently.

The door opened. Lena could hear the quick footsteps before they reached her bedroom. Thomas stood in her bedroom doorway and gave Lena an evil look. Without another word he approached her. Lena closed her eyes and waited for whatever was to come. Thomas backhanded her, Lena's hair fell down. She fell backward on the bed. The sugar bowl flew out of her hands and exploded as it landed on the floor. Thomas was on top of her now, choking her. Lena wouldn't speak. She allowed the tears to flow down the sides of her face. Thomas drew back a fist and gritted his teeth. "You didn't believe me when I said I would kill you if you as much as let Jasper near you, did you, Lena?" He brought his fist down directly in the middle of Lena's face with force. She screamed and threw up her hands before the blow landed. Thomas was breathing like an angry bull as he grabbed her skinny wrists. Holding them together with one hand, he began slapping and landing incomplete punches anywhere he could, and whenever he could get control and his balance. Lena continued to struggle as Thomas hit and held her awkwardly. Thomas lost his balance altogether and fell on the bed. Lena rolled away from him onto her stomach and began to holler and wail. "Just go get the knife out the drawer and kill me, Thomas! Don't beat me to death! You done caused me enough pain and grief! Just git it over with, *please*! Just help me to die! Don't keep on punishing me for what I done before you was even born! Just kill me and make it quick!"

Thomas lay on his back, out of breath. "Why, Lena? Why? We just talked about Jasper the other day. Why you keep on making me do this? Why you come to my house in front of my mama, huh?"

Lena sniffled and spoke from a grief-stricken heart. "You let everybody else come there. Jasper, my granddaughter, and that little black gal I saw you walkin' through the alley. I figured if nothin' else, before I died, I'd come to your house. Um dressed tuh die, Thomas. Um dressed tuh die."

Thomas pulled on Lena's rigid body until she was close to his chest. "She ain't nobody, Lena. She ain't nobody."

"Then why she been to your house *twice*!"

"Lena, when I first seen that girl, I had to have her 'cause she looked so much like you. She completed some kind of fantasy that I had about you, and that was all. To keep her comin' to me, 'cause I was so mad at you, I gave her some money the day you saw her come up to my fence. Yesterday she came without an invitation and I had to whip her ass. I saw you in the window, figured I'd get a chance to explain it all to you today. Believe me, I wasn't trying to hurt you, Lena, not that time. What you do for me—ain't no way in this world I would purposely let you know about some other woman—and bring her in your *face*. Only if you made me angry enough to do that, and you haven't so far."

"Thomas, I don't want to do this no more. If you kill me, you just do it, but you tearing my heart in pieces. I got to get over you, Thomas! What I'm feeling for you is killing me!" Lena clutched the front of her dress as if she could hold her heart. *"You killin' me. . . ."*

Thomas held Lena closer, tighter. "Baby, baby, baby, baby, please. Don't say that—"

Lena tried pushing away from Thomas, but she couldn't. He held her tighter and wrapped her arm around his waist. "Come on, Lena. You know you don't wanna leave me."

"I can't do this no more, Thomas. At least Jasper pretended to love me—"

Thomas squeezed Lena so tightly, she had to scream.

Thomas relaxed his hold. "Didn't I tell you about mentioning him to me?"

"But you don't love me, Thomas. You say you ain't mad no more. Why you doing this? Why don't you just let me go?"

Thomas closed his eyes so that the tears that had formed in them wouldn't drop. He didn't want to tell Lena that he had feelings beyond love for her, that he felt a connection. But he knew that he needed to say something to make her stay. It seemed as though Lena was the only one of his women who could keep his attention.

Thomas put his open hand on the back of her

head and held her face into his chest. "I don't think that I ever told you that I didn't love you, Lena."

Lena tried to look up. Thomas held her head. He didn't want Lena to see what he was feeling.

"Do you care anything about me at all, Thomas? Anything? Just give me a reason to wait on you when you ready for me. Anything, Thomas! Anything at all!"

Thomas closed his eyes again. "I care about you, Lena." Thomas could no longer hold back the tears. "Just don't leave me. I'll try to do better. I swear to you."

"What about when Kerrissy git back?"

"What about her, Lena?"

"Don't you miss her—and your baby?"

Thomas wouldn't answer.

"Thomas, don't you miss her—them?"

Thomas shook his head slowly from side to side.

Lena gasped and forced her hand up to her mouth. She needed to know more. "Do you love her?"

Thomas shook his head again.

Lena was a little frightened. She knew that what she was doing with her granddaughter's husband and her great-granddaughter's father was wrong, but she couldn't stop. At the same time she loved Kerrissy and didn't want her hurt. She wouldn't be with Thomas if the situation wasn't forced.

Lena's shock subsided, "Thomas. Maybe—"

"Don't say it, Lena. *Don't say it!* You ain't going nowhere, and I mean that! *And I will beat you to death if I have to!*"

Lena cringed from the tone and sound of anger in Thomas's voice. She buried her head into Thomas's chest. "You know I love you, Thomas. You know I ain't gonna try and go nowhere. Please just calm down."

Thomas grabbed the back of Lena's head. She jumped from his sudden movement. Thomas held her to his chest and laid his head on top of hers. "Um glad you ain't gonna leave me, Lena. You the only one that I couldn't live without, the only one."

Lena could hear the strong beat of Thomas's heart—it comforted her. She held him tighter and closer.

Thomas closed his eyes and sighed. Lena still loved and wanted him; Jasper was no longer a threat to their relationship. He had only been a temporary diversion, but it was Thomas whom she wanted. She accepted her lot in life as a woman, with all its limitations. The truth was that Thomas made her feel young. Unfortunately, if some pain in the form of a fist accompanied his love, she accepted that as part of the territory. He began to remove Lena's formfitting wool dress. Lena didn't stop him. She loved Thomas and everything he did to her. She would no longer pretend like she had done for so long just because of their age differences and her granddaughter.

Thomas wiped his face on the sleeve of his coat as he headed toward his house from Lena's in broad daylight without taking his secret route.

Venn was surprised to see him coming from the direction of Lena's as she headed out her front door to go back to work. Thomas didn't usually get home until way after her lunch hour was over—something was very wrong. Looks of fear, concern, and panic covered her face as she headed in his direction. She knew how mean Thomas could be at times, and she spoke before reaching him. "Thomas? Why you coming from Lena's? You didn't do nothin' to her, did you?"

Thomas instantly turned red, his eyes stretched wide, and he couldn't speak.

Venn pushed his upper arm in a mild attempt to move him out of the way, broke into a run up to Lena's front door, and began pounding on it.

Lena was still lying on her bed, trying to get herself under control. The pounding frightened her, but she had to lie for a while to get over her and Thomas's encounter. She prayed that it wasn't his angry fists at her door. She quickly searched her mind to sort out what she could have done wrong as she slowly adjusted her clothing. She slid off the bed and walked to the door. She was tired of fighting with Thomas about her belonging to him. Maybe he had run into Jasper as he left her house, maybe she had said or done something distasteful before Thomas had left. Whatever she had done wrong, she would just have to deal with it—cooperate and not make him any angrier. She had no business messing with Jasper in the first place. Thomas wouldn't be so angry with her if she hadn't gotten involved.

She took a deep breath and opened her door.

Venn and Lena stood, face-to-face, with their mouths open.

While holding the screen door open, Venn put out her trembling hand and grabbed Lena's. "Did he hurt you, Lena? Did he hurt you?"

Lena squinted in confusion. "Did who hurt me?"

"Thomas, my son. Did he hurt you?"

"No, Venn. I don't even know what you talking about—"

"Then why is your makeup and hair looking like that? Look like you been crying, too. You trying to cover for Thomas? You afraid of him? I swear, Lena, if that boy—"

"Venn, he didn't do nothin'. I was asleep when he came—"

"I thought you said Jasper was taking you to the store, Lena!"

"He was, but I fell asleep lying across the bed, waiting for him—"

"Why Thomas just leave here? *And don't lie!* I saw him coming from this way!"

"That's what I'm trying to explain, Venn. Thomas just come to apologize to me for talking to me the way he did."

Venn put the flat of her hand on her chest and took a deep breath.

Lena thought it somewhat amusing and couldn't help but smile. "Venn? Do you think your son that violent?"

Venn looked back at Thomas, causing Lena to see him, too. He stood in the circle, watching the whole incident. Venn shook her head. "He got a bad temper. If he was to hurt you or anybody, I just don't know. I guess I just raised him selfish 'cause he all I got. But I love my baby, Lena. More than anything else in this lousy old world, I love my son."

Lena put her head down. She wanted to say, *"I love him too."* But she knew that Venn would never understand their feelings. She was more than twice Thomas's senior.

Venn released Lena's screen door and hand, and dropped her head. "I'm sorry, Lena. I try to teach Thomas respect. I just couldn't have him disrespecting people and know about it."

Lena smiled. "Um okay, Venn. Thomas was a perfect gentleman the whole time he was here."

Venn walked over to where her son stood, draped her arm around his shoulder, and walked him back to their house. She was more than proud after Lena told her that he had apologized and had been a perfect gentleman.

Lena turned up her nose. The mushy mother and son sickened her. She was jealous of Venn's and Thomas's relationship; she always had been. Thomas hadn't as much as looked back to see if she was okay after she had lied for him, but he naturally respected his mother, and he let her treat him like a child. If Lena as much as raised her voice, there would be a problem between her and Thomas.

Frustrated, Lena stepped back inside her door and pulled it open extra wide so that she could slam it shut. However, she thought about the consequences if Thomas heard the force of the door closing, and if he believed that she was really slamming it in his mother's face as a nasty gesture. She gently closed the door and went back to her bedroom. She lay across her bed and wondered when Thomas would return to her.

Chapter 45

Thomas lay on his bed, fingers locked together under the back of his head, as he looked up at the ceiling. He was thinking about Lena, Kerrissy, and Sable. He wondered why he really hadn't missed Kerrissy, and why he hadn't seen Sable in a few weeks, and hadn't tried. He was thinking about breaking off with her, knowing all the wonderful things she did for him, and how much time and patience it took him to teach her. He couldn't figure out why he felt so close to Lena, nor the reason why he wanted to be so sexual with her so much, and in so many ways. She looked exceptionally good for her age, since she'd lost the weight, but he had felt that way about her before the weight loss. She hadn't looked nearly as good as Sable or Kerrissy, although he always thought she had a pretty face and nice hair. He actually loved the way it fell in the somewhat thin, curly ringlets whenever he shook her up to let her know who was in control. He knew that she didn't need to straighten it, and he would fantasize about her being younger whenever they would lie together. Kerrissy—

well, he had lusted after her, although he had used
the excuse of Lena not having time for him, but
Sable completed his Lena fantasy. He no longer had
to dream, think, or imagine how it would have been
with Lena in her prime—not after he taught Sable all
of what he wanted, and needed, to quench his sexual
appetite and fantasy.

Thomas rolled over onto his side and laid his
head in the palm of his hand. He wanted Lena. He
wanted to be with her that very moment, but it
wasn't really about the sex. She just made him feel
comfortable. She made him feel as if he was away
from trouble and the rest of the world, which he
never mingled with much, anyway.

The phone rang. Thomas called out for his
mother, but he remembered she had gone back to
work. He jumped up, ran downstairs, and grabbed
the phone. "Hello!"

Breathing was on the other end.

"I said, hello!" Thomas was becoming irritated.

The caller held the phone.

Thomas held the phone for a second and listened. When he heard the voices in the back-
ground, he knew who was on the other end. He
smiled. "Sable, why you playing on the phone—and
don't try to hang up or you'll regret it!"

Sable's voice was meek. "Thomas, I just wanted to
hear your voice—"

"Sable, what the hell you doin' callin' here—and
from your house? You tryin' to get me in trouble.
Ain't that your parents and little sister's voices I
hear?"

"Yeah, Thomas, but they ain't in the same room
with me! They can't hear what um sayin' or who um

talking to—and you won't meet me no more, Thomas! You just forgot about me! What's wrong, huh? Is it over between us, or what? That's all I wanna know, Thomas. Is it over?"

Thomas wanted to say yes and ask her to call his wife in California and tell her the same, but he just held the phone and thought before he spoke. "Look, Sable, you know why you ain't seen me. Because you always getting on my nerves. Just when I feel that I done punished you enough, and decide that you done learned your lesson, and decide to come to the parking lot, you start doing things like this. . . . How did you get my number?"

Sable began to lie. "It's—"

Thomas stopped her. "It's what, Sable?"

"Somebody who work for the phone company gave it to me."

"I won't ask you who it is, Sable. But if you call here again, I will have to do something about it. Do you understand me?"

"Yeah, I understand. I won't call again."

Sable started to hang up; Thomas stopped her. He might need her. He was getting too hooked on Lena. "Wait, Sable. . . ."

Sable's heart began to pump with excitement.

"I want you to start calling me every night before you head to the lot. Give me your number. If I'm going to be there, I'll call you back and let the phone ring twice."

Sable was happy. He still loved her. She quickly whispered the numbers into the receiver. She looked around the room. "Can we see each other tonight, Thomas?"

Thomas smirked. "I don't feel like doing nothing, Sable."

Sable cleared her throat and looked around the room again to make sure that she was alone. "All I wanna do is make sure that you okay, Thomas. I wanna make sure that I'm pleasing you. I don't want you to leave me just because you mad at me and we been apart. I just love you so much, Thomas." Sable began to cry.

Thomas felt a little sorry for her, but he really didn't want to see Sable. She only made him want Lena each time they were together, but he wanted to stay away from Lena for a while. She was occupying too much of his heart. He found himself hiding women and explaining himself to Lena—something he hadn't done for any other woman, not even his wife. Thomas couldn't figure out what was wrong with him. Lena was making him crazy, without doing much of anything. Each time he thought about Jasper being with her, he wanted to kill them both. He had already vowed to stay away from Jasper. He had unknowingly tread on his waters, but Thomas couldn't forgive that. Jasper was a discomfort.

Thomas put his head down with the phone to his ear, listening to Sable sniffle.

"Sable, I'll meet you at the house in about an hour."

"Okay, Thomas! Okay! Please, please, please. Don't stand me up!"

Thomas hung up the phone without answering her and prepared to meet Sable, against his better judgment.

Chapter 46

As Sable saw Thomas approaching, she stood up and headed for the rear of the abandoned building. Thomas followed her at a distance and prayed that Lena hadn't seen him leave the house. After what had happened between them the day before and earlier, she would be constantly questioning him about his whereabouts.

By the time Thomas entered the building, Sable was naked and lying down on the mat, with the fire lit. Thomas frowned and wondered how she knew how to get it started.

Sable reached out to Thomas.

He stood and looked down at her. "I didn't come here for this, Sable, and you know that. Why don't you have any clothes on?"

"It's much more romantic this way, Thomas. Come to me, please."

Thomas walked over to Sable and stood across her body. "I'm here, now what?"

Sable reached up and hooked her hand inside his waistband, pulled him to the floor with her, and began to undo his pants. Thomas grabbed her wrists and watched Sable's dazed expression through the flickering shadows of the fire, which danced on her face. She looked different now, so different. Thomas jerked and made a sound like he'd been stabbed. He looked down and realized that somehow Sable had quickly released him. Anger filled him as he thought about the way Sable had attacked him the last time he was there, and now she was *in control again*. Why hadn't he forced himself on her the day she made her way to his house? She would have more than deserved it. She'd respect him now. Thomas's facial expression changed. He grabbed a fistful of Sable's hair, pulled her upward, and growled: "You still wanna be the man, huh, Sable? You still wanna be the man?" Thomas put both arms around her and held her firmly. Sable tried pushing away.

Thomas laughed nastily. "We won't stop until you done took advantage of me, Sable." He slowly descended, holding Sable tightly in his arms. He didn't want to hurt her, just her ego. She had to realize that he was the one in charge. She'd gotten too bold for him, and he wouldn't tolerate that from any woman. He wouldn't feel raped when he left a woman, only satisfied.

Sable couldn't understand Thomas. He had too many personalities for her. The nice Thomas, the supernice Thomas, the fatherly Thomas, the Thomas that wanted to be her husband, the mean Thomas, but the one she hated most was the one she was dealing with now. The superfilthy, nasty Thomas—and she couldn't understand how she'd brought that

one out of him. How could he treat her so
dirty? Didn't he realize how much she loved him, that
everything she had ever done was for him? The
change in Thomas frightened her. She began talking
inside of her head and praying that he would let it be
over. She began to whine with the little breath she
could release as she tried to release the hold Thomas
had on her.

Thomas ignored her. She had to be taught a
lesson.

After being abusive in so many ways with her,
Thomas lay on his side, breathing hard and watching Sable with wicked eyes as she cried and tried
collecting herself. He ran his hand through her
hair. "I want this to be your last time trying to be
the man, Sable—trying to take advantage of me.
Your last time, you hear me? You wait for me. Um
in charge! You hear me?"

Sable nodded.

"Good, because I don't like doing those things to
you. Do you think that I like the way I have to
punish you?"

Sable shook her head from side to side. Her hair
made a swooshing sound on the plastic mat.

Thomas reached for her and held her close as he
stroked her hair and kissed her on the forehead.
"Look, we ain't havin' no sex. That ain't why you
called me here. You called me here for just what I
got, and that's all that's going to happen, Sable.
Why you get naked, anyway?"

Sable coughed and continued to cry. "I don't
know. Um sorry."

Thomas could feel her full breasts against him. He
became tempted and wished he'd taken a drink of
his courage before he'd come to meet her. It always
made him less conscious of what he did. He could go
back to Lena's and make her miserable for all the
wrong he'd done—the wrong she had taught him—
and he wouldn't feel the least bit guilty, not even
after the high wore off.

Thomas held Sable close so that his feelings
would subside. Impulsively he lowered his head to
her breasts.

Thomas walked back to his house, with his head
down and his hands in his pockets, feeling guilty.
Why did he have to take Sable, and in so many
ways? Why didn't he just leave after she had finished what he'd come for? Why didn't he just avoid
her entirely? His intentions were to only punish
her, but his flesh called out for her as long as she
was near, and he had done too much and stayed far
too long. If Lena saw him come home, she would
be tapping on the window, summoning him to
come to her. If she did, he would have to go to her
right away to prevent her from being curious and
going to Jasper. She'd smell another woman on
him, and that would make her talk about Jasper
again. And if she did, he would have to do something drastic. He had claimed Lena, he'd consum-
mated their passion; she belonged to him, and he
wasn't nearly ready to let her go.

Thomas made it into the house. He looked out
his front door's window to see if Lena had been
watching him. She hadn't. Her lights were off.

Maybe his treatment of her earlier in the day had put her to rest.

Sable sat in her room, thinking of Thomas. She pulled out the ring he had given her and tried it on again. She wondered why he never mentioned it since he'd given it to her. It was very apparent to her that he loved her. He had just treated her the way he had the first time they'd been intimate, and relived their various successions. He seemed so greedy and hungry for her. *He loves me.* Why didn't he just marry her?

Chapter 47

Kerrissy had been greeted with open arms by her mother. Her mother had even taken the news of her baby's marriage—and her firstborn—graciously. She had begged Kerrissy to stay, or at least try to talk Thomas into coming to stay in California. Kerrissy had wanted to, but she knew how bullheaded Thomas was. She had slowly packed her belongings; she and her mother had a tearful departure. They had hugged so tightly that they thought they would squeeze the life out of each other. Now her plane was landing. As she entered the terminal, she looked around for Thomas. She saw him leaning against the wall, near the magazine station, and smiled. As she and the baby approached, Thomas felt something in his stomach that he had never felt before: dread. He couldn't smile, frown, or pretend. He continued to stare Kerrissy down. When she approached him, she could see the look on his face and summed it up as Thomas still being angry with her. She nervously looked up at him. "Hi, baby."

Thomas leaned down and kissed her forehead.

"Hey, how was your trip?" His voice was smooth, more mature.

Kerrissy slightly jerked her neck back and frowned a little in shock. She looked in Thomas's eyes to make sure that he was the same Thomas she'd left a few weeks ago. She could see the change in his eyes and on his face. Something was different. She swallowed. "My trip was a good one. My mother ain't mad at neither one of us. She said that she wish that you would have come with us so that she could apologize for everything."

Thomas took the baby from Kerrissy and led the way to the luggage pickup. He spoke without looking back at her. "She don't have no reason to apologize to us. We need to be apologizin'. We was wrong. I can accept that. I wish it had never happened."

Kerrissy was stunned, and somewhat hurt. The tone in Thomas's voice seemed to tell her that he wished they'd never happened, that their marriage and the baby were big mistakes. She wanted to snatch him around to face her, but she knew better. Although he seemed more mature, if she made the wrong move, the only people who could stop him would be the police. She swallowed her pride and continued to tag along.

Thomas loaded the bags in the taxi as Kerrissy sat in the backseat with the baby. When Thomas entered the cab, he sat away from Kerrissy, as close to the window as he could. He wouldn't look in Kerrissy's direction, make conversation with her, nor join in as she talked. When Kerrissy finally decided to give up, Thomas blew out a low, disgusted breath of air and rolled his eyes upward. *Why didn't she get the hint sooner?* Even the cabdriver nervously looked back at him through his rearview mirror every once in a while, trying to see Thomas's facial expression.

They reached the house. Thomas quickly unloaded. He needed to find a way to get away from Kerrissy before he did something that he would regret. "Baby, I know that you just got in, but I gotta get me a drink. They worked me so hard, um edgy. I need something to relax so that I can get a good night's sleep, something that I ain't got since you left."

Kerrissy smiled. He did miss her. Kerrissy looked up. "Okay, baby. I know how hard you work. See you later. Okay?"

Thomas half-smiled. He felt a little guilty. Kerrissy was sweet. She always tried to make sure that he was never disturbed by anything. She was a good mother and wife. She had even been willing to stay away from her mother for him. Why was he acting like suck a jerk?

Thomas left the suitcases in the living room, promising to remove them upon his return. Kerrissy and the baby headed upstairs. Kerrissy decided that when Thomas came home, she would look extra special for him. When she was certain that the baby would remain asleep, she went downstairs into the kitchen, washed her hair with her fragrance-scented shampoo, conditioned it, and used the vacuum cleaner to dry it. She loved the fresh scent that wafted in the air from her barbaric drying method—the *only one* available to her. She smiled—almost giggled—as she took out the straightening comb and proceeded to get rid of her oversized Afro. Patiently she maneuvered the hot comb through her hair until her hair shone and fell over her shoulders like silk, then shook her head to see if it would wave like it did before the Afro. She put a small amount of fragrant hair lotion on her hands, rubbed them together, and applied it to her hair to get rid of traces of straightening-comb smell. Then she dented the ends with the curling iron. Cautiously she wrapped her hair in a scarf, towel, rolled her ends, pulled them back, and covered them the same way. She could barely see her way to the bathroom, but she clumsily managed to fill the tub with warm water and get in. She used all of the body products her mother had given her as a wedding gift so that she would smell exceptionally nice for the man she loved.

Kerrissy thought she would get a cramp in her neck from sitting in the tub and trying not to get her hair wet or steamed.

She clumsily climbed out of the tub and retrieved the new negligee from the suitcase downstairs. She thought about bringing the suitcases up, but that might cause Thomas not to come up right away when he came home. She removed the towel, scarf, and rollers from her hair and slipped into her negligee as she stood in the living room. Then she made her way back up the steps, with her rollers and scarf wrapped in the towel.

Kerrissy stood on the bed and looked at herself in the dresser mirror. She was definitely a fox. Thomas wouldn't ignore her tonight. She looked good enough to be on television.

Chapter 48

Thomas sat next to Lena on her bed with his hands folded between his legs. "She back, Lena. She back, but I ain't gonna stop coming here. I can't stop coming here."

Lena closed her eyes, took a deep breath, and let Thomas talk.

Thomas looked up at her. "Did you hear what I said?"

Lena nodded her head like an obedient pony.

"Then talk to me!"

Lena jumped. She knew that Thomas needed to take out his frustration on someone. He was in one of his moods and he wasn't drunk. Why didn't he find the little whore she had last seen him with? She searched her mind to say the right thing, then nervously looked up at him. "Thomas, I love you. Whatever you want, that's what I want."

Lena screamed as Thomas jumped up and shouted, *"Then I wanna go home, Lena!"*

Thomas headed for the door. Lena leaned forward

and touched his arm, only to stop his violence if he felt neglected. "Please, Thomas, why?"

"Because, Lena, you don't give a damn!"

"I do, Thomas. You know how much I love you. Don't you know it take a lot for a person to do what um doing with you, and know that you married to my flesh and blood?"

Thomas turned to her and began punching the inside of his hand as he spoke evenly. "You doin' what you doin' because you my woman, and you do whatever I tell you to do, Lena."

Lena dropped her head.

Thomas walked over to her, grabbed her chin, and pulled her face up. "Um goin' home, Lena. Don't have Jasper here or nobody else at no time. Do you understand that?" Thomas let go of Lena's chin.

Lena put her head down and nodded.

"I'll be back, Lena. You just better remember what I said."

"I will."

Thomas looked at her again. "Did you git them keys made for me that I asked for?"

"What keys?"

"The ones to your house, Lena! Don't act stupid!"

"I don't remember you asking me for a key—"

"Um your man. I shouldn't have to ask you for nothin'! You shoulda give me a key when we first laid together, Lena!"

Thomas walked over to her again and grabbed her hair. "I should break your neck for tryin' to play with me!"

"I'll get you a key, Thomas! I'll get it tomorrow, okay?"

Thomas let go of her hair. "See that you do."

Thomas backed away from Lena and reluctantly walked out the door.

Lena gently exhaled, then eased off the bed to lock her door. When she got to the kitchen, Thomas was sitting at her table, looking at her, grinning and taking sips out of his bottle. Lena knew this meant trouble.

"Where you going, Lena?"

"I thought you had left. I was gonna lock my door—"

"Why you in such a hurry for me to leave, Lena?"

"I ain't, Thomas."

Thomas stood up, took another swig from his bottle, walked toward her, wrapped his arm around her waist, and pulled Lena close to him. "How come I can't git enough uh you, huh? Why can't I just leave you alone and just say forget it, Lena? What you done did to me? Me wantin' you like this can't be right. *It can't be!*"

Lena was more frightened of Thomas than she had ever been. She wished again that she had never turned Thomas out. She loved it when he was treating her good, like he had just a short time ago, but when he went into his rages of regret, she never knew what would happen. She could only offer him sex, hoping that would calm him down, but Thomas never seemed pleased—satisfied. What would happen tonight?

Thomas laid his head on Lena's shoulder as she trembled like a leaf. "I ain't gonna hurt you. I just need some answers, Lena—I just need some answers. Um just so tired of feeling like this!"

Lena slowly raised her hand and cradled the back of Thomas's head.

"Sh-sh-sh. We gonna git through this together, Thomas. It's gonna be okay, baby. I promise you that."

"How do you know that, Lena?"

Lena jumped and gripped Thomas's head tighter, closed her eyes, and rocked him. "Because . . . you all I got to love."

"Then let's go to bed. I just wanna spend the night here. I can't go home to her. I gotta be with you."

"Whatever you want, Thomas. Whatever you want."

The pain Lena felt was almost unbearable. Not only had she ruined Thomas, she'd ruined her only granddaughter's marriage. She wondered how she was going to live with herself after what she had done.

Chapter 49

Kerrissy woke up to Thessia's crying. She lay on her side for a while, trying to wake up before handling her baby. She rolled over to lean on Thomas for leverage, but he wasn't in bed with her. Instantly her heart began to beat with such force, her body seemed to vibrate with each *thump*. Where was he? Did he get hurt? Should she call the hospital, the police? Should she alert Venn? Kerrissy was too frazzled and dizzy to make a decision. Staggering like a drunk, she jumped up and ran to Thessia's bedside and picked her up in her shaky hands. Kerrissy was afraid, alone, and out of choices. She had visited her mother to let her know how well she was doing, and now she'd awakened to a nightmare. She sat on the bed, breathing hard, and rocked Thessia as she held her tightly in her trembling arms. Somehow, someway, she would get through the terrible ordeal. She had to. If Thomas didn't care, she had to care about her baby. Kerrissy's panicking stopped when she heard the footsteps on the stairs. Boldness leaped into her. As soon as Thomas reached the doorway, she would let him know exactly how she felt, maybe even leave him. When Kerrissy saw the figure in the doorway, she thought she was dreaming. Kenneth leaned against the frame of the door and held his stomach as he took Kerrissy in with his eyes.

"Damn, you look beautiful!"

Kerrissy began to cry. "How you get in here, Uncle Kenneth? What you doing here?"

"Venn left the key. I called her early this morning. Told her I was gonna stop by. Once I made sure Thomas wasn't gonna be here, I come on in."

Kerrissy was now trembling all over. "You better leave! You know what happened when Thomas caught us—"

"Um gonna take that chance, Kerrissy. I need to be with you so bad. All I been thinkin' 'bout is you—"

"*No!* You see I got this baby here. *No!*"

Kenneth walked closer. "Gimme the baby so I can lay her down, Kerrissy. She done gone to sleep."

"*No! No! No!*"

Kenneth began to pry the baby out of her arms.

"Wait a minute, Uncle Kenneth, wait!" Kerrissy was still crying, but she relaxed her arms so that her baby wouldn't be jerked to the floor during the struggle, allowing Kenneth to take her. He smiled down at the baby as he cuddled her in his arms and walked toward the crib. "This shoulda been mine." He laid the baby down, turned to Kerrissy, and walked toward her. When he leaned over, she dug her fingers into his face. He quickly stood up. "Watchoo do that for?"

"*Just leave me alone and get out!*"

"Not until we done been together again—"

"That was in the past! That was before! Me and Thomas doing good now!"

Kenneth wiped at his face, where Kerrissy had struck, and looked at his hand. "You really got me good, didn't you?"

Kerrissy leaned away from him in fear. "You shouldn'ta been messin' with me. You should just leave."

"You know—even the way you talk always turned me on." He stepped closer. "You know he out with that little gal, don't you?"

Kerrissy frowned. "I don't know what you talking about."

"Um talkin' 'bout that no-good husband uh yours. He out with that gal, 'cause his mama told me he ain't been home all night."

Kerrissy's face turned red with anger. She jumped to her feet with her fists balled up, then relaxed her hands. "Git out! *Now!*"

"Okay, if that's the way you want it." Kenneth turned and walked out the door.

Kerrissy immediately fell on the bed and began to cry into the mattress. The sudden weight on her back made the air rush out of her body. Kerrissy tried to scream, but nothing came out.

Kenneth put his hands under her, cupped her breasts, and laid the side of his head on hers. "Girl, you know I couldn't leave here like that."

Kerrissy tried twisting her body away from Kenneth. He slid down her body, slowly releasing her breasts, allowing his hands to travel the length of her body as he did. Kerrissy didn't fight Kenneth. She wanted him, had acquired feelings for him, and needed to be loved—the same as her cheating husband.

Chapter 50

Kerrissy lay on the bed, staring at the ceiling, and thought about Kenneth. She disgusted herself for enjoying him and allowing him to take her, and release and mix his liquid feelings with hers. She thought she would never willingly lay with him again. She thought the day Thomas had caught them together had killed the memory of Kenneth's touch—the perfect rhythm that she could not resist, and had begun to become accustomed to, once he'd infected her with it. He was much older than Thomas. He was much older than them both. He was hers and Thomas's uncle. Why did he do it? Why did she let him? Why did his touch make Thomas's feel so mechanical? How did he do it? And what did he do to make her accept him when she felt as if she really hadn't wanted him? Why did she quickly reject and loathe him, but was still not able to stay away from him? And why did she suddenly yearn for the warmth of Thomas's arms around her, and for Kenneth's to be chopped off?

What was Kenneth doing to her to make her take him and respond passionately?

* * *

Kenneth sat on the bed and watched Kerrissy cry. She tried to pull her head away as he ran his fingers through her long, soft hair. She let out an agonizing whine as Kenneth leaned over and clasped one of her nipples with his lips, then the other. He sat up straight. "You gonna love me one day, just like the rest. Just watch and see."

"Just git out and leave me alone before my baby wake up again. I swear to God, Uncle Kenneth. If you come back or touch me again, um goin' just tell Thomas—I don't care! Just don't come back here to me again! You hear me?"

Kenneth stood up. *"Kerrissy . . . !"*

Kerrissy jerked her head rapidly in Kenneth's direction. "What?"

"You gonna tell me you don't like what happened, after the way I had you moanin'?"

Kerrissy became angry and began throwing pillows, and anything that she could get her hands on, at Kenneth, causing him to stumble backward.

"You just tryin' tuh deny your real feelings, Kerrissy!"

Kenneth walked out the bedroom and headed for the front door.

Kerrissy followed behind him, shouting, "Don't come back, or I'll make sure Thomas kills you next time!"

Kenneth slammed the door behind him.

Kerrissy immediately headed for the bathroom, kneeled over the toilet, stuck her head in it, and spewed out the nauseous feelings that her indiscretions caused. After she clutched the bowl with both arms, to give herself leverage to stand, she staggered up the stairs. She changed out of the soiled negligee, put her robe on, then picked up her baby. She looked around the room, loathing the terrible things that went on in that house, in their room.

The front door slammed again. . . .

Chapter 51

Kerrissy sat on the bed and nervously rocked Thessia as she heard the footsteps approaching the stairs, then heading upward. She closed her eyes and sighed with relief when she saw that it was Thomas. He quickly peeked in the door without a smile or any further acknowledgment of her, then went back downstairs to bathe.

Anger surged inside Kerrissy. Her nostrils flared. How could he? Who did he think he was? This man had been out all night long, leaving her vulnerable and wanting to be with his uncle again. Only this time, it was while their baby slept less than a foot from their bed, and all he could do was take a quick look at her and his child and say nothing! Although Kerrissy knew she had feelings for Kenneth, and had wanted him, she rocked and hummed to keep from jumping up in anger.

Thomas entered the bedroom but wouldn't give Kerrissy the slightest glance. He walked over to the dresser, began picking his hair so that he could head back out to work. When he splashed on cologne, Kerrissy jumped up off the bed, holding Thessia in one arm. She made a fist with her free hand and began pounding on Thomas's back, head, and shoulders. Thomas spun around and caught a fist in the face. His eyes bulged with anger. Kerrissy didn't care. She was too filled with resentment and rage to care. Thomas made a fist but looked down at Thessia, who was now screaming at the top of her lungs. He allowed Thessia her freedom of expression, and Kerrissy to beat him, as he pried Thessia out of Kerrissy's arms. He gently laid Thessia in her bed, then walked back over to his wife.

"You wanna fight? You wanna fight with me?"

Kerrissy charged at Thomas, screaming, both arms whirling.

Thomas thought that he was faster than Kerrissy, but she caught his cheek between her fingers and dug in. She tried biting Thomas in the face. He grabbed her throat and held it until she could only do one thing—calm down.

When Thomas saw her arms drop, and that she could barely breathe, he released his grip. "You wanna talk? You wanna talk about somethin'? Or you wanna continue this?"

Kerrissy was still breathing hard. *"I hate you, Thomas! I hate you for what you did to me!"* Kerrissy brushed her thick, long hair away from her face. "If you wanted this to be over, all you had to do was say so! When I went to my mother's, I woulda stayed there, but you wasn't man enough to allow me my freedom and serenity." Kerrissy fanned her hand around. "You had to go and do this!" Kerrissy fully calmed down. "Oh, yeah, and by the way, your uncle came by again this morning and raped me in front of your daughter."

Thomas's mouth flew open.

Kerrissy knew that she had an option, but she grinned nastily at the lie she told, then continued. "Oh, yeah, it's true. He called your mom to make sure that you wouldn't be here so that he could." Kerrissy walked over to the hamper and retrieved the soiled gown. "You need more proof, Thomas?" Kerrissy threw the gown at him. "He raped me in the *Adornment* that I had worn *especially* for you! That my mother had bought me for you—as a first year anniversary gift! You see my hair. It was s-o-o-o-o-o pretty! But guess what! I'm married to a coward who was too afraid to tell me that he no longer wanted a wife or his own child!"

Thomas stepped toward Kerrissy.

Kerrissy threw up her hands. "Don't touch me. The next man who touches me is going to jail, Thomas, going to jail. *I'm tired!* You don't have to treat me like I'm in the way any longer. I'm calling my mom to send for me." Kerrissy walked over to Thessia's bed, picked her up, sat back down on hers and Thomas's bed, and began to rock her.

Thomas had been so sure just moments ago that *this* was what he wanted, but the way Kerrissy looked—the way she had chastised him—his helpless baby, and what his uncle had done to his wife, again, made him melt. He fell down on his knees and crawled over to the bed. "Please, Kerrissy, please. I thought you didn't love me no more. I wanted to make you miss me the way I missed you, baby. Please. Don't do this—"

"Why did you tell me to go, Thomas, if you didn't want me to?"

Thomas hunched his shoulders before he lied again. "You was gonna leave me forever if I hadn't! You was so dead set on it, Kerrissy! What else could I do?" Thomas laid his head on Kerrissy and his baby. He punched the mattress with his fist. "When I catch Uncle Kenneth, um gonna kill him! And you better call me if you see him before I gonna do, 'cause um definitely gonna tell mama to let me know next time he come around here or call—"

"Please, Thomas, don't tell your mother that he raped me—"

"Why, Kerrissy? Did you like it?"

Kerrissy was glad that her eyes were also wet. They might tell the wrong story, dry—the true story. She sniffled. "How can you ask me something so nasty, Thomas?"

"Then why don't you want my mother to know?"

"It's too embarrassing to be telling everybody, Thomas! You just don't know how it is to have some old man—some old person—take advantage of you practically in front of your whole family!" Kerrissy burst into fake tears.

Thomas held her and Thessia close to him and cried with Kerrissy. He did know how Kerrissy felt, although he had gotten his revenge. It hurt him more than Kerrissy would ever know. He took the baby out of her arms. "Go ahead and get her bottle, she hungry."

As soon as Kerrissy left the room, Thomas hugged his daughter and cried. He'd created a situation that didn't look so easy to correct, now that reality was on the table. He searched his feelings. Could he

live without Sable and Lena? He thought about
Lena with Jasper and became angry. He shook his
head to clear his thoughts. He thought about Sable
with a new man; that made him jealous. And trying
to see his uncle doing things to his wife made him
want to tear the room apart, then go looking for his
uncle. They were *his* women. He had initiated them
all. They all belonged to him, and they'd better be
there for him no matter how long it took for his
return, and they'd better not allow another man to
taint them. That was a definite no-no, but what,
could he do about his uncle and his wife? He would
have to accept it for now, after all, he had just been
out all night with his uncle's ex-wife, his wife's
grandmother.

After quieting Thessia down, Thomas helped Kerrissy to clean herself up. He washed her back as he
kneeled beside the tub and talked to her to soothe
her feelings. Another tear slid down his cheek. "Um
sorry, baby. Don't open that door for nobody, you
hear? Um gonna tell Mama not to let nobody else in.
That Uncle Kenneth come in here and went straight
upstairs lookin' for me and caught you naked."

Kerrissy cringed, not from disgust but pleasure.

Thomas whispered, "Don't be shamed. It wasn't
your fault. It was mine and Kenneth's. You ain't do
nothin' wrong."

Kerrissy could only blink. She knew that she had
enjoyed what had happened with her and Kenneth.
She was sure of his return, although he had left in
a huff. She told Thomas about him mostly out of
anger—anger of enjoying the feelings, and at

Thomas for staying away so that she would be in that position again. Her real motives were to be with Kenneth, pretend each time that she hated him, but to have him around to keep her satisfied. She'd keep up the shy, mistreated act until she was ready to take their meetings where no one else would know. Thomas had already stayed out all night. At the time she was sure he'd been cheating and would continue this pattern. If that happened, she would surely find out what Kenneth did to escalate feelings in her that she fought to resist, but that she found missing from hers and Thomas's intimate encounters. Not only would her desires be satisfied, so would her curiosity.

Chapter 52

Kerrissy woke to darkness and a distinct, distant voice quietly arguing. She looked around the room, trying to perceive its contents. She felt around for Thomas. He wasn't there. She got out of bed and followed the hallway light to the bedroom doorway. The voice was coming from downstairs and it was Thomas's. Fear went through her as she thought of Thomas arguing with Kenneth and possibly hurting him—if he could get near him. She headed downstairs to stop Thomas from taking action, then stopped as Thomas's voice grew louder. "I thought I told you not to call here again, Sable! Didn't I teach you about calling my house the last time we talked?"

Thomas's voice was quiet. Kerrissy waited and listened.

"Sable, I don't wanna hurt you. But I will if you keep on talking—"

Thomas was cut off. He was listening again.

Kerrissy's knees grew weak, her stomach ached, her body went cold.

Thomas started up again. "Meet me at our spot"—

Thomas was cut off briefly, then somewhat shouted in frustration, "You know what spot! The abandoned house by the playground! Bet you won't be playing when I see you, Sable!" Thomas slammed the phone down and headed back upstairs.

Kerrissy quickly ran back into the room, jumped back into bed, and pretended to be asleep. Thomas came back up the stairs, sat down on the bed in the dark and nudged her. "Kerrissy. I gotta go out and take care of something that I thought was fixed. I'll tell you all about it when I get back, okay?"

Kerrissy kept her back to Thomas and tried to sound sleepy. "Yeah, Thomas. Okay."

Thomas went to the kitchen, snatched open the freezer, emptied the cubes from the ice tray into a plastic bag, stuffed it into his jacket pocket, and headed out the door. He was going to break it off with Sable. She was getting too desperate. He had told her about not calling his home.

Kerrissy lay in bed trying to decipher Thomas's movements and debating on whether or not she should follow him. She wanted to know exactly what was going on. But was she ready . . . ?

Thomas was in a huff by the time he reached Sable. He stared at her coldly as she stared back at him expressionlessly. Her seemingly fearless gaze angered Thomas. He grabbed her wool scarf with one hand and dragged her inside of the abandoned structure. Sable stumbled and tripped but didn't whimper. She had already slipped out of her house in desperation to see Thomas. She no longer cared what happened to her.

* * *

Thomas pulled the board back for Sable to enter the structure. He immediately pushed her to the floor, once inside. Sable sat where she landed, emotionless, no tears.

"So you big and bad now? You a woman."

Sable wouldn't answer. Still. No tears.

"Okay. We'll do it your way, Sable."

Thomas removed his belt.

Sable still refused to show emotion.

Thomas picked Sable up in his arms. She wrapped hers around his neck and buried her face into his chest as he carried her over to the mat. As he lowered her, he allowed her to roll onto her stomach, squatted across her body with his back to her head, pulled up her tight miniskirt, pulled down her underwear, and began to massage her. Sable stretched her arms out in front of her, closed her eyes, and relaxed. All she wanted was Thomas's touch—a little of his time—some attention from him, even if it was negative. Why didn't he just meet her earlier, tell her to meet him sooner in their conversation?

Sable moaned, then screamed.

Thomas talked. "You actin' like a child, um gonna treat you like one, Sable! When I tell you something, that's what I want you to do!"

Thomas brought his belt down, over and over again, stinging Sable's bottom until he forced the sounds of mercy from Sable that she knew he demanded when things weren't right.

Sable lay facedown on the mat crying like a baby. Thomas took the bag of ice out of his pocket, which he had prepared earlier to combat Sable's swelling. He gently laid it on her rear end, causing Sable to jump and shiver.

"This could have been avoided, Sable. All you had to do was wait for me and you couldn't do that." Thomas continued to stare at Sable's nakedness. He licked his lips, then shook his head to clear his indecent thoughts. He was only going to whip her, then leave, making sure that she wouldn't want to contact him again, but he found his lustfulness getting away from him.

Thomas finally rolled away from Sable. He reached inside his coat and quickly drank from his bottle. It didn't dilute the guilt. He lit up a joint and smoked it. He pulled out the sack of cocaine for backup but used it before he could think twice. Finally the pain was gone. He handed the bottle to Sable. Lit another joint, smoked it with her, and did more cocaine until they were both too high to care as they continued to indulge in more forbidden activities.

Chapter 53

Using the limited light that poured through the window, so she wouldn't wake her baby, Kerrissy felt around in the dark until she found something to put on. This wasn't a mission of beauty—it was one of resolution. She made it to the closet and grabbed the nearest coat. Once downstairs, she peeked in at Venn, who was fast asleep. Kerrissy quietly headed out the door to find Thomas. . . .

Kerrissy walked hastily through the brisk late-night air. She caught a glimpse of herself as she searched for her lapels to pull her coat tightly around her. She almost giggled at the outfit she had fused together in semidarkness on short notice. Her sockless feet in her boots, the large T-shirt she had worn to bed, and the short, wrinkled wool skirt. As she approached the vacant structure that Thomas had mentioned over the phone, she began to lose her nerve. Maybe she was stupid or crazy. Maybe she should have waited for Thomas to take care of the person who was on the other end of the phone. She stood in the cold, listening for sounds, then proceeded toward the structure. She stood at the rail looking—hoping to see Thomas and his appointment standing outside. She could run away as soon as she saw them, heard them talking angrily, and was certain that he'd come to rid their family of this enemy.

Kerrissy suddenly became frightened when she realized that she might be at the vacant structure alone. Maybe someone else was lurking in the darkness with her—some stranger. A warm tear escaped her left eye and turned cold as it slid down her cheek. She wiped it away, stepped over the railing, and headed for the rear of the structure. She needed answers and wouldn't leave until she got what she came for. When she saw the boarded back door, she became angry. Had Thomas already come and gone? He should have been home by now. They would have crossed paths. Could he have taken his date to a secret love nest? Tears began to flood her eyes and fell with a will of their own. Kerrissy leaned against the building to collect herself and almost fell when the board on the back door shifted. She turned and gently pushed it to see how far it would go. She could see some type of light inside, but what if there were vagrants in the building? She walked up the stairs and stood at the top step as she held the board and looked inside. The only life visible was the burning fire. She wiped her nose and eyes on the back of her sleeve and began to back away until she heard the voices, and one of them was Thomas's. Kerrissy's heart thumped so hard with anger she was ready to kill. She entered the structure without trying to silence the board. There he was—standing against the wall, naked—with the same whore kneeling in front of him that she'd seen him giving money to. The same whore who had caused her and Thomas to have problems, and Kerrissy to allow Thomas's uncle privileges that should have been only for her husband. As Thomas ordered, the girl was trying to fulfill his every command, his needs. Needs Kerrissy knew she would never want to satisfy.

Thomas opened his eyes and saw Kerrissy. Before she could get out a sound, he began to back away from Sable, dragging her along.

The look in Kerrissy's eyes was murderous. Thomas could feel the hairs on his body stand at attention from fear. He could see her tightened lips, chest heaving. Her hands opened and closed as if they were trying to make a decision.

Thomas gripped Sable's shoulders as tight as he could and pushed her away, causing her to hit the floor with a thud. Sable lay on the floor, dazed. Thomas stood naked, dangling, and out of fables. His mouth hung open. Kerrissy's fists tightened. Thomas began walking toward her. She met him halfway and landed a punch square in his face as soon as they reached each other. Then her fists began to move like a whirlwind as she screamed, *"I'll kill you,"* shouting loud obscenities. Sable crawled backward in confusion. Thomas finally got a grasp on Kerrissy's wrists and held them as he stuttered and tried to explain his indecency. Kerrissy kicked him in the groin. Thomas let go of her wrists and was now bent over, holding himself, as Kerrissy landed blows to his head. Thomas became enraged. He stood up, reached behind Kerrissy, and wrapped his arm around the back of her waist, turning her upside down as he lifted her off the floor. Kerrissy kicked, screamed, cried, and beat on Thomas as he walked with her body in that awkward position. He dropped her on the mat and drew back a fist. Kerrissy put up her hands to block the blow. Thomas put his hand down. He looked around the firelit room but couldn't find Sable. Kerrissy fought, kicked, and screamed some more.

Sable sat drunkenly in the corner as she watched Thomas and Kerrissy fight, until she realized Thomas was messing around with another girl. She slithered behind Thomas and bit him in the rear. Thomas let go of Kerrissy and held his bottom as he cried out in pain, while Kerrissy lay on the mat, crying from defeat and shame. Thomas walked over to Sable and jerked her up off the floor. Kerrissy jumped on his back and told Sable to run, but she was too foolish to take the advice—high or sober.

Chapter 54

Thomas had gotten himself together and had gotten the best of the two, thanks to the help of Sable. Because Sable did not run, Thomas felt he remained in control of the situation. As sick and perverted as it was, he was able to fulfill his lustful fantasy where he had sex with one woman, while the other one watched—even if it was his wife. He dragged both girls outside by their wrists as he argued angrily. He made Sable walk home alone and chastised Kerrissy all the way to their house while dragging her by the arm.

She snatched away from Thomas and looked up at him. "Why, Thomas? Why?" Thomas snatched her arm again and kept moving.

They stood in the yard, and Thomas tried to make her quiet down. They both entered in silence and headed up to the bedroom.

Kerrissy walked over to the dresser and began to pack. Thomas grabbed her by the back of the neck. "What the hell do you think you're doing, Kerrissy? Do you want me to kill you?"

"You already did, Thomas. If I can't see or breathe, then I won't have to think about or remember what you did to me tonight. I didn't ask you for nothin', you sent for me, remember?"

"Kerrissy, I went there to break it off with that girl—"

"Sure, Thomas! Sure you did! And then all of a sudden your clothes fell off, right?"

"Kerrissy, if you woulda just waited—"

"Waited for what, Thomas? For her to finish giving you what you really want? *I don't have to live like this!*"

"Lower your voice, Kerrissy, before you wake the baby and Mama."

"You know what, Thomas? You might care about your mother, but you don't give a damn about me or that baby!"

Thomas stepped closer to Kerrissy.

"Go ahead. Finish destroying me, Thomas. It don't matter no more."

Thomas relaxed. "Kerrissy, you don't understand. I got a problem."

"I know you do, Thomas, and that problem is me. Once I'm gone, your problem will disappear, too."

"Kerrissy, no, it ain't you. It's me—"

"*Thomas.* After all you've done to me, and with that girl practically in front of me, there ain't no story you can tell me. *I mean no story that can keep me here!*"

"But I was raped—"

"*Raped!*"

"Kerrissy, please stop being loud. I don't want Mama to know about everything, including Uncle Kenneth, unless you do."

Kerrissy quieted down.

"Kerrissy, I know people don't believe this, but a man can get raped. This woman was older than me and she had sex with me. I thought she was being nice, but it turned out she was just softening me up to get at me and my mother. I stayed away from her a long time after that, but what she did, made me crave her. When I met you, I fell in love. My friend Jasper had showed me how to get you, like that lady had got to me—"

"You told Jasper about you and that woman?"

"No, Kerrissy. He was always trying to teach me about sex 'cause he older than me. Sometimes, when he got drunk, he would be doing things—you know, like making gestures that he didn't know I was catching on to. That's how I learned what to do to you to get you. I wanted it to make you stay with me 'cause I loved you so much. Then that young girl looked so much like the woman who took advantage of me I had to have her. I wanted to see what she would feel like so that I could fantasize about that woman in her young days, and I just can't stop doing the things I do. I was pretending to be angry about you following me to that place, but the truth is—I was, but not that angry. You catching me only aroused me. . . . You see, my appetite for sex is out of control, Kerrissy. It feel dirty now that it's over, but that's only because you my wife and I ain't as high. But to be honest with you, you better off leaving me. You need to go, 'cause with them other women I mistreat, it don't feel dirty no more—even after I'm sober." Thomas sat down on the bed and held his head. "I had tuh git real high after I touched that girl, 'cause I felt so guilty about betraying you so fast, Kerrissy!"

Still holding the garment in her hand, Kerrissy stood and stared at Thomas. Now she wasn't so sure if she should leave. But how could she stay after what he had done just moments ago?

Chapter 55

Kerrissy lay on the bed, exhausted after taking the baby to the doctor and shopping. Suddenly the door opened and slammed. Knowing Venn was at work, and no one was on the first floor where her mother-in-law's bedroom was located, she became tense. She thought it was Kenneth coming back to finish what they had started. How would she resist Kenneth today? She was too tired to fight with him—he somehow always caught her off guard when she was well rested, and even then she could only resist his touch for so long, no matter what.

Kerrissy looked over at the crib. Thessia was sleeping like an angel. Maybe she could crawl between the bed and wall and hide from Kenneth. "No, he would look for her after he saw the baby. She walked over to the crib, gently picked Thessia up, walked over to the bed, slowly slid between the wall and bed, reclined, snuggly lay Thessia on her chest, and waited. She heard Venn's downstairs bedroom door open, then close. Kerrissy threw her hand over her mouth. Was Kenneth messing around with Venn, too? Kerrissy could hear them talking and lay perfectly still. Thessia stirred. Kerrissy looked down at her, smiled, and gently brushed her curls back. She jumped when the shouting began. She could hear their argument through the floorboards. She was wondering what the argument was about so she put her ear to the floor.

"I come home early, go to borrow some sugar to make you a cake to surprise you, 'cause I couldn't make it to the store, and you answer the door in your drawers. What the hell was you doing up in that old-ass woman's house?"

Venn couldn't get an answer. She put her hand on her hip. "I know you can hear me talking to you! Answer me or you out of here today, Thomas!"

"I love Lena, Mama—"

"Boy! Have you lost your damned mind!"

"But I can't help it! I love her like a homosexual man who done tried women and couldn't *change*! That's how I feel about Lena! I done tried younger women to get over her, but I can't—I can't! I thought I was lovin' her 'cause she was my first, but it ain't that! Um in love with Lena! I went there to tell her it was over, but I couldn't!"

Up until this point, Kerrissy had no idea that Thomas was having an affair with her grandmother, Lena. Suddenly Kerrissy understood why her mother-in-law was so angry with Thomas. Then she thought back to a recent incident where Lena had come to borrow sugar from Venn. Although it was customary for neighbors in Hussey Place to borrow sugar from one another, Kerrissy now understood Miss Lena's visit had been a cover-up for her husband's affair.

Venn became dizzy. She had to lean on her dresser to keep her balance. "What about Kerrissy, Thomas? You tradin' in new for old—hell, I don't want that old-ass woman for no daughter-in-law! What about Kerrissy?"

"She done been with Uncle Kenneth—"

"Thomas!"

"I caught them together, Mama! I caught them right here in our house. I ain't gonna lie! I had been messin' around with this other girl, she even come by here and got money from me, but I ain't never done nothing with another woman in our house, but Kerrissy. And Kerrissy couldn't really prove that nothing was going on between me and that girl until lately!"

Kerrissy now lay on the floor relaxed as tears ran down the sides of her face. How could Thomas be so dirty? He was laying with her and her grandmother and told his mother about Kenneth as if she didn't matter. Why didn't he at least keep that part to himself? Couldn't he have at least let his mother and her relationship remain cordial? She was going to take her life back. Thomas had helped her to make that decision, and no one would control her ever again. She lay quietly as she continued to listen. . . .

"Thomas, why you make such a mess of your life—and Kerrissy's—and the baby's? If you didn't love that girl—I mean, um crazy about her—Kenneth a whore! Always been one! He had to do something to get that girl to lay with him! She's a good person, Thomas, and a good daughter-in-law and mother. How could you do this to her—to them—to all of us?"

"Mama, I do love Kerrissy—"

"Thomas, how can you love all these women? Do you know what 'love' is?"

"Yeah, Mama, I do now."

Venn shook her head. "No, you don't. If you did, you wouldn't be having this conversation with me. You wouldn't be trying to use what happened between Kerrissy and Kenneth to cover up for you coming from being with Lena's old raggedy ass."

Thomas became angry and flexed his fists.

Venn stepped closer to him with a look of murder on her face. "What the hell you flexin' your hands like that for, Mr. Thomas? You ready to die today? You know that I ain't nothing like none of them women, *boy*. I will kill you where you stand and won't think twice—*and you know it!*"

"Sorry."

"You gonna be more than sorry if you ever act that way toward me again, Thomas. And I mean what I say!" Venn opened the door and walked out of the bedroom. Thomas slowly followed behind her, feeling empty. He touched his mother's shoulder and spoke quietly. "She enjoyed him, Mama. Kerrissy was letting Uncle Thomas have her. We both done wrong, not just me. We forgave each other—"

Venn looked back at Thomas, rolled her eyes, and jerked away from him, but she couldn't resist the urge of slapping him so hard, he fell on the floor.

Kerrissy heard the *thump*, covered her mouth, and couldn't help but snicker and think, *I need a piece of that action.*

Venn continued out the door.

Thomas's eyes flooded with tears as he calmly stood up and headed upstairs.

Kerrissy slowly crawled from behind the bed,

gently laid Thessia in her crib, and jumped into bed, pretending that she had been asleep.

When Thomas saw Kerrissy lying on their bed, his heart raced in fear from the thought that Kerrissy had heard his and his mother's conversation, and Venn knocking his hateful ass to the floor. He thought she was still at the doctor's with the baby. His legs felt like lead as he approached her. He sat down on the bed to see if she was awake. When she didn't move, he sighed in relief.

Chapter 56

Thomas wouldn't take another chance—like the onc hc had taken the day Venn caught him at Lena's. He pretended to go out with Jasper. Actually, he went to Jasper's house, so he could wait for it to get late and dark enough so that his visit with Lena would go undetected by his mother and Kerrissy. Kerrissy was seething with anger, but remained calm. She sat up in the bed and wiped her eyes when Thomas announced that he was leaving. "Have a good time, baby." The words almost made her heave. She lay back down and turned her back. Thomas brushed her hair back and kissed her ear.

Kerrissy cringed from disgust as he walked out of the bedroom.

Thomas sat at Jasper's house, visiting and making idle conversation, until it was late enough for him to sneak off to Lena's house. He drank from his bottle and smoked his joint on the way. Anger filled him as his memories led him back to Venn catching him in his underwear at Lena's house. It was Lena's fault. If she hadn't made him so paranoid of Jasper, he wouldn't have been in that position. He wouldn't have gone to the door, half-naked, trying to expose to Jasper that he and Lena were sleeping together. He wanted to rub it in his face. Lena would pay for his mother finding out her original scheme.

Thomas leaned against a lamppost, took a snort of his cocaine, and proceeded to Lena's. His nostrils flared as he walked up her steps. He clutched the knob. The door was locked. He shook the door, then pounded. Lena's face suddenly appeared from behind the curtain. She could see the look on Thomas's face and instantly became frightened. She snatched the door open.

"Hey, Thomas." Her voice was shaky.

Thomas brushed past her as he walked inside. He went over to her refrigerator, opened the freezer, and filled a plastic bag with ice. He glanced at Lena. "Come on."

Lena wanted to cry instantly. She swallowed hard and followed Thomas to the bedroom.

Thomas sat on the bed. Lena stood in the doorway, picking her thumb, watching him.

Thomas patted a spot on the bed as he set the bag of ice down on the nightstand.

Lena went over to him and sat.

Thomas sighed. "You know what's wrong, don't you, Lena?"

Lena swallowed hard enough for Thomas to hear, but she wouldn't answer.

"You hear me talking to you, Lena?"

Lena nodded.

"Then answer me!"

Lena jumped. "Thomas, I don't know what's wrong—"

Thomas grabbed her chin with his fingers. He stared coldly into her eyes. "You got this comin'."

"But, Thomas—"

"Take your clothes off, Lena."

Lena began unbuttoning her dress.

Thomas continued to sit next to her but wouldn't look her way.

Lena stood up and stepped out of her dress, still hoping that Thomas would change his mind.

Thomas remained quiet—until Lena was naked. He scanned her now-sleek, somewhat shapely body and found himself becoming rigid, wanting to connect with her. He suppressed the feelings. "Come—lay across this bed on your stomach."

Lena cried as she slowly crawled upon the bed and lay facedown.

Thomas straddled her, the way he had Sable, partially supporting himself with his knees. Lena could feel Thomas's fullness in her back and became more confused of his intentions.

Thomas removed his belt and proceeded to deliver lash after lash as he watched Lena's motions, making sure that her muscles flexed and tensed with pain.

Lena clutched her pillow and groaned.

Thomas brought the belt down a little harder.

Lena bucked and held up her head. "Please, Thomas! That's too much!"

Thomas brought the belt down firmer.

Lena screamed, "Ah, Thomas! Ah!" She twisted, trying to free herself.

Thomas hit Lena several more times, then held the belt up and looked at it. "Why did you make me do this, Lena?"

Thomas held the cold ice pack against Lena's tender bottom, causing her to flinch.

"You know what I told you, Lena."

"But I didn't do anything, Thomas—"

"*Shut up!* If you hadn't made me so jealous of Jasper, my mother wouldn't have caught me up in here naked, and I wouldn't have to be here settin' you straight!"

"But me and you done straightened all that out, Thomas."

"You think I trust you just because we had a little talk, Lena? You didn't lose all that weight for nothin'. What you take me for—a fool?"

"Thomas, I ain't got no interest in nobody else but you. You know how I feel about you."

"Lena, you kin whine all you want, but I don't trust you. Now you just lay still till um done here, okay? Um tryin' to keep you from being all bruised up and swollen right now, but you gonna make me much harder on you. Just keep still till um done."

Lena lay facedown and cried silently.

Thomas lifted his head and wondered how it had happened again. He was angry—there to punish, not to please. He crawled away from Lena and went straight to his bottle, then his weed, then his cocaine again. He was going to end his party right. He had already gone further than he'd intended. Now Lena would prove how much she loved him before the night was over.

* * *

Lena continued to lay facedown. She knew that Thomas's actions weren't out of anger alone—this was a new phase of lust. She'd realized long ago that Thomas did things from experimenting, and if he liked it, it would become a routine. He would now be making up something to become angry about so that they could indulge in the new behavior—without him admitting to having a problem.

Chapter 57

Thomas slapped Lena for not showing the emotions he wanted while they were being intimate. He gazed into her eyes and growled, "You too good, now that you done lost that little bit of weight?"

Lena shook her head feverishly from side to side. She could see the dark look in his eyes. The same look that he'd had a few times before when she thought her life was truly over and Thomas would be her assassin. She hugged him tightly, like she could never enjoy anything or anyone more.

Thomas smiled. Lena wanted to scream as she thought about the first time she'd encouraged Thomas to use her like a toilet. It was to catch him and keep him. It was only supposed to be the two of them. Now she had become a part of, and was consuming, whatever Thomas lived.

Lena sat on her bed unsteadily, with her head hung and legs dangling over the sides. Thomas stared into the mirror as he dressed, watching her reactions with a cheap smirk on his face. He threw on his jacket, walked over to Lena, kissed her on the forehead, and lifted her chin with his fingers. "You gonna be good from now on?"

Lena blinked the tears out of her eyes as she nodded in agreement.

Thomas stepped away from her. "Good, 'cause I don't like what you make me do to you, Lena!"

Lena remained quiet.

Thomas raised his voice. "You ignoring me!" He touched his belt. "Maybe I didn't get my point across!"

"Um sorry, Thomas, um sorry. I didn't mean for none of that to happen!"

"Good, 'cause you know how I feel about you, Lena. And now that you do, I ain't so sure you ain't trying to take advantage of my feelings!"

"I wouldn't do that, Thomas. You know um in love with you!"

Lena burst into tears.

Thomas kneeled down and laid his head in her lap. "Don't cry. It hurt me when you cry." Thomas looked up at her. "Come on now. Don't do this. Um so sorry. I just can't control myself when um around you. I don't be wantin' tuh hurt you. It's like I can't help myself, like um competing with Jasper every time um with you now. Just don't make me hurt you again. Okay, baby?" Thomas laid his head back down in her lap.

Lena rubbed his curly head. "You ain't got to compete with nobody else, Thomas, no matter what. I done told you that over and over. I don't want nobody else but you."

"That's good, Lena. 'Cause before I let you go—

before I let you leave me—I'll take us both out of here." Thomas could feel Lena's heart pounding through her stomach. He stood up and left without looking back.

Lena sat on the side of her bed, thinking about all that had gone on. She would never be able to deal with Thomas so intensely as time went on— her age would not permit it. The words of her mother rang through her head: *"Lena, you want Kenneth too bad. I told you I would help you with that baby. But if you wanna marry Kenneth, I ain't gonna stop you. But I gotta warn you. The way you start out with them men is the way you gonna end up with um, and it ain't no different with a woman."*

Chapter 58

It was midnight when Thomas entered his house. How could he have stayed out so long, again, after the conversation he and Kerrissy had just one day ago? He'd felt so sure of himself, so in control, but he'd felt that way the night he'd gone out to punish Sable. He took a deep breath and headed upstairs. He would have to cry his way back into Kerrissy's life again.

Thomas switched on the light before entering the room. His mouth flew open in astonishment. No Kerrissy. No Thessia. Just a note hanging from the crib with a small piece of tape attached to it. Thomas ran over and yanked it off.

Thomas,
  I know all about you and Grandma. It was bad enough what your uncle did, but my grandmother? How could you be so disgusting? How could you set me up that way? How could you be that kind of no-good person for your daughter? I hate you, Thomas, and I don't ever want to see you again, and if you

come near me in any way, I will have you arrested.
Forget me and your daughter.

—*Kerrissy*

Thomas quickly sobered. He flopped down on the bed. *How did she find out?* Thomas remembered the argument he and Venn had. Kerrissy must have heard them. How could he have been so stupid—so trusting of her? How did he allow this situation to leave his control? He wanted to call Kerrissy's mother, but he wasn't ready to confront the reality of the fierce argument that would ensue. Maybe Kerrissy hadn't gotten there yet, anyway. Maybe she hadn't gone there. Maybe she had left with Kenneth. Thomas became enraged as he thought of how Kerrissy was enjoying Kenneth the day he had caught the two of them together.

He had tried to dismiss it as payback only, but deep within he knew. He had seen and felt something coming from his wife that he had never gotten from her. If he saw her again, he would ignore all that Jasper had taught him. Kerrissy would be taught the lesson—the same one he was teaching her grandmother and Sable. He ruled and *only him.* He was the only man in the relationship.

Chapter 59

Thomas felt listless all day. He had almost changed his mind about going to work, and had worked slowly from the time he entered the building. When he heard himself being paged over the intercom, he dreaded going to the plant floor to answer the phone. He removed his gloves, lay them aside, and slowly headed to answer the page. He perked up when he thought that it might be Kerrissy calling to reconcile. He anxiously snatched the phone up. "Hello!"

"Thomas?" The voice was gruff. Definitely not Kerrissy's.

Thomas swallowed. It was Mr. Decker, the big boss. "Yes, sir?"

"Thomas, you need to come to my office right away."

"Yes, sir. I'll be right there."

Thomas's stomach knotted as he walked what seemed like ten miles to the office. When he reached it, the door was open and he could see Mr. Decker sitting at his desk, wearing an unpleasant expression. Mr. Decker waved his hand. "Come on in, Thomas."

Thomas walked into the office.

Mr. Decker folded his hands on his desk. His expression didn't change. "These gentlemen need to speak with you, Thomas."

Thomas hadn't seen the two men who were standing behind the door, both white, one a little taller than the other. The taller one was somewhat on the heavy side. They both flashed their badges.

The taller one spoke. "Are you Thomas Bazedale?"

Thomas swallowed. "Yes."

"Do you know a young lady by the name of Sable Mae Tutor?"

Thomas began to sweat. He looked at Mr. Decker, back to the officers, then at the door.

The officer repeated himself as he moved toward Thomas. "Do you know Sable Mae Tutor?"

Thomas nodded and stuttered. "Y-y-yes, sir."

The officer cleared his throat. "We need to take you to the police station and ask you a few questions."

Thomas was now sweating profusely. "About what?"

The officer didn't hesitate. "Her parents are accusing you of statutory rape."

Thomas's knees buckled. His face turned red. "I—I—I—I didn't rape her—"

"You can come with us and answer some questions now, Mr. Bazedale, or we can come to your house and arrest you in front of your family."

Thomas looked at Mr. Decker for support—for confirmation from him of his innocence and good character, or something. He had always been the image of pure respect. Why didn't Mr. Decker speak on his behalf? He just sat quietly and watched.

Thomas agreed to go to the station. The officer gave the signal for Thomas to lead the way as they both followed. As his shaky, sweaty hand gripped the doorknob, then pulled the door open, Thomas prayed that no one else would be in the hallway. Mr. Decker got up, walked around his desk, and raced over to where the three stood before they stepped over the threshold of his office. He pointed to the rear exit, indicating that they should use it on their way out. The officers gave compliant gestures and left with Thomas still leading the way. Mr. Decker shut his door as soon as they left. He hoped that whatever was going on wouldn't get out among the other staff.

Chapter 60

Thomas was detained after being questioned. He had no other recourse but to call Venn to bail him out of jail. Venn wondered when and how Thomas had done so many things to Sable. He was at home most times when she got there, even if he was asleep or in his room, except for the time Kerrissy left for California— but she knew that was about Lena. And that was another thing, he'd claimed to love Lena and he had a wife. Guilt engulfed her. What hadn't she done for Thomas? She had always treated him good. Sure, she had spoiled him. He was her only child, but she had never let him get away with being disrespectful.

Maybe she should have had the sex talk with him that she thought was only meant for a father to give. Maybe she should have been home more, but she had to work to take care of him and the house. Maybe she should have had more conversations with her one and only son, *period*. But he was grown now and she had done the best she could as a single parent. Venn put her unsettled thoughts to rest and began to focus on her son's upcoming court date. *If only he hadn't kissed Sable when she was only sixteen, he'd still have his freedom.*

Chapter 61

Thomas stood at Mr. Decker's desk. He was holding his baseball cap in his hand. He looked down at it, then up at Mr. Decker. "Sir, if you would just please give me my old job back or another one, I would really appreciate it. Everybody deserves another chance. I swear, Mr. Decker, I'll never as much as go near anything illegal again."

Mr. Decker stood up and came around his desk. He closed the door as he spoke. "Thomas, I know how hard it is for a good-looking young man like you to stay away from the women." Mr. Decker smiled and patted Thomas's shoulder. "You were a good worker. I've been in contact with your mother. There's still a job here for you whenever you wish to start. Besides, you have done your time. Four years is time enough for someone to realize their mistakes, and the fact that your sentence was cut short for good behavior proves that you have good intentions—integrity!"

Thomas wiped his eyes with the back of his hand that held his cap. "Thanks, Mr. Decker. And um really sorry for shaming you—"

"Forget it, Thomas. No one here knows what

happened. They think that your wife had you falsely
arrested for beating on her because she thought
you were cheating. The police took her word over
yours—that's common. Here, take this slip to the
manager and he'll see to it that you start at your
earliest convenience."

"Thanks, Mr. Decker. I won't let you down."

"No, Thomas. Don't let *yourself* down."

Chapter 62

Seventeen-year-old Sepia lay on the floor of the abandoned building. She closed her eyes as the head lowered toward her lips. She moaned loudly from the contact and held on to him tightly.

Her lover looked up. "I been gone a long time. I was waiting for you to grow up, to be mine, and now that day is here. You won't be like your sister, she betrayed me. When you get old enough, we gonna git married."

Sepia looked up. "I love you, Thomas. I'll never betray you like they did. I love you and I always will."

Thomas grabbed her throat. "What you mean by 'they'?"

Sepia held his wrist with both hands, swallowed, and closed her eyes. She liked the aggressive contact. It meant Thomas loved her. She had heard the older ladies talking about this with her mother. She spoke and began to breathe more seductively. "I know you had a wife and another woman. I heard my sister telling my parents, but I don't care about that. She was stupid to leave you, Thomas. She should have waited for you to get it all straightened out."

Thomas grinned. "You do understand me."

"That's what love is all about. Understanding."

Thomas slowly released Sepia's throat and lowered his head again. He mumbled into her body, "Sable didn't deserve me, Sepia, but you do. And um gonna give you all of what I gave her and more—even teach you more. I was trying to make her special. She was too stupid to know how to accept it, but you all woman, Sepia. You more woman than that stupid-ass sister of yours will ever be."

Sepia held Thomas's head and cried as she allowed him to further impair her body chemistry; his words of flattery traveled through her mind and touched each one of her nerves. Sable was a fool to leave. How could anyone give up what Thomas was filling her with? Yes. Her sister had been foolish.

Sepia had been following them when she was little. Had seen Thomas giving her sister money. Saw them kiss and hold hands. Saw them going into the vacant building. Imagined them together in the darkness. She'd even thought that he was cute and had fantasized about him, hoping to get a man like him someday. She'd been a tattletale, but that was her big secret. The one she would never tell anyone else. She kept it locked away for her own personal obsession.

When she saw him go past the playground on his way from work four weeks ago, she couldn't help but stand in his path and show off her figure, which was similar to her sister's. Thomas couldn't help but go for the bait. She was Sable and Lena all in one, and, on top of that, he could get back at Sable. She had tried getting back with him, although she'd had a baby by someone else and was responsible for Thomas going to jail. Thomas was more than ready to mess with Sepia and let Sable know about the relationship. She wouldn't dare tell her parents. She wasn't supposed to be near Thomas, and to keep her away from him, Thomas had threatened to tell her parents that she was begging him for sex, and was lying about him and Sepia for revenge. Sepia would back up his story 100 percent. Sable's parents would be more than displeased.

A jealousy grew in Sable that she couldn't explain. Many nights she wouldn't have dinner with the family to avoid her little sister, and she would only speak to her if they crossed paths and their parents were around. They walked around with a harsh secret between them that kept them from being sisters. Sisters should love each other—no matter what the outside world did.

Chapter 63

Thomas saw Sable pushing a baby stroller toward home. He slowly slipped up behind her and put his hands over her eyes. Sable screamed and turned around. Thomas grinned. His teeth still sparkled. His physique was still irresistible, and he was more handsome than ever. Thomas licked his lips as he watched Sable's breasts heave up and down.

Tears formed in Sable's eyes as she stumbled over her words. "Just leave me alone. You told me you didn't want me no more—to stay away from you—why you gotta mess with my little sister?"

"You didn't want me. Had me put away like you some kind of little fool or somethin'. You knew I had things to take care of before me and you could be together the right way."

"But you lied to me, Thomas! You lied about everything!"

"That wasn't 'cause for you to do what you did to me, Sable. You didn't have to mess with me."

"But I loved you—I still do. . . ."

"You don't love me. You don't even know what love

is. Now, your sister, she know how to please a man. You'll never be the woman she is, Sable, *never*. Look at you. Couldn't wait for me to go away before you cocked your legs open for another man."

Sable lowered her head and let the tears flow.

Thomas brushed past her and headed in the direction Sable was traveling.

She followed behind him. "I was missing you—"

"You wouldn't have had to miss me if you hadn't gotten me locked up. And you ain't miss me that much. If you had, you wouldn't have that baby in the stroller. Now would you, Sable!" Thomas headed for the parking lot.

Sable followed behind him. "It wasn't like that—"

"Like what, Sable? He wadn't that good?"

Thomas looked around. They were alone. He stepped close to Sable. "You want me, Sable?"

Sable looked down at her infant baby. "I—"

Thomas put his hand on her lower back and snatched her close to him. Sable held on to the stroller with one hand and dragged it along with her as she was being jerked. Thomas ran his hand up under her skirt and into her underwear. Sable closed her eyes, but she grabbed his hand.

Thomas continued to stare at her without changing his facial expression. "See, I told you. You ain't as much woman as your little sister."

"Thomas, please. Don't do this to me."

"You grown now, Sable. What am I doing that you can't stop? Why you always trying to act like a victim, huh?" Thomas stood closer and whispered in her ear as his hands roamed Sable's body. "You want more, or you want me to stop?"

Sable wouldn't answer.

Thomas gently pulled her private locks with his fingers.

Sable squealed, then quickly put her hand over her mouth.

Thomas began whispering all the things they had done in the past.

Sable's eyes went from Thomas to the vacant structure.

Thomas grinned. "You wanna go in there with me?"

Sable trembled, moaned, and moved with the massage. "I can't—My baby. I can't—Jayzell. My baby."

Thomas continued to tease her nerves as he spoke. "That baby shoulda been mine, once we got ready, and as far as I'm concerned, this still is. Come on, Sable, I need you."

"But my sister—and we ain't supposed to be together—"

"Whose fault is that, Sable? And why didn't you feel that way when you was supposed to be too young to be with me, and a while back when you asked me to git back with you? And your sister ain't none of my wife. She can't treat me nearly as good as you can, Sable, and if you don't tell, neither will I."

"But I got my baby, Jayzell, with me—"

"He sleep, how he gonna know? Besides, if he wake up, he too little to understand. . . . And do you really want me to stop what um doing?"

Thomas could hear Sable let out a defeated breath. He lifted his head away from her ear, removed his hand, and took hold of Sable's. "Come on, Sable. Let's not keep on doing this. You know we want each other."

Sable cried as she slowly shuffled along with

Thomas—he pushed her baby's stroller with one hand.

Thomas cautiously lifted the stroller, with Jayzell in it, over the steps and took the baby inside as Sable followed. She was more anxious to be with Thomas than she wanted to portray. She wiped her eyes and sniffled as she pretended to hesitantly walk through the door without giving the old place a second glance.

Thomas secured Sable's baby in a corner, near the fireplace, with him facing the wall; then he went back over to Sable. Thomas brushed her shiny hair back. "If you wanna leave, just let me know. You don't have to do this."

Sable dropped her head. She knew that she should leave, but she really didn't want to. She didn't have the strength to terminate the memories of her and Thomas's past, nor consider Sepia's and her well-being.

"You taking birth control pills?"

Sable shook her head no.

"Then what we gonna do about that, Sable? You already got one kid."

Sable stood quietly, hoping that Thomas would just make the decision so that she wouldn't have to be responsible for whatever happened. She'd abort or take care of another baby if that was what came out of it, but she didn't want to make that decision and lose Thomas altogether. She just stood silently and waited.

Thomas kneeled in front of her, wrapped his arms around her legs, and pulled her close, causing a gush of air to escape from within Sable. He lifted her skirt and let her feel his hot breath. Thomas loved the sounds Sable made. She always made him want her in ways that he knew were taboo. She made him feel overly masculine.

Sable squealed when she felt Thomas pull the leg band of her panties. Thomas slightly lifted her as he teased and strained her until she begged for closure. Thomas allowed it, but started again. As he did, he led her over to the old mat, removed his jacket, and laid it down. Then he pulled Sable on top of him, turning her upside down. Sable immediately tore at Thomas's clothing. She had missed so much of what she thought they had discovered together.

Sable walked ahead of Thomas, feeling light and brushing dirt out of her hair. Thomas pushed her baby's stroller as they exited the abandoned structure. She turned to Thomas as soon as they stepped on the ground. "You gonna tell Sepia it's over?"

Thomas gave her a dirty look. "What's over?"

"You and her, Thomas. I can give you more than she can—"

"*Sable!* You betrayed me once. I ain't gonna give you a second chance to do that. Besides, what you just did for me, I can teach anybody to do."

Sable's mouth flew open. Thomas mimicked her as he held his hands out to the side with his fingers open, and shook his head sarcastically.

Sable squinted evilly.

Thomas returned the look. "What, Sable? What? You wanna go back inside with me so that you can teach me a lesson?"

Sable tried to control her racing heart and

the warm air of anger that filled her. She stood breathing heavily.

Thomas pushed her baby to her. "Here, take your baby and go on home. Your services are no longer needed at this time."

Sable took the baby's stroller, then looked up at him. "She's only seventeen—"

"Get out of my face, Sable. And stop pretending that you care about your little sister. If you really did, you wouldn't have gone inside with me, knowing what I wanted."

"It won't happen again, Thomas."

"It may not need to, after today."

Sable charged at Thomas with her fists closed.

He grabbed her wrists and slung her around. "You want me to take you back inside, don't you?"

"Just let go of me, Thomas."

Thomas pushed her away from him. "You'll pay for that later. Right now I got better things to do."

"What better things? My sister?"

"You are jealous. Look at you poutin'. . . ."

"Ain't nobody jealous—"

"What if I told you it is your sister? Would that make you feel better?"

Sable put both hands on her baby's stroller and began to move away from Thomas without saying a word.

He grabbed her arm. "You ain't gonna let me see you no more?"

Sable was relieved that he still wanted her, but she refused to show it. "Just teach Sepia what you want her to know, Thomas. I don't even care anymore."

"Yeah, sure you don't—until you start thinking about me and you again." Thomas leaned in close to her. "Start taking them pills so that we can get acquainted the way we were before." He released Sable's arm.

She headed out of the parking lot. Thomas wasn't quite ready to let Sable go. He was on her heels. He squeezed her from behind as she walked away.

"Stop, Thomas!"

"Baby, you know you don't mean that." Thomas continued to massage her. "You too mad to keep on seeing me, Sable?"

"This just ain't right, Thomas. You seeing my sister. She just a baby—I should be looking out for her. I shouldn't be having nothing else to do with you. Me or her."

"You were mine long before she was, Sable. If you hadn't sent me to prison, you'd still be mine."

Sable dropped her head. "You know um sorry for that. I told you so. I thought you was using me. I told you that, too—"

"And you know what I told you. There ain't no excuse for what you did to me after I had been so good to you. You sent me to jail over a kiss. If only I hadn't kissed you before your seventeenth birthday."

"I swear to you, Thomas, I didn't know that would happen—"

"Let it rest awhile. What I wanna know right now is, when can I see you?"

"I don't know, Thomas. This don't feel right."

"Then stop talking about it and just don't come back."

"Thomas, you the one come up to me. I wouldn't have messed with you if you hadn't touched me, and stuff."

"Sable, I ain't the fool you seem to keep on thinking I am. If you really don't want me, you wouldn't mess with me—no matter what I did. You sent me to jail without a second thought."

The spring light hadn't completely gone. Sable looked around for eavesdroppers, no one in sight. She stared down at the ground. "I ain't comin' back."

Thomas pulled her closer to him. "You see what you do to me. Sepia can't do this."

Sable could feel him against her and let out a deep sigh. Her voice squeaked. "It ain't right."

"How does it feel when we're together?"

Sable hunched her shoulders.

Thomas kissed her neck. "You don't know how my lips feel?"

"Please, Thomas." Tears welled up in Sable's eyes again.

Thomas pulled her back into the parking lot and hid her behind the big tree. He held Sable close as he talked her through the journey. Whispering all the things he liked doing with her, admitting to lust not love.

Thomas stood back and adjusted his clothing. "See, I knew you was lying. You can't stay away from me."

"Thomas, why you got to hurt me? Why you got to keep on hurtin' me?"

"Sable, hurting you makes me feel so good. Why when you tell me you gonna walk away from me you don't do it?"

"I still love you."

"You don't really love me. You like all of what we do. You ain't gonna find nobody else 'round here to satisfy you the way I do, and you know that. It just make me so mad when I think about what you did to me and you, and I have to make you hurt like I do. Maybe someday I will forgive you, Sable, but I don't know when. Now go on home. I'll see you tomorrow—"

"I ain't doin' this no more, Thomas!"

"I'll see you tomorrow, Sable. Don't be late. And take them pills so I don't have to keep on pulling away from you."

Thomas left Sable standing in the parking lot, watching him walk away. He laughed out loud and shook his head as his thoughts of Sable changed. She didn't care about being in that building with him. She must have known that's where he took her sister. Where else would they go? Sable hadn't even questioned him, just pretended to hesitate before going inside after she had given him the idea with her eyes. Thomas let out an exasperated breath. *Women. Why do they always play games, but want an honest man?*

Chapter 64

Thomas removed Sepia's clothes, then his own. This was the big day. She would give him her biggest treasure. He had been seeing her every Friday for six months, spending hours at a time trying to train her on what to do for him, but Sepia couldn't get the hang of it. Sure, she was young, but her sister had caught on like a woman of age. Thomas was getting sick of Sepia. She seemed to deliberately do everything wrong each time they were together. Thomas had a solution. Instead of allowing her to feel her way through the experience, he had her lay on her back, then crawled across her—like he had done her sister. Reality struck as he looked into Sepia's innocent eyes and face. Her thin lips and small mouth made her look much younger. She was much more petite than Sable, lighter, and a little prettier. Thessia's face replaced Sepia's. Thomas felt sheepish. He shook his head, closed his eyes tightly, then opened them. Sepia was back.

Thomas rolled away from Sepia and stared up at the ceiling. Why had it taken him so long to realize that he was ruining a child? What had he done? His own daughter might be Sepia someday, then what?

Sepia rolled toward Thomas and ran her fingers down his bare chest. "Did I do something wrong, Daddy?"

Daddy? Why did he order her to call him that? The word made Thomas want to scream. That was exactly what he could have been to the little girl he had planned to take advantage of a few seconds ago. He wanted to scream, but he stared at the ceiling, motionless, and allowed tears to stream down the sides of his face.

Sepia laid her head on his chest. "What's wrong?"

Thomas wrapped his arm around her. "This gotta stop. I can't see you anymore, Sepia."

"Why, Thomas? I know it took me a long time to learn, but I'm ready—"

"Sepia, I messed up. I messed *you* up. I don't know what made me just realize it. . . . Yes, I do. Just now when I looked down at you, I saw my daughter's face—"

"But you ain't even seen your daughter since she was a baby—"

"I know. But that don't mean I don't love her, don't wanna see her, and want some man like me to be laying up with her like um doing with you right now. Sepia, um gonna let you go before I take the last important thing that me or you could possess."

Thomas turned his head away from Sepia.

Sepia touched his face with her fingers and turned his head toward her. "What, Thomas? What?"

"Your virginity, Sepia. I definitely don't deserve it."

"But I love you, Thomas!"

"Sepia, you deserve better."

"I don't care, Thomas. I love you enough to do anything you want! Anything!"

"No, Sepia. That ain't right. 'Cause if I was to tell you to sell yourself, would you?"

"If you really needed me to, Thomas."

"Sepia, me or nobody else is that important or special, and if I ever catch you on the streets, um gonna whip you good. Now you listen to me. Um gonna explain something to you that a friend of mine explained to me. When you drink from a person's body, you drinking all of what that person is now and before. I was gonna let you do that for me once you learned, then get you pregnant and finish ruining you. I hated Sable just that much— at least I thought I did, but I don't—"

"You love her, Thomas!"

"Sepia, I don't know that. I don't know what I feel right now. Since I was seventeen, I've been having sex almost every day, and a lot of it until I was locked up." Thomas wiped his eyes with the backs of his hands. "While I was locked up, all I thought about was sex and how I was gonna get back here and get back at Sable for putting me there—knowing that I had a problem."

A confused frown swept over Sepia's face. "Problem?"

"Yeah, um a sex addict that never could admit it."

"Thomas, ain't nothing wrong with liking sex— no matter what all these old folks be saying. They just don't want us to have no fun. I like what we be doing. I want you to take me, Thomas—"

"No, Sepia. No, you don't. Once somebody take you, it seem like your soul is lost, if you ever think about it the right way. You don't want just no any old body taking your gift away from you! I know, I been there!"

Sepia's stare drifted away from Thomas. "I want you inside me so bad, Thomas. Sometimes I want it so bad I feel like running away from my home—"

"If you ever did that, Sepia, I'll make sure you never did it again."

"But you say we can't be together—you don't want sex with me. If you don't, who else you got? Why do you even care? What you do in prison?"

Thomas looked away from Sepia. "Most times I fantasized and made what I wanted happen, then . . ."

Thomas paused.

Sepia leaned on one elbow. "Then what?"

"Some men be there that look and act like ladies. We do them, they treat us."

Sepia, who was still a virgin, looked confused again. "What can you do with a man, Thomas?"

Thomas was tired of explaining, and blurted it out. "We have anal sex with them! They give us oral sex!"

"Stop lying, Thomas. How a man know how to do that to another one?"

"Sepia, that ain't my business to know. All I was looking for at the time was relief."

"Can they make you feel good like a woman?"

"Sepia, you talking about some full-grown men who done been practicing that shit a long time. They got it down pat, better than most women."

"They better than me, Thomas?"

"Yeah, Sepia. They better than you."

"But how—"

"Sepia, shut up. If I was to tell you everything, it would make you sick."

Sepia looked at Thomas arrogantly. "No, it won't!"

Thomas grinned. "Oh? So you think you so grown now, huh? You think you can do it all, don't you?"

Sepia batted her eyes defiantly and raised the tone of her voice. *"Yeah."*

Thomas turned onto his stomach and laid his head on his folded arms. "Get started."

Sepia looked at Thomas. "What?"

"I said, get started. You said that you was ready for it all! Get started!"

Sepia began to crawl over Thomas's body.

Thomas pushed her. "What the hell do you think you doin', huh?"

Sepia jumped. Thomas had never talked to her like that before.

Thomas grabbed her arm, whispered in Sepia's ear, then shouted, *"What you waitin' on!"* He whispered in Sepia's ear. "You know where I want your tongue." He pointed to his anus.

Sepia began to cry.

Thomas let go of her arm. "You said you was grown enough to do it all, that you was ready and would do anything for me—"

"I bet you didn't do Sable like that!"

Thomas grinned nastily. His voice turned evil. *"Don't bet on it."*

Sepia was outdone. She began crying hysterically. Thomas sat up, crossed his arms, and watched her. She reached for him. He pushed her away. "If you was my whore, really my whore, I would give you something to cry for, Sepia. So now you know that you wouldn't want to turn no tricks for nobody, especially after you couldn't follow my last command."

"But that was disgusting!"

Thomas stared at her. "Some people think giving your virginity away is too."

"People do that for *love,* Thomas."

"Sepia, people do it all for love and pleasure. But that don't make it right. And I ain't even got around to discussing anal sex with you yet."

Sepia's eyes widened. "Anal sex?"

"Yeah, I love doing that, but I mostly pretend it's punishment when I want it. I don't want my women to think I'm a faggot or nothing." Thomas ran his hand under Sepia's naked bottom, and allowed his finger to touch her opening. "You gonna let me have that?"

Sepia jumped, reflexively pushed Thomas's hand, and stared at him in fear.

Thomas touched her chin with his fingers. "I ain't gonna make you do it. But if we continue seeing each other, I know that we'll get around to that. And if you don't want to, I'll eventually force it on you, Sepia. If my old appetite for sex come back, I'll have to have it all, and I like it dirty when the other stuff don't work for me." Thomas could feel himself becoming excited, and he had to remind himself of his daughter again. Thomas quickly grabbed his pants off the floor. "I gotta go."

Sepia yanked his arm. "No. No. Please. Don't stop seeing me, Thomas, please."

Thomas immediately became angry. He pulled both of Sepia's legs straight out and flipped her onto her stomach. "So you really wanna be my faggot!" Thomas lay on top of Sepia and whispered what would happen to her if he was to go further.

Sepia began to squeal.

Thomas grabbed the back of her head with his

palm, turned it toward him, and stuck his tongue in her mouth. He could hear Sepia gagging from just the thoughts he had put in her head.

Sepia lay facedown crying, too ashamed to look at Thomas.

Thomas massaged her back as he spoke to her and allowed her to cry. "Is this what you want the rest of your life, Sepia? You want a man to please himself in any way without any concern for you? Corrupt your body till there ain't nothin' left of you? Do you know that almost anything we do sexually can send you to the hospital?"

Sepia shook her head from side to side. Thomas looked down at her round brown firmness and licked his lips. He lay across Sepia. Sepia looked back at him and pleaded, "No, Thomas. Please—"

"Sh-sh-sh. I ain't gonna hurt you."

Sepia fell back into the mat. Thomas ran his penis up and down Sepia before lodging it between her legs. He made swift thrusts until he felt himself expand again. Sepia could also feel the sensation and clutched the mat tightly. Before Thomas was satisfied, Sepia let out a scream, trembled, and writhed. Thomas moaned loudly.

Sepia could feel the warm wetness between her thighs. It was uncomfortable and she didn't like the smell, it made her gag again. Something about what had just happened between them just now made her want to get away immediately, but she was too afraid to say how she felt. She remained quiet and waited for Thomas to dismiss her. The romance had definitely gone out of it for her. She had made up her mind that she never wanted to see him again right after he had explained it all to her. If he could hurt her with something that pleased her, she didn't want to even imagine what would happen if she was to indulge in the rest. How had Sable handled it? Once those words rang out in Sepia's head, she felt stupid. How had she been so blind about Thomas being with Sable? How could she possibly ever lay with a man, be with a man—in any sexual way—who was probably still in love with her sister and sleeping with her? Was this the dog-eat-dog thing she'd overheard her parents laughing and talking about? Had she and Sable swapped blood sexually? Had Thomas done things to her sister, then kissed her? Had he done things to her, then kissed Sable? Did this heighten his sexual fantasies? Sepia was so sick, she wanted to vomit, but she wouldn't allow Thomas to see her disgust. She was afraid that he might feel insecure and force her to be like him for his own self-assurance.

Thomas let Sepia leave. She felt very fortunate as she walked home. She was still young, had regained her freedom, and had kept some of her innocence. She had another chance to somewhat live the life of a child. She would talk to Bobby Meyer, one of the cutest boys at her school, who had tried to date her, if he approached her again. Her latest encounter with Thomas made her feel so dirty, old, and out of touch that she never wanted to go in his direction again. She would definitely stay out of his way.

* * *

Thomas stuck his hands in his pockets. He shook his head as he laughed. *She almost didn't get away. But she'll be back. They all come back. There's no way she can resist me. She's just like all the rest. She'll ignore my lecture and come running right back.*

Chapter 65

Lena held on to her lover as she sat on the side of her bed, as erect as possible—the way she had been ordered to do. Her eyes puffy, face swollen. Her body rocking from weakness and contact. Her sounds of pleasure were more like grunts of pain. A figure appeared in her bedroom doorway. Lena stared, but she wouldn't give caution. Her eyes watered as she stared at the fuzzy structure and thought about how she had been whipped with fists of fury for being honest, after being told to do so. Things needed to be clarified for the new relationship to grow.

Lena jumped and squealed as the figure in the doorway seemed to reach for her. As her lover was snatched away from her, she collapsed sideways on her bed. She lay there and watched the struggle, the surprised look in her lover's eyes as he was pulled to his feet. His voice squeaked. "Man! What the hell is wrong with you? We kin both git this! This ain't nothin'!"

Thomas punched Jasper square in the mouth. "Man! What you done did to Lena? She too old for you to do that to her!"

Jasper held his mouth, squinted evilly, then lunged at Thomas. "Man! You must wanna die!"

Thomas stepped back. "Naw! You the one wanna die!"

The two men tussled and went blow for blow. Jasper, out of breath, tried to reason with Thomas again. "Man, look! We kin both have her! You know she ain't no good! You know that better than me! You done already raped her for what she done to your aunt! Why we can't do this, man?"

Thomas wouldn't answer. The fight continued. There was no way he was sharing Lena with Jasper or anyone else. Thomas would take all of what Lena had to offer—and their secret affair, which only his mother knew about—to his grave.

Lena lay helpless as the two fought through her house before they ultimately rolled down the steps. Both men ended up sprawled out on their backs, looking up, watching the ceiling spin, then darkness.

Chapter 66

Jasper was treated and released. Thomas lay in bed with a broken leg, ribs, and wrist from tripping over Jasper as he tried standing up during the fall and trying to catch the railing before they both went tumbling downward.

Thomas was happy that Venn wasn't at home when the incident occurred. Lena told the story that a large man had broken into her house, beat her, and was trying to rob her when the two came by to visit on a whim. They both agreed to the story. Neither wanted their families to know that they were really fighting over the sexual favors of an older woman, but Venn questioned Thomas, now and then, and gave him strange, unsure looks.

Thomas called Sable to his bedside to deter Venn's suspicions. He even married her after Venn brought him his last mail, which included a divorce from Kerrissy. Venn argued that it was too soon, but Thomas convinced her that he had been without a woman for a while, and he had matured considerably since he and Kerrissy were together. He even promised to buy a house if his boss gave him a full-time job.

It would take Thomas weeks to heal. His boss allowed him the time. Thomas was somewhat of a hero to him. Protecting a helpless lady from a would-be predator was as honorable as a person could get.

Chapter 67

Thomas had accomplished the ultimate American dream. A new house built from the ground up, with two bathrooms and four bedrooms. Mr. Decker had given him a higher-paying full-time job so that he could afford it, and Sable was having his baby. Sepia had tried talking to her sister about Thomas, explaining that he was just getting a freaky fantasy out of being with two sisters, but she didn't want to hear it. She knew that Thomas was a good man and would never hurt either one of them again. Besides, they had moved out a ways and Sepia would never have to see her or Thomas, unless she wanted to. Sepia gave up trying to talk to Sable. She came to the conclusion that the girl was just plain old love-struck or just stupid.

After working late, Thomas removed his gloves and washed off the factory residue in the employee shower, got dressed, and headed out of the building. The night air was so pleasant, Thomas whistled and smiled as he walked. He looked down at the shiny new key as he stood on the porch and smiled even broader before sticking it in the lock and heading up the stairs. He stripped naked and slid under the covers next to the nude, warm body waiting for him there. She reached back and hugged his head. He moved closer. "Nobody ain't gonna keep us apart. I'll do whatever it take for us to be together. You the one I wanna be with and always will be. And as soon as I convince my mother that ain't no other woman right for me, she gonna see it, too. . . . You know I love you, don't you? You know I only married Sable and got her pregnant to throw my mother off our track?"

Lena nodded.

Thomas leaned up on his elbow. "If Jasper ever come around here again, um gonna kill him, Lena. By this time next year, you gonna be my wife forever. I won't need that key I had you make, and I won't have to sneak around and pretend that um on no weekly business for my boss, to hide what we got. We goin' leave here to make sure of it." Thomas laid his head on Lena's, hugged her tighter, and began to cry. "I can't stand being away from you, Lena! I just can't! I almost died in jail without you! If me and Jasper hadn't fell down them stairs, I'd be there again! I was gonna kill him after I had whipped him enough! Please, please, please, Lena! Let's not let nothing else but what we got to deal with now come between us, please! I know you probably git jealous of Sable sometimes, but I swear to you, baby, you all I want! You all I ever wanted! I just got to git rid of her and it'll be me and you from now on! Just please trust me and go with the flow! All we need is a year or so, and she'll be out of the picture, too."

Lena was also crying. She wiped the tears from her eyes. "Thomas, we done come this far. Ain't no sense in me doing nothing else but waitin' for you. I already know down deep that gal can't satisfy you. Never will, and can't learn. Our ages may be different, but we is soul mates. I love you. Ain't nobody else for me. I love you."

Thomas relaxed and fell back in bed. Lena eased under the covers.

Chapter 68

Sable was so happy. She hummed as she carried her new baby inside her house and pushed the other in the stroller. Tovia had been born four months ago and the delivery had been swift. Thomas had held Sable's hand all through it, until they rushed her into the delivery room.

Sable continued to hum as she went through the mail, although Thomas was away on another business trip. She smiled as she ripped open the big brown envelope. Thomas always sent her something in large packages whenever he was away. Sable pulled out the thick contents. Her hand trembled. She left her sixteen-month-old toddler Jayzell in the stroller, slowly walked into the living room, over to the sofa, and laid six-week-old Tovia down on it. She sat down next to her and began to read. It was a letter of divorce. Thomas had had their marriage annulled. They had only been married one year. Sable sat on the sofa and stared into space until she was ready to admit to herself that the letter was real. Why would he do this to her?

Chapter 69

Sable went home and cried on her parents' shoulders and took blame for the entire separation. Her parents thought that she should try again. They hadn't liked Thomas in the beginning, but he showed promise after marrying their daughter and putting her in such a beautiful home. She didn't have to work or worry about money. Sepia just shook her head. She knew that Thomas had somehow gotten rid of Sable and forced her to make up a bunch of lies so that he would come out smelling sweet. Looking back, she remembered that Thomas had been charged with rape, but yet his boss gave him his job back. She also knew that Thomas had served four years. He claimed he went for kissing Sable at sixteen. He also told her that everyone else was of legal age when he started or had affairs with them, including Sepia.

Chapter 70

Thomas carried Lena over the threshold of the newly built house that Sable had believed was for her.

He set her feet on the living-room floor, her suitcase next to her, and patted her on the butt. "Go get your shower so that we can start our honeymoon—and don't forget that lingerie I bought you."

Lena grabbed the suitcase and rushed into the bathroom. Like Sable had, she hummed with joy. As she showered, she thought about how many women didn't have a man like Thomas. How young, virile, and fine he was. Most of all, he wanted her openly. He didn't see their relationship as taboo. Older men could have a younger woman. That was normal. But the young girl was still considered a tramp for dating the older man. An older woman was considered the same for dating a younger boy or man, and the younger male was almost always blameless and looked upon as more virile because of the involvement. It was believed that women matured faster, and the young male didn't know any better. And like any man, he was just taking what was offered to him, but the downside was that young girls shunned him after that. He and Lena both would be isolated in some way and treated as if they had the plague.

Lena stepped out of the shower and headed upstairs. Thomas called out to her from the kitchen. Lena walked softly toward his voice. Thomas was seated at the table. Before he could conceal his bottle, Lena saw it.

Thomas looked up. "Come here to me."

Lena's heart pounded heavily. She was going to pay for something that had happened months and months ago, maybe even longer, and she knew it. She knew his tones, his actions, his body movements. She took a deep breath and walked over to Thomas. As soon as she got close enough, he pulled her over his lap and proceeded to spank her. He watched as Lena's muscles flexed through her sheer gown. "I don't know how Jasper got into your house that day, Lena, but ain't no man gonna come up in there without you lettin' him in. You must have been messin' around with that nigga all the while I was away. You think um some kind of fool or something? Huh, do you? Do you?"

"No, Thomas, no!"

"So you admittin' that y'all had been doin' things all along, then—"

"He just come up there that day! I had forgot to lock my door after coming from the store! I tried to make him leave, then he started beatin' on me!"

Thomas stopped the whipping and began massaging Lena. Out of his jacket, he pulled the ice pack, which he had made ready, and continued his routine.

Chapter 71

Thomas kept his arm around Lena's waist until he snorted his cocaine and smoked his joint, filling his mind with more hate and resentment while planning revenge for his suffering. As he rose from the chair, Lena slid off his lap. She was too afraid to turn too quickly and look at him. She hated his high expression. It was menacing. She hoped that he hadn't gone that far yet. Timidly she cut her eyes at him. It was there. His eyes bulging and red, his lips twitching. She could hear his tongue clacking inside his closed mouth. She knew it was time for the most torturous round. He was going to finish abusing her. She hated his intoxicated regimens of lewd torment. Her heart pounded fiercely as she thought about her fate and his grueling, harsh stamina. Sure, he was a young, handsome, virile prize, who more than satisfied her when things were right between them. He'd married her and put her in a dream house. He had even defied his mother and his younger women for her. But had she won or lost? Was she the lucky one or the most unfortunate?

* * *

As Thomas pulled her along to the bedroom, she
looked back at the kitchen door, wanting to run.
Nothing had changed about him, and now he had
her trapped. This wasn't love; it was lust. He was obsessed with her and she knew it. He had fooled her
until he could get her all to himself—isolated. He
didn't love her. He was obsessed with her and she
had just realized it. She remembered the many days
she had stayed inside her own home, just waiting
for him. She had been too afraid to leave in fear of
the punishment he would inflict on her if she
wasn't available to him. Lena dropped her head in
defeat. He'd caged her so that he could feast off
her whenever his appetite craved her. Lena lifted
her head again and tugged slightly in resistance.
Thomas whirled around and quickly lifted her up,
holding her tightly in his strong young arms. Lena
squealed and shivered. She could smell his drug-
charred, alcohol-tinged breath. Thomas's breathing was now angry and coming out in drunken
wheezes. He kicked the bedroom door open. Then
he chuckled at the screaming he caused from his
actions. He walked over to the bed and threw Lena
down. Lena opened her eyes and she, too, began to
scream as she focused on Sable sitting next to her.

Thomas kneeled in front of Sable. "Um glad you
decided to be with us, baby. I thought you would be
too uptight."

Sable rubbed his head. "You know how much I
love you, Thomas. I'll do whatever you want. It ain't
too much for me to help you fulfill your fantasy. If
you want an old and young twin, then that's wha

you gonna git. Um your wife. Um gonna stay your wife. Um gonna die your wife."

Lena was now standing on the other side of the bed. She had backed into the wall, near the window. "You ain't none of his wife no more! Um his wife! Um his wife now!"

"You just what you always been to Thomas, Lena. What Thomas crave when he don't want me. When he tired of young women."

Thomas slapped Sable. "Shut your mouth! She my wife!"

Sable jumped up. Before she could swing, Thomas grabbed her throat. Lena eased the window up. Thomas slapped Sable, pushed her down on the bed, flung his body across it, and grabbed Lena by the wrist. "Where you think you going?"

"You don't need me here. Please, Thomas, let me go."

"You the last one I'd let outta this room, Lena. This girl here good, but you better." Thomas gently kissed Lena's lips.

"But—"

"Sh, Lena, sh. It's gonna be okay, baby." Thomas pulled Lena back onto the bed. "Just stay put till um done."

Thomas went back to Sable. She was crying and still holding her face. He pulled her hand away from her face. "What the hell wrong with you?"

"You told me that we wasn't really divorced. That you was only with her when you couldn't get with a young woman. That's why I agreed. . . . " Sable lowered her head and continued to cry.

"So what you goin' do, Sable?"

Sable looked helpless.

Thomas stepped between her legs. "Come on. Let's do this."

Sable sat emotionless as Thomas kneeled in front of her. Lena covered her mouth and held her stomach, trying not to vomit as she watched her husband with his ex-wife.

Chapter 72

Thomas and Sable had fallen into a medicated sleep from all the drugs they had done together while Lena slept. This gave Lena the chance to sneak off. When she first woke, she thought everything was normal and had almost decided against leaving, until she discovered Thomas and Sable sleeping, hugged up in each other's arms. Lena became jealous. Thomas was her man. She watched them with squinted evil eyes, wanting to kill Sable and hurt Thomas. Lena had shaken the thoughts out of her head and had quietly slipped off. Thomas would definitely continue to force this on her, again and again. No matter what she had ever done for Thomas in the past, she had always been willing and had enjoyed most of it. But what had just happened to her in the past few hours of her life was just too devastating. She walked down the lonesome road in the early-morning light, barefoot. She carried her suitcase after quickly throwing on what she could find, then casually walking out the front door of Thomas's lifelong dream house. She hopped on the first local bus she saw and headed downtown to the national bus station.

Chapter 73

Lena rode silently in the cab she had hailed from the station. Her body moved with every bump and bounce. She stared out the window in awe at the farms and motels that lined the dusty highways and wondered why they were so close to each other.

The cabdriver pulled up to the private road and let Lena out at the curb as she had requested. She quickly handed the driver the money over the front seat. She grabbed her suitcase, once her feet hit the ground. The driver nodded and waited to see that Lena was going to be okay. He smiled as he watched Lena open her suitcase, take her beige wedding slippers out, slide them on her feet, close her suitcase very casually, then proceed to walk toward the mansionlike structure. Once Lena was out of sight, he drove away.

Lena gripped her one piece of luggage tightly, and swallowed hard as she stood at the door, trying to find the nerve to ring the bell. She closed her eyes and gently pressed the chime. She could hear the bong through the thick front door. An older white woman answered. She was wiping her hands on some sort of rag. She frowned with confusion. "May I help you?"

Lena cleared her throat and spoke as clearly as she could. "Yes. Please. Um—um . . . I'm looking for Gweneth."

The woman smiled slightly. "May I ask who's calling on her?"

Lena began to cry. "It's her mother."

The woman instantly choked. Lena patted her back. "If this ain't a good time—"

"No, no, no. She's just never mentioned you—" The woman wheezed. "I mean, she's here—hold on." The woman stepped back inside and closed the door.

Lena stood in the yard and looked around at all the beautiful greenery.

Gweneth snatched the front door open, expecting to see another useless person claiming to be a relative, begging for food, money, or something.

Lena jumped.

Gweneth stumbled backward at the sight of Lena and had to throw her hand over her mouth. She mumbled through her hand, "Mama?"

Tears instantly welled up in Lena's eyes. Gweneth grabbed her and hugged her tightly. They both stepped inside.

Lena set her bag down. "Where Kerrissy?"

"Mama, Kerrissy don't live here with me. She came here, met some old-ass man named Kenneth, and took off again. I don't know when we'll see her. That old man must be puttin' somethin' with her. She don't even call."

Lena wanted to pass out. "Kenneth? What's his last name?"

"Mama, to tell you the truth, I don't even know. I ain't never even seen that man. The neighbors told, Kerrissy admitted it, and that was all. I ain't gonna keep on worrying about that girl. She a grown woman now—all I can do is pray."

Lena wiped her eyes. She was surprised that Gweneth hadn't put the name with her stepfather's. The man whom Gweneth had known as her father. Lena continued to question. "You know what he look like?"

"Yeah, but only from what the neighbors say. He kinda tall, brown-skinned, wavy hair. I heard Kerrissy telling one of her other fass friends he got some pretty eyes and can put it on her like Thomas never could, or never would. Mama, the young girls real sick now. Just wanna run the streets, party, and get a man's money, *tch, tch, tch*. I don't know why Kerrissy wanna waste her life with some old man like that. The young ones flock around her and give her whatever she wants, too."

Lena couldn't give Gweneth eye contact. She knew that Kerrissy's Kenneth was the same Kenneth that had been her husband, Gweneth's stepfather, and Kerrissy's step-grandfather. Why hadn't Gweneth figured it out?

Gweneth shook Lena's shoulder, bringing her out of her daydream. "Mama? You okay?"

"Yeah, yeah, baby. Um okay. . . . Kin I stay here awhile just till I find me a place?"

"Mama, you mean you ain't here just to visit? You gonna stay? But why? Did something happen to your house?"

Lena lowered her head. "I sold it."

"But why, Mama? Why?"

"I got married again. It didn't work." Lena began to cry. "He took everything!"

"We can get it back, Mama—"

"No! I don't want it! He did leave me a little somethin'. Besides, that house wasn't worth much."

"But it was all you had, Mama. It was all you had, and it was paid for. And we had fixed it all up." Gweneth broke down.

Lena hugged her. "All you bought me is put up for later. I kin git that anytime I want. It's time for me to move out from that old alley, anyway, Gweneth. It's just God's way of telling me that."

Gweneth felt better. She had never heard her mother speak of God before. Everything had to be okay. She took her mother's bag and led her to the guest room and bath. Lena was in awe again. She had never seen a place so big and so many bathrooms. She wondered why Gweneth needed so much room.

Chapter 74

Lena settled in quite nicely. After four months with her daughter, she had SSI checks, since she was now sixty-two years of age, found a new subsidized complex that would take her, in a few weeks, and had retrieved the furniture that she had actually stored back home. Kerrissy hadn't stopped by once since she had been there. Lena was disappointed and relieved at the same time. Although Gweneth didn't know their secret, Lena and Kerrissy did. Things would have surely been awkward and tense.

Lena sat at the kitchen island as she did every morning, reading the paper and drinking her coffee. She jumped at the sound of the phone ringing. As she scurried over to the phone, she cursed at the distraction that made her spill her coffee. She smiled at her silliness and took a deep breath. "Hello."

The other end was silent.

Lena spoke up. "Hello!"

"Lena, baby, why you leave me like that? You know I can't live without you!"

Lena screamed and dropped the phone. She

could hear the chatter continue as it hung by the cord. She slowly picked it up. Her voice was pleading. "Thomas, please. Just leave me alone—"

Thomas raised his voice. "Not until you tell me why you left me!"

"Thomas, you brought that other woman in our bedroom and was doing all them thangs with us. That ain't right, Thomas. Our marriage supposed to be sacred—"

"Lena, baby, listen. I done stopped drinkin', sho 'nuff. For real, honest! I done quit. When I realized you was gone and wasn't coming back, I stopped—" Lena would never forget all the violent episodes she'd suffered at Thomas' hands on Hussey Place. Nor could she forgive how he had violated her, both physically and emotionally.

"Thomas, if you started back drinking, then you done had that woman back in our house, too, since I been gone. With the one habit, you always start the other. They go hand in hand with you, and so do them drugs. You done been with that woman since I left."

"Baby, I swear I ain't had that woman here—"

"Then how you gittin' 'long, Thomas? I know you, Thomas, I know you!"

Thomas remained silent.

Lena closed her eyes. "Thomas?"

"Lena, I told you. I ain't been with that woman— no woman!"

"But you done slept with her, Thomas, after your annulment to her. After you promised me and brought me to that house!"

"No, baby, no—"

"How you know I was here, Thomas?"

"I tracked you down from the storage people. I had been sittin' 'round thinkin' 'bout you and lookin' for you, and then I remembered your furniture and stuff in storage and went down there, askin' around. All I had to do is tell um I was your husband and was making sure our furniture got to the right place and they gave me everything, even the contact number in case somethin' was tuh go wrong. I'd memorized this number, anyway. . . ."

"Suppose my daughter or Kerrissy woulda been here—"

Thomas became furious. "See! That's what make me so crazy with you! You always got to hide what we got! Why we always got to hide, Lena?"

Lena fell quiet. Something that had been hidden inside of her, and that she was almost too ashamed to even remember, let alone talk about, burbled up inside. She finally spoke on it. "Why you got to bring other women into our bed, Thomas? Why you got to have them touching me and you and all, huh?"

"Lena, I swear I love you. You seen what I did when she tried putting you down. You heard me tell her you my wife. It was our wedding night. I ain't had no bachelor party or nothing, Lena. All I wanted was that one time—*one time*, Lena!"

"Oh, and it didn't matter how much I was put to shame. Right, Thomas?"

"I swear to you, Lena. If you come back home, won't nothing like that never happen again. *I swear.*"

"I ain't coming back there, Thomas."

"Then um gonna come git you, Lena."

"Thomas, my daughter got all kinds of security 'round her house. You ready for that?"

"Lena, come on now. Don't you miss me? The

way I kiss you, run my tongue up and down your neck? When we make love?"

Lena closed her eyes as she imagined Thomas and her together. She opened them. "You sure you ain't drinking? You sure you ain't gonna bring that woman back to our bed?"

Thomas grinned and crossed his fingers behind his back, as if Lena could see him. "Um positive, baby."

"Okay. But how you gonna git me? I mean, you so far—"

"Um only a few blocks away in a motel. I got one more night here. We can celebrate our honeymoon right, since I messed the first one up."

Lena smiled. "What time you gonna come git me?"

"I kin come now, Lena."

"Naw. It's gonna hafta be late. I can't let my daughter know what's really going on. If she find out about you, she might flip, 'cause of you and Kerrissy. Then she might find out the rest that happened before I got here. People git weak in time of pressure and start talking. I might say the wrong thang, Thomas."

"What time your daughter go to bed, Lena?"

"'Bout eleven."

"I'll be there at midnight." He hastily hung up.

Lena went to her room and busied herself with packing. She would sneak out of the house as soon as Gweneth fell into a deep sleep. Lena knew that would be when Gweneth began to snore.

Chapter 75

Thomas smiled as he watched Lena quietly hurry to his car with the suitcase she'd left with. The closer she got, the better she looked—and Lena had lost even more weight. All of her stomach was gone and her extra fat had been replaced by curvaceous hips. Her legs had always been smooth and pretty even for a woman Gweneth's age. He could feel himself rise. He could also feel himself become angry. He tried not to let his eyes bulge with anger as he thought of Lena with another man. There was no way all the men out in California weren't trying to get with his wife.

Lena opened the car door and got inside. Thomas put on a fake smile. "Ooh, baby, you look so good. I gotta have you now!" Thomas leaned over and began biting, licking, and kissing Lena's neck. She could feel herself get excited. When Thomas got to her breasts, she held his head. She really didn't want to, but she couldn't allow him to go any further in front of her daughter's house. Her voice shook in fear. "Thomas, please. Let's go to your motel room.

My daughter and the neighbors might see. They put
you in jail for thangs like this out here."

Thomas sat up without another word, put the car
in gear, and sped out of the large, brushy private
road. He stopped a block away from Gweneth's on
the dusty, dark road. He slowly drove the car onto the
shoulder and into the shelter of the trees. He pulled
Lena by the leg as soon as the car stopped. When he
discovered how light she had become, he smiled. He
jerked her harder. Lena reclined.

Thomas climbed on top of her and spoke passionately into her ear, "Why you leave me, Lena?"

"You hurt me so bad. Why you had to hurt me
like that?"

Thomas didn't answer. He wanted Lena to suffer
and crave the way he had. "Tell me what you want,
Lena! Tell me how much you love me or um gonna
take you back where I got you from!"

Lena submitted.

Thomas sat up. He looked over at Lena. She was
still breathing hard, trying to catch her breath, with
her eyes closed. Thomas reached inside his jacket
and pulled out his bottle. Before he could twist the
cap off, Lena opened her eyes and caught him.

"Thomas, you said you was done with that."

"Lena, I don't drink as much as I did before." He
held up the bottle. "Look here. This just a small
bottle, see."

Lena finished sitting up. "You goin' hurt me if
you drink that. You goin' hurt me."

She tried reaching for the bottle.

Thomas pulled it away. "Didn't I tell you I wasn't gonna drink much? Now stop 'fo I git mad, Lena."

Lena sat quietly and waited. Thomas pulled out his drugs and began rolling down the window with one hand as he rolled a joint with the other.

Lena knew that she had made the wrong decision again. As soon as Thomas was high enough, his fun would start with her. Thomas had plans to whip her, but she would be beaten if he thought in any way she had been with another man. And Lena knew the difference in Thomas's whippings and beatings.

Thomas sat quietly as he thought about how quickly his wife had made him react. He was too proud to let Lena know that he had lost control. That right now he was so high, he couldn't distinguish that it had really been Lena controlling him during their passion. That's when Lena knew Thomas had more than a problem. Thomas had always been sharp, even when he was high. He would have instantly cussed her out for not letting him totally humiliate and control her.

Thomas got out of the car and went over to Lena's side and opened the door. She reluctantly stepped out. She looked down the long, dark road and wanted to take off running. Thomas grabbed her arm, opened the back door, got in, and pulled her with him. His drunken head bobbed. "Why you, um, um . . . why you always trying to embarrass me, Lena?"

"Thomas, I don't—"

"Sh, just answer the question so we kin git this over with real quick. I ain't got no place to go. You ain't got no place to go. I ain't gonna let you go no place. We kin be here all night, *bish*." Lena wanted to giggle at the way he called her the foul name drunkenly, but she remained solemn.

"Lay cross my yap, Yena."

Again, Lena wanted to laugh, but fear stopped her. She looked down at the cooler Thomas had on the floor and hesitated to obey his order.

Thomas shook his head. "You must love doing things the hard way."

"Wait a minute, Thomas. Why we can't never talk about—"

Thomas snatched the breath out of Lena as he pulled her over his lap. He pulled her skirt up. "Damn, Lena, your ass so pretty. You know what? I don't beat you nearly as hard as I do them otha hoes. You know why?" Thomas looked down at Lena as if he expected an answer. Lena shook her head from side to side. "'Cause your ass so pretty. I don't wanna mess it up, Lena. You know what else?" Lena shook her head. "I love doing all kinds of things with you, 'cause you turn me on so much. Was it so bad what me, you, and Sable did?" Lena shook her head again, too fearful of telling the truth. Thomas massaged her. "Damn, you pretty for an old lady. How you turn me on like you do? Make me do so many things? Make me want more and more? More than I know you kin give?"

"I don't know."

"You know why you 'bout to git punish, Lena? You ready for that?"

"Thomas, please. Why you gotta hurt me? You supposed to love me."

"I do love you! Punishment the only thang you seem to know! You must like it, you keep leaving me and doing things you know I don't like! Why?"

"I wouldn't have left if you hadn't had another woman in our bed—"

"That ain't your choice, Lena! You my wife! You do whatever I say! Give me what I want! You hear me?"

Lena nodded.

"Say somethin', Lena!"

"I hear you, Thomas."

Thomas's hand went down. Lena squealed, it stung so badly. He proceeded to spank Lena and watched her muscles flex. He enjoyed her reactions and the sounds of her agony. "I can't wait for you to do something else after this, Lena."

Lena cried and screamed until it was over.

Thomas collapsed from their lovemaking. He kissed Lena's ear. "Baby, you the best thing that ever happened to me. You know. It ain't so bad with Sable in the bed with us sometimes, is it?"

Lena couldn't believe that he was still talking about sleeping with her and another woman as he lay on top of her. Lena broke down and cried like a madwoman.

"You'll get used to it. Watch and see."

Lena continued to cry.

Thomas sat up. "You might as well stop crying,

Lena. We going home. Sable gonna be there. You gonna be there. Um gonna be there. Both them kids gonna be there. We gonna be a family. I done thought about all this, long and hard, even about messin' with you tonight, and when and where and how I was gonna do it. Thought I could wait till I got you home. Was even gonna make Sable stay in another room of the house, her and the kids till I had filled myself with you, but I couldn't wait, Lena. Soon as I saw you, I knew I wasn't gonna be able to wait. You got to me before you even sat down in this here car."

Thomas stared straight ahead like an obstinate child.

Lena's crying lessened as she thought about Thomas's confession. She tried reasoning with him again. "Why you can't just let me go, Thomas? I don't want no part of that mess. If somebody don't want somethin', you shouldn't make um do it, Thomas."

"Did you think about that when you got me hooked on you, Lena?"

"But what you need me for now? That girl do everything I do, and some, and she like it! *I don't!*"

"Ain't no way I can be without you, Lena! I'd git rid of her first!"

"Then let her go, and be with me—and only me—like you promised me, Thomas."

"I can't!"

"Why, Thomas?"

"'Cause I like havin' the both of y'all when um high like this! I wanna be with both of y'all right now! And don't threaten to leave me no more, Lena! You gittin' too old for me to really whip you, but I'll think of somethin' if I have to!"

Lena lowered her head in obedience, put her hands in her lap, and picked her nails.

Thomas could hear them click. It irritated him. He put his hand over hers. "Stop that! It ain't gonna change nothin!" Thomas got out of the car and straightened up his clothes. Lena looked around for her skirt.

Thomas peeked in the back window. "What you doin'?"

"Um lookin' for my clothes—"

"Leave um! I ain't done! And stay in the back, till I say you kin git out!"

Thomas got back in the front and began to drive. Lena continued to watch the dark as they moved farther and farther away from her daughter's house.

"Thomas, where we going?"

"Um trying to find a gas station so that we can make it to the exit."

"I think I saw one up the road a piece when I come in here. It ain't much farther. . . . Yeah, there it is."

Thomas could see the lights before he got there. Before he exited the car, he grabbed Lena's chin and stared into her eyes, looking for traces of another man. Lena could not match his stare and closed her eyes.

Thomas shook her chin. "Look at me! Look at me!"

Lena opened her eyes and stared at Thomas with fear in her eyes.

Thomas didn't blink. "You think you better than me, since you been out here with the movie stars and that stankin' uppity daughter of yours, don't you?"

Lena shook her head fervently from side to side. Thomas held her chin while he stuck his tongue in her mouth. Lena's stomach began to bubble. She could taste the alcohol and marijuana. She held down the nausea until Thomas drove to the gas station. As soon as Thomas went inside the store to pay for his gas, Lena opened the car door and threw up. She saw Thomas come out of the store and walk around the building to the bathroom. She quickly put her clothes on, grabbed her suitcase, jumped out of the car, and headed down the road to the motel that was close to her daughter's house.

Chapter 76

Thomas grinned his usual arrogant grin and leaned his head back in relief as he emptied his bladder, then walked out of the bathroom, around to the front of the store, stretched, and headed to his car. He squinted his eyes as he got closer to his vehicle, believing that the darkness was playing tricks on him. He snatched open the back door. "What the f—Lena! Lena! Lena! Where you at? If you come back now, I won't be mad! I won't punish you! If you keep hidin' out here, um gonna be forced to beat you instead of just the whippins I been givin' you for disobeying me! Come on now, Lena! Stop playing games! We gotta get home to Sable and the kids!"

Thomas walked up the road a little ways and searched the bushes before thinking that Lena might be in the store. But when he walked back to the store, the owner was turning off the lights. Thomas was furious. He snatched open his car door so hard, it closed shut by itself. Thomas began to curse up a storm and stomp. He eased the car door open again and sat in his car. *Um gonna sleep here at this station till the mornin'. I'll see her at her daughter's house tomorrow. She'll be sorry she ran from me. She gonna be real sorry.*

Chapter 77

Gweneth snatched her front door open. It was only 6:00 A.M. Who would be stupid enough to be ringing her doorbell at that time of morning? Everyone who knew her well was aware of the fact that her feet did not touch the floor on Saturday mornings until far into the afternoon.

She wiped her eyes and squinted. "What!"

Thomas stood nervously on the stoop, twisting his hat in his hands. He stepped back a little, trying to make sure that Gweneth didn't recognize him, as he prayed that Kerrissy didn't come to the door—although Lena had informed him of her running off with Kenneth. Thomas kept his head lowered, pretending to be shy. "I hate to bother you. But is Lena in?"

"Shit! Hold on a minute. Mama! Mama!" Gweneth closed the door and went to Lena's room. She wasn't there and her bed was made. This wasn't unusual. She always went to the farmers' market early-morning Saturday, and kept a made bed. Gweneth hunched her shoulders and walked back to the front door. "She ain't here. Try the farmers' market."

Before Thomas could speak, Gweneth slammed

the door in his face. Thomas turned red with anger. Lena would get whipped—no, beat for running away, and for her daughter's insolence.

Thomas stomped back out to the curb, where he had left his car parked so that Lena wouldn't hear or see him coming. He spun around in confusion, trying to figure out which way Lena had gone, before dropping to his knees. *"Lena! Where are you?"* Thomas dropped his head and cried.

A police car pulled up next to him. "You okay, mister?"

Thomas sniffled. "Um okay."

"Sir—do you need anything?"

Thomas wouldn't look up. "No. Nothing."

"Sir, this is a restricted area. You're going to have to move it along then."

Thomas held on to the hood of his car as he pulled himself up off the ground. "Okay, Officer. And thanks. I'll be okay."

The officer watched Thomas pull off.

Chapter 78

Lena smiled as she walked in the beautiful California sun back to her new apartment, holding her bag of produce tightly in her arms. Thomas stepped in front of her. "I told you I would get you!" He began choking Lena, shaking her wildly, causing her fruit and vegetables to scatter about. Lena finally dropped the bag. Thomas drew back a fist.

Lena jumped straight up in bed and switched on her lamp. She clumsily reached for her calming pills and drank the water she always left on her nightstand. Without looking, she searched for the latest letter her daughter had saved for her, which she always left beside her sedative. It crumpled in her hand as she grabbed it off the nightstand. Lena's hands shook vigorously as she put on her glasses and read the letter for more than the tenth time.

Lena,
*   I could not go on without you. All I could do was drink and get high. I tried to make Sable enough for*

me, but she couldn't replace you. I just wish so hard
now that I would have never tried bringing her into
our bedroom and trying to force you to accept it. Well,
Sable got sick of me, too, when I stopped touching her.
She left me and married her son's father. All I did was
go to work and drink. Stopped paying my bills alto-
gether and lost the house.

I am back with Mama. I swear, Lena. I swear this
time on all that's sacred to me, if you come back, I
won't ever touch no liquor or drugs no more. No more
women, just me and you. I am even going to an alco-
hol program for help. If you don't believe me, I put
proof inside the envelope. You can call them if you
want. I swear, Lena, I didn't mean to hurt you. It's
just that you always made me feel so good and made
me want more and more. God, you a good woman,
Lena. If you come back to me, I'll do whatever you
want. I love you, Lena. You the only woman I have
ever loved. No matter what happen, you will always
be my wife. My one and only love.

Thomas . . .

Lena began to sob uncontrollably. Why did he
keep on writing her? Why did he continue bothering
her? Why didn't he just leave her alone? All she
wanted was peace. She only kept the letter available
as a reminder that he was far away and living with his
mother again. Sometimes the pills alone didn't work.
The letter always helped to put her at ease whenever
she read it. It helped her to fall asleep after having
the nightmare and knowing that Thomas would
never leave Venn's house to come looking for her.

"Baby, you okay?"

The deep voice made Lena snap back to reality.

"Yeah, I'm okay."

"Was it that dream again, the one about your ex-husband?"

Lena nodded, put the wrinkled letter back on the nightstand, and lay down.

He brushed her hair with his hand.

It felt good. She sighed and closed her eyes. She could feel her body being pulled and didn't resist. Feeling his warm, taut flesh against hers made her smile. This time he was in his late fifties, closer to her age. Lena was now almost sixty-three, and she was collecting social Security Supplemental Income, known as SSI. She'd only worked as a domestic so she couldn't get Social Security Retirement or Disability. James Baker was big and black, with toned muscles from lifting in the warehouse. He appreciated her—had even fought for her when another man tried stepping to her. She had smiled like a schoolgirl, even when he had threatened to hit her if it ever happened again. Lena wasn't worried. He wasn't a nut like Thomas. Nope.

James Baker was a good man. He didn't drink, smoke, use drugs, or sleep around. She was happy, very happy. She smiled as she remembered James calling out to her from the docks where he worked. She was apprehensive at first. It had taken her forever to get rid of Thomas; she wasn't ready to entertain a new madman. But James wooed her until she gave in. She and James had a long courtship, and after finding out that she was older, James hadn't batted an eye. Lena had a very young-looking face and body, and James couldn't wait to see all of her.

He spent his money freely on Lena so that he could. When he felt the time was right, he and Lena discussed their lives and intimacy, with James talking freely about it and initiating some of the things that were socially considered taboo. Lena wanted to please James, and he had responded with much affection, but she never let on to how much she knew, until a few nights ago. The dream had made her blurt out the one thing she never wanted James to know about. He reassured her that it was okay. That he thought no less of her. That he, too, had indulged in the same things, and if she didn't condemn him, he wouldn't condemn her, because he found nothing wrong with the way a person chose to show his or her love. He could see how Thomas could be so obsessed with her in so many ways. There weren't many women Lena's age so pleasing to the eye, and looked as good as she did without plastic surgery.

He had told her how proud he was of her, her beauty, the way she always let him lead, never stopping him—no matter what he asked for or how he wanted it.

"Lena, I don't wanna hafta kill nobody over you. We gotta get married before I lose you. You let me be the man. You let me be the man, and that make me love you more. Make you even more valuable to a man. You let me lead. That's what a man like. All these men around here see that and be droolin', but we gonna get married and let um all know. We gonna let um all know."

In Lena's opinion, there was no way around the control issue if you wanted to keep a good man.

You had to always let him lead. But lately, Lena was feeling a bit uncomfortable. Things seemed to be slowly changing. She even felt caged at times. Some of those times were when she was locked in James's huge arms. On occasion he had seemed to purposely hold her extra tight, like a primate showing his mate who was dominant. And it seemed to have gotten more frequent within the past two days— even his appetite for her had heightened. This frightened Lena a little, but she was always able to talk to James and he'd loosen his hold a bit, stating that he was unaware of how tight he was holding her. It was just his way of feeling her more, because he loved her so much. Lena accepted this.

James put one of his huge arms around Lena, brought her even closer to him, and hugged her tightly. There was that caged feeling again. Lena accepted it.

He put his lips to Lena's ear.

She smiled.

James whispered, "Mmm, baby. Since you up, I wanna go again."

Lena looked back at James with fear in her eyes. He looked like an imp. Lena wanted to scramble out of bed. Before she could think twice, she was wrestled down.

"This won't happen again, Lena. I just couldn't bear to hear you say no to me right now. I love you so much."

Lena smiled pleasantly. She became confused from the tugging on her hair, her head being jerked up, the painful blow to her face. "Who you thinkin' 'bout, Lena? Why you smilin' like that? You thinkin' 'bout that otha nigga!"

With the strength of a bear, Lena pushed James away from her, jumped out of bed, pulled out her father's treasured razor strap from the closet, and began whipping James until he curled into a fetal position on the floor, rolled him into the hallway naked, and threw his clothes out after him.

Chapter 79

Gweneth called for her helper, having forgotten that it was her day off. The sudden perception made her jump to her feet. As she also remembered the package she had been waiting for, she rushed to her front door, sipping from her cup of coffee. She quickly flung the front door open, ready to sign. The cup seemed to fall from her hand in slow motion. Pieces of glass went sailing, causing the coffee to splatter everything that it came in contact with. Gweneth put her hands over her mouth as she stood in her corridor and stared at her visitor. A tear slid down her cheek. Lena stood there, face swollen, eyes half-shut. With the back of her hands, Gweneth wiped at the tears she'd allowed to fall. "Mama? Mama? What happened?"

Lena stood in the doorway, holding two cloth suitcases, one in each hand. She looked like a little child who had run away from home. She looked down at the ground, embarrassed by Gweneth's stare. "James. He whupped me. He was jealous. He whupped me last night. I had to leave. He told me he would kill me if I so much as looked at another man, since we gonna git married." Lena was too ashamed of the truth.

Gweneth's hands shook. Her voice filled with desperation and fear. "Don't he know where I live, Mama? I mean, your mail. It's on the letters you've been getting from back home!"

Lena still hadn't shed a tear. Her heart and eyes felt dry. She stared blankly. "No. He know I get them. He even seen me read them—know what's in some. But I never let him see them letters, Gweneth, or them envelopes—"

"Don't leave here again, Mama! Next time some man may kill you!"

Lena nodded in agreement. She'd come to that conclusion the night before, along with many other things. It was good to have someone who loved you, but love shouldn't come with the price of lost dignity, physical pain, the loss of family, or certain freedoms. She had lost all of that. Lena had also lost precious time, and so much more. Her recklessness had ended. She gently set her soft flowered bags on the floor in the hallway, and walked by Gweneth into the house. She headed straight to her old bedroom to think and finish unraveling her mind. Gweneth stood silently. Her tear-filled eyes followed Lena . . . until she was out of sight.

Lena sat at the end of her bed and looked out the window. She stared up at the beautiful bright blue sky with admiration as she thought. She would write Thomas and apologize again for what she had put him through when he was a child. It was wrong.

Maybe she would tell Venn the story and apologize to her, too. She smiled as she watched a bird fly into the trees, sit there alone, and seem content. It was small but looked so confident as it just sat there alone, looking around appearing to enjoy all the scenery. Lena folded her arms and sighed.

That's it. That's the way life is supposed to be—so filled with freedom you feel light enough to fly. So pain-free you care about all the pretty things around you and take your time to enjoy them. Lena smiled broader as she slowly reclined, put her hands under her head, and tried to drift off to sleep in a relaxed state. It was over, truly over. No more unwanted dreams, pain, worries, or fears.

She was no longer anxious just because the world had programmed her to believe that her age, gender, and the supposed male drought were factors to rush her life and accept whatever came. It had always seemed odd to her how whenever she went out to the juke joints, there were more men than women, but she had always been told that there was a male shortage. As far as she was concerned, this had been a male conspiracy. Men did the news, data collections, and statistics for those reports. She'd constantly wondered if the male shortage reports that came from men were merely lures for women to accept more down than up in relationships, and to be thankful just to have a man—any man.

But was it really better to have a no-good man than none at all? Did she need a man to keep her feet warm at night, like she'd been often told? 'Cause she sure as hell never had one long enough to keep hers covered. Why had she always heard these crazy things from her parents and other women? Had they been desperate, or did they actually believe these little clichés?

1970

Lena hunched her shoulders and shook her head as she allowed new tears to flow from her eyes. Tears that expressed her certainty of freedom. At last she was free—and she felt it. She never had to go back to being a slave to negative love. Her world had changed for the better, and she would begin living it to the fullest at the next rising sun.